"Mara, I want you..."

Shane murmured against her hair.

"I know" was the only response that would pass her lips. His hands on her shoulders were enticing, inviting.

"You're beautiful," Shane coaxed, and his fingers tickled her neck. "I know this is crazy—I don't know how to describe it—but I need you, Mara. Not because you're a woman, but because you're unique...special...captivating. You're you, and I want the most intimate part of you."

"You don't even know me," she whispered in a feeble protest, knowing she was succumbing to the magic of the seductive night.

LISA JACKSON

THE SHADOW OF TIME

Silhouette Books

Published by Silhouette Books
America's Publisher of Contemporary Romance

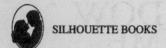

SILHOUETTE BOOKS

RECYCLED PAPER

THE SHADOW OF TIME

ISBN 0-373-21824-9

Copyright © 1984 by Lisa Jackson

This edition published by arrangement with Harlequin Books S.A.

® and TM are trademarks of Harlequin Books S.A., used under license. Trademarks indicated with ® are registered in the United States Patent and Trademark Office, the Canadian Trade Marks Office and in other countries.

Visit Silhouette Books at www.eHarlequin.com

Printed in U.S.A.

To Nancy

Chapter One

Shane Kennedy had been wrong. Dead wrong. He didn't make mistakes often. In fact, he very rarely made mistakes, and the realization that this morning was not only an error in judgment but also an exercise in frustration made him clench his teeth and jut his jaw against the early November morning air. He prided himself in his ability to think clearly, solve problems, handle any situation, *and* avoid costly or time-consuming errors. Yet here he was, doing exactly the opposite of what all of his instincts instructed him to do, caught up in the enticing but bitter nostalgia of the past, acting the part of a fool!

As he leaned against the moss-laden trunk of a barren oak tree, he wondered what had possessed him to come here— it wasn't as if he were welcome. He muttered a silent oath under his breath and watched the scene before him with fascination…and contempt. He must have been out of his mind, driving most of the night just to…what? he asked himself. To see her again? Talk to her…touch her? He snapped his mind closed at the thought with another oath. Damn! He closed his eyes as the cold, familiar sense of betrayal crept silently up his spine, and he hiked the collar of his coat up more closely to his throat as if to ward off the chill of the early winter morning.

Perhaps it was because four lonely years had passed, and time has a way of twisting memories to make them appear more captivating than they actually were. Or perhaps he had just forgotten how mysteriously beautiful she could be. Or, more likely, even in Shane's own estimation, he had secretly hoped that the years would have begun to take their toll on Mara's winsome features and that the signs of age would have started to weather the regal loveliness of her face, making him immune to her beauty. But he had been mistaken— and a fool to even believe that the passion she had once inspired would have died within him. It was a false hope on his part, nothing more. Even now, in the cold, misty morning, cloaked in an unflattering black coat, Mara appeared more serenely beautiful than he had remembered. And if age had caught up with her, it was only to add a determination and a maturity that increased the seductive quality of her elegant beauty. The memories that her presence evoked shattered Shane's resolve.

He had come to the lonely cemetery on impulse, and now he realized the gravity of his mistake. One look at Mara was not enough to satisfy him. His fists balled at his sides as he discovered, to his disgust, that despite the pain of the last four years, he still wanted Mara as desperately as he ever had. The thought made his black eyes spark with contempt. The feeble excuses that had propelled him to the well-manicured cemetery on the hillside were already fading. It was an inexcusable mistake; he should never have come, never have broken into her privacy. But, still, he lingered, unable to take his eyes off of the attractive new widow.

The cold, gray morning was clouded in mist, giving the ceremony an eerie, uneasy quality, and the light dusting of dry snow that lightly covered the ground added to the ethereal feeling that captured Mara. A light breeze tossed the few remaining dry leaves into the air in frozen, swirling circles that spiraled heavenward.

Behind the flimsy protection of the black veil, Mara's cobalt-blue eyes stared down at the gravesite, unseeing. The usual sparkle that lighted her face was gone, replaced by a serious cloud that made her delicate features more tightly pinched than normal. Her skin was still flawless, and her high cheekbones were as regally sculpted as they ever had been, but there was a determined set to her jaw that stole the usual softness from her face. Unconsciously, she licked her arid lips and stared down at the brass casket with dry eyes. In one hand she clutched a single white rose to her black-draped breast, in the other, she clung firmly to the tiny fist of her dark-eyed daughter.

At the final words from the preacher, Mara dropped the snowy blossom onto the coffin and coaxed her reluctant child to do the same. The mourners began to disperse slowly, with only an occasional hoarse whisper of condolence cast in her direction. She smiled grimly behind the thin, black veil and nodded briefly at each of the sympathizers before making her way back to the black limousine that was idling quietly nearby.

Once inside the luxurious car, Angie looked at her mother in a childish imitation of concern. "Is Daddy gone forever, Mommy?"

"Yes, honey—I'm afraid so," Mara responded, and placed a comforting kiss on the child's forehead.

"Good!" Angie snorted.

Mara felt a dry tightness in her throat at the stinging words of her daughter, although the outburst wasn't totally unexpected. She closed her eyes and in a soft, consoling voice replied, "No, Angie, it's not good...why would you say such a thing?"

"Because it's true! Daddy don't like me!" The little girl crossed her chubby arms over her chest in an attitude that dared her mother to argue with her.

"No...oh, no...that's not the way it was, honey. Not at all. Daddy loved you very much."

The child puckered her lips before shooting Mara a knowing look. Mara swallowed with difficulty and bit nervously at her thumbnail. She wondered how she was going to stave off the inevitable argument that was brewing. How could she lie to her own daughter? Although only three years old, Angie had a keen sense of perception—so like her father's. Once again, Mara tried to reason with the child. "I know that Daddy...was a little...gruff with you at times, Angie. And, maybe, he was overly grouchy. But honey, you have to remember that Daddy was very, very sick. Sometimes...the things that he said, well, he just didn't mean them. You have to believe that Daddy loved you very much."

"Why?" Angie demanded, imperiously.

Mara hazarded a quick glance at the chauffeur, whose bland expression told nothing about his thoughts on the difficult conversation between mother and daughter. "Because...oh, honey, Daddy's gone. Can't you just forget the times that you and he quarreled?"

"No!"

"Look, Angie—" Mara's voice became a hushed whisper "—there are going to be a lot of people at the house this afternoon. Please promise Mommy that you'll be good."

"Who?"

"Who?" Mara echoed, confused for an instant. "Oh, you want to know who will be at the house today?" The impish child nodded, tossing her blond curls. "Let's see," Mara began, placing a comforting arm around her wayward daughter's small shoulders. "I know that Grammie and Aunt Dena will be there. Maybe cousin Sarah and…" Mara's voice trailed on tonelessly while she listed all of the relatives who would attend the intimate gathering of those closest to Peter. She was relieved that she had managed to change the course of the conversation with Angie, and fervently hoped that the little girl wouldn't bring up the touchy subject of her father for the remainder of the day.

As Mara thought about the afternoon ahead of her, she mentally groaned. It would be trying, at best. The thought of all of Peter's friends and relatives trying to console her made Mara's weary mind whirl. Couldn't they just leave her alone and let her deal with her grief quietly and in solitude? No matter what kind of a marriage she and Peter had shared, being a widow was a new and frightening experience. She needed time alone.

When she thought about widowhood, Mara felt her throat become dry. Although she was relieved that Peter's suffering was over, she felt guilty at the thought. It all seemed so senseless—the malignancy that had forced him into an early grave. Now, after all of the tears had been shed and the suffering had ended, she wondered uneasily if it had been her fault that the marriage had been foundering. Why was it that the only thing that had held Peter to her in the end was the devastating news of his terminal illness? Peter had been kind to her, at least in the beginning, and she couldn't forget that kindness, even if in other ways he had failed. She sighed despondently to herself. What was the use of dredging up old, unwanted memories? Poor Peter was gone, and if it hadn't been for him, what would have happened to her and Angie? Mara looked anxiously at her bright-eyed daughter sitting on the velvet gray upholstery of the long, black car. Angie's eyelids drooped, and the tangled mass of golden ringlets sprang out discordantly from beneath her tiny black hat. It was a shame to dress such a lively child in black, Mara thought, but after all, this was Peter's funeral, a time for mourning, and if Peter hadn't married Mara four years ago, what would she have done? Mara closed her eyes and pushed the nagging question aside. It wouldn't do to dwell on the past. Not today, not ever. How many times had she given herself that very same advice—always for the same reasons.

The driver eased the sleek ebony car through the twisted road of the graveyard, and the motorcade followed his lead. A long, flexible line of cars wound its way past the cemetery gates and down the hill toward Asheville and the Wilcox Estate that bordered the western North Carolinian city.

If Mara hadn't been so distracted with her daughter, perhaps she would have noticed the one mourner who stood slightly apart from the crowd. She had been too busy with Angie to realize that the tall man with the brooding black eyes followed her every move. Even now, as the large limousine made its way toward the city, the man waited and watched. His eyes, dark as obsidian, held a quiet flame in them, and although he tried desperately to deny the urges within him, he knew that he would find a way to get close to Mara again. He would see her again—if only for a short while, he vowed to himself. It had been four long, agonizing years, but Peter Wilcox's untimely death had ended Shane's tormented vigil. Unfortunate for Wilcox, but quite the opposite for Kennedy, Shane thought grimly. His speculations were ruthless, and he felt a slight twinge of conscience but ignored it. He reminded himself that Mara had it coming; nothing could alter that fact and the quiet anger of betrayal smoldering in his mind.

The burning picture of the suffering widow stayed with him and played dangerous games with his mind. The heavy black coat and gracious veil that Mara had worn couldn't hide her serene beauty from him. He could still visualize the slender curve of her calf, the bend of her knee, the swell of her breasts, and the perfection of her face. It was an image that had tormented his nights for over four years. He had been patient—a gentleman in all respects—but now the waiting was over. A slight gleam of satisfaction stole across his angled features.

Shane stood watching the procession of cars, mesmerized. The wind, promising still more snow for the Blue Ridge Mountains, ruffled his thick raven hair, but still he stared into the breeze, mindless of the chill, until the last vehicle passed over the crest in the road and was no longer in view. Damning himself for his own impetuous desires, he strode to his car. It would be better to wait, and he knew it, but there was an urgency to his movements. Once inside the silver Audi he turned the ignition key, and the sporty car roared to life. He paused for a moment, his hands poised over the steering wheel, and uttered a curse at his hesitation, which seemed, somehow, to be a sign of weakness. It was a mistake, but to hell with it, he had to see Mara again, face to face, and find out why she had deceived him four years ago. But it was the day of her husband's funeral, his conscience argued with him—anyone would need a little time to adjust. He ignored the thought, and muttering a low, self-derisive oath, he cranked the wheel of the car to follow the funeral procession.

The limousine carrying Mara and Angie headed up the slight incline toward the gracious Wilcox Manor. Small by genteel southern standards, it was nonetheless impressive and stately. The circular drive was long and guarded by ancient white oak trees. Though the onset of winter had left the giant oaks stripped of their once lush leaves, the tall trees added a royal dignity to the estate.

The house was a white clapboard structure which seemed larger than its two stories due to the knoll on which it stood. With a backdrop of pine trees and gently rolling hills, the clean white exterior of the manor seemed to reflect the pristine brightness of the new fallen snow. Teal-blue shuttered windows and a broad front porch of polished red brick enhanced the gracious, colonial house. The grounds, now blanketed with the new snow, were only a portion of the original, vast country estate. Most of the acreage that had been used for farming and timber had been parceled off to neighboring farms as the cost of machinery and taxes had escalated over the past few years.

Even in the severity of winter, rhododendrons and azaleas peeked through the mantel of dry white snow, exposing their still green leaves. Tufted grass pierced through the icy drifts to remind Mara of warmer days, and Mara's words vaporized in the air as she whispered to her child. It was a bitterly cold day, and yet, even in the dead of winter, the Wilcox estate held the easy Southern country charm of North Carolina and welcomed the grieving family and friends of Peter Wilcox.

Fortunately for Mara, Angie had fallen asleep in the car. Lovingly, Mara carried the child into the house and headed directly up the sweeping staircase that flanked the elegant, marble-tiled foyer. Polished oak and rosewood gleamed as she cuddled Angie more closely to her. On this day, as she had often in the past, Mara felt a deep melancholy which made her cherish her child as if Angie were the only child in the universe.

Although Peter's mother protested, Mara stood her ground and insisted that the tired child rest. Mara didn't want to chance another outburst from Angie about her late father, especially in front of the mourning guests. There was no need to add any further tension to the already gloomy and uneasy afternoon.

"Please explain to the others that I'll be upstairs with Angie for a few minutes," Mara pleaded with her mother-in-law.

June, usually agreeable, touched a nervous finger to the

collar of her tidy, black silk dress. "But don't you think that Angie should stay down here and..."

"No, I really don't," Mara interrupted, as kindly as possible, as she began to mount the ancient, curved staircase. "I'll be down later, as soon as I'm sure that Angie is comfortable." With her final statement, Mara continued up the stairs, carrying her limp child to the bedroom.

As Mara laid the girl on the bed, Angie's eyes blinked open for just a moment, and once again Mara was reminded of how much her eyes were like her father's. A hot pain seared her heart at the memory. Angie sighed deeply, her eyelids dropped reluctantly, and she snuggled contentedly into the blankets. Mara gently lifted the hat from Angie's head. Golden curls splayed in unruly ringlets around her face, and Mara thoughtfully brushed the blond hair away from Angie's cherublike cheeks. Despite her tension, Mara couldn't help but smile down on the sleeping child—her only physical link to the girl's father.

It took her nearly half an hour to descend the stairs and face the rest of the family, but Mara had taken time in preparing herself for the onslaught of condolences from bereaved family and friends. The funeral had been a draining ordeal, and Mara was beginning to feel the exhaustion of the day and the worry of the last six months wearing upon her. Her normally wholesome appearance paled, her color was washed away, and the skin over her high cheekbones was stretched tightly. Even the sparkle in her clear blue eyes had faded, and the smile, once quick and elegant, had seemed to disappear. The torment of Peter's illness had affected his wife deeply. No matter how difficult the marriage had been, Peter's painful death seemed brutal and senseless to Mara. So unfair! Now she wanted to be alone. She didn't have the strength to smile or speak to any of the guests, especially Peter's sister, Dena, whom she had been avoiding for the past few days. Dena had made it clear that she wanted to talk to Mara and discuss Peter's will, and Mara could feel the inevitable confrontation in the air. She only hoped that Dena would have the sense and common courtesy to bring up the subject another day, in more private surroundings.

As Mara descended the stairs she realized that some of the guests were already leaving. June was escorting a young man, whom Mara recognized as a business associate of Peter's, out of the broad front door when Mara joined her to smile politely at him and accept his condolences. Mara couldn't help but notice that June's nerves were tightly drawn and that the older woman's eyes, though dry, were slightly swollen and red rimmed. There was a dead look of weariness in her face and her normally full lips had pulled into a tight, thin line that was neither a smile nor a frown. June Wilcox was a very private person, but Mara knew how devastated the older lady was over her only son's death. Nervously, June fidgeted with the single strand of pearls at her throat.

The door closed as one of the last guests departed, and Mara and June were alone together for the first time that day. Mara gently touched her mother-in-law's frail shoulder. "Why don't you go upstairs and get some rest," she suggested. "It's been a long day."

"I'm fine," June insisted staunchly, dismissing Mara's advice with a wave of her finely boned hand.

Mara wasn't convinced. "No one will miss you. Most of the guests have already gone."

"I know, but…" June wavered for a moment and managed a stiff smile for Dr. Bernard, the family physician and old friend.

"You should take Mara's advice," the kindly old man stated authoritatively. "It's been difficult for you." His brown, knowing eyes traveled over the strained features on

June's face. "And don't be afraid to take any of those pills I prescribed if you feel that you need them."

"I won't," June agreed hastily, but the doctor raised a suspicious gray eyebrow as he shrugged into his raincoat.

"Good day," Dr. Bernard said with a wave of his broad hand, and once again Mara was alone with her mother-in-law.

"Pills?" Mara inquired.

"Oh, you know," June responded with a shake of her perfectly coifed gray hair. "Tranquilizers, or some such nonsense."

Mara pulled her eyebrows into a single line of concentration. "I didn't know you were on any medication."

"Don't be silly," June interrupted a little crossly. "It's not medication—not like you mean. They're just nerve pills. Doctor Bernard passes them out to half of the women in the county."

Mara was about to disagree but was forced to let the subject drop as several of the remaining guests filtered into the hall and extended their final condolences to the family. She acknowledged the sympathy before making her way as gracefully as was possible through the open doors and into the drawing room, where only a handful of guests remained. She spoke quietly to some of Peter's friends before they, too, excused themselves.

Fortunately, Angie, exhausted from the long ceremony earlier in the day, slept through most of the afternoon. By the time she did awaken, only the most immediate members of the Wilcox family were left in the house: Peter's mother, June, and his sister, Dena.

The argument was just beginning to boil when Angie, dragging her favorite tattered blanket behind her, crept unnoticed down the stairs.

"I don't even know what you're talking about, Dena,"

Mara was saying in a tight but controlled voice. "*What* man was here?"

"It was really nothing," June began, but was silenced by Dena's icy stare.

"Oh, so now you're pretending that you don't know him?" Peter's auburn-haired sister asked insolently.

"Don't know *whom?*" Mara repeated. Her slim hands were turned palms upward in a gesture of complete bewilderment.

"Look, Mara, if you think you can pull the wool over my eyes the way you have with the rest of the family, you're wrong. Wrong as hell!" Dena snapped, her green eyes glittering with an unspoken challenge.

"Dena!" June gasped. "Why must you be so crude?" she asked, before spotting a groggy Angie on the stairs. "Uh-oh...look who just woke up! Did you have a nice nap, precious?" June asked, turning all of her attention to her grandchild.

The blond girl rubbed her eyes with her small fists and then held out her arms expressively to her grandmother. June bent down and groaned slightly as she lifted the child into her arms. Mara wondered fleetingly to herself if her mother-in-law should overextend herself—Dr. Bernard had mentioned something about pills. But Mara's thoughts were interrupted as June smiled at Angie and continued talking to the girl as she carried the small, sleepy child out of the room. "Why don't you and I go outside for a while," she suggested, reaching for Angie's coat. "Mommy and Aunt Dee Dee have some...er, business to discuss."

Dena visibly cringed at the cutesy-pie name that Angie had bestowed upon her. After grandmother and child were safely out of earshot, on the opposite side of the French doors, Dena whirled back on Mara.

"I mean it, Mara!" Dena hissed. "I want to know all about that man!"

"Dena!" Mara's thin patience snapped and the tone of her voice chilled. "For the last time, *what* man?"

The redhead paused and let her clear green eyes reappraise Mara. Her full lips pursed and the finely plucked brows drew together thoughtfully. As if finally understanding that Mara knew nothing of the stranger, she began to explain in a decidedly calmer voice. "There was a man here today—a tall fellow. Good-looking, but unconventional, if you know what I mean. He asked to see you, practically insisted!" Green eyes watched Mara closely, as if gauging her reaction. "Mother refused to let him in because she didn't know him, and he declined to introduce himself— said his business was with only you! You were with Angie at the time. I thought that perhaps he might have been your attorney," she suggested.

"You know that I use the family attorney! Are you sure that he wasn't a business associate of Peter's? I certainly don't know anyone—"

Dena cut in. "Well, he acted as if he knew *you!* He became demanding, insisting to see you. When mother refused he stormed off in a huff. Now, are you sure you don't know him?" Dena inquired, arching her eyebrows suspiciously as she studied Mara's pensive face.

"I really couldn't hazard a guess," Mara said evenly, but a puzzled expression crowded her features. "Must have been a friend of Peter's," she mused, half to herself.

"I doubt that," Dena disputed and walked lazily over to a table laden with uneaten appetizers. She regarded Mara with feigned innocence as she popped a shrimp canapé into her mouth. "This man, he wouldn't fit in with Pete's usual crowd, if you know what I mean."

"That's just the point," Mara sighed. "I don't know what you mean. As a matter of fact, I really haven't understood anything that you've been saying, *or* implying," she admitted, and touched her suddenly throbbing temple. Any discussion with Dena seemed to always end in a headache.

"Well," Dena said, fingering several different hors d'oeuvres and stalling for theatrical effect. "This man, he was different." She thought for a moment and a smile curved her full lips. "A little rough around the edges…"

"Coarse?"

"Hmmm…no," Dena shook her deep-red curls, absorbed in thought. "Just, how can I explain it? Tougher, I suppose. He looked as if he knew what he wanted in life and wouldn't let anything or anyone get in his way!"

"Nice guy," Mara murmured sarcastically.

"I wouldn't know," Dena rejoined, and shrugged her slim shoulders, "but he was definitely more interesting than the usual crowd that Peter hung out with." She let a polished fingernail linger on her lips as if savoring a very pleasant thought.

Mara was tired of the game playing, and Dena's interest in the stranger didn't concern her. "It doesn't matter, Dena. I've no idea who that man was or is. If he wants to see me so badly, then he'll certainly be back. If not—who cares? Honestly, I don't see why he should upset you so much."

"He's not the reason I'm upset, and you know it!" Dena shot back at Mara, her pensive smile dropping from her face.

"The will?" Mara surmised, and Dena's spine seemed to stiffen slightly.

"I mean it, Mara," Dena threatened. "Peter may have inherited the bulk of the company shares from Daddy, but I still have some say in what goes on!"

"And I'll bet that you'll say plenty," Mara returned ruefully.

"You can count on it! Imagination Toys is as much a part of my life as it was Peter's. And if you think I'm going to sit idly by while you turn a profitable toy empire into a…a…"

"A tax loss?" Mara prompted. "As Peter was doing?"

"Peter was sick!"

"Yes…that he was," Mara agreed in a controlled and unwavering voice. "But not in the beginning, when profits first began to fall off."

"That's not the point!"

"Then what exactly is the point, Dena? I'm tired, and I want to spend some time with Angie. So why don't you get right to the crux of the problem?"

"Angie! Angie! It's always that kid with you, isn't it? I really wonder why you married Peter in the first place. Oh, yes, now I recall. You were pregnant, weren't you? But why in the world did you have to marry Peter, for God's sake? It's not as if Angie was his child!"

"That's enough!" Mara felt her cheeks begin to stain with unwanted color at Dena's cruel supposition. "Let's leave Angie, and for that matter, Peter, out of this argument. I'm going to take a few days off—maybe even a week or two. I'm not really sure. But I'm going to spend that time alone with my daughter!" Mara's voice was stretched as tightly as a piano wire, but she tried to keep her rising temper under control. "It's been a long, hard day, and we've both said some things that we shouldn't have. When I get back to the office, you and I will talk about the company. We'll settle our differences then."

"And who will run the company while you're off vacationing with the kid?" was the insolent inquiry.

"Don't worry about it. It's all been decided. John Hammel is perfectly capable…"

"The accountant?" Dena was incredulous, but Mara firmly stood her ground.

"That's right."

Dena's eyes flashed emerald fire, but she let the words that were forming in the back of her throat die. She could see that it was of no use to try and talk to Mara now. Dena knew her sister-in-law well enough to realize that the determined line of Mara's jaw meant business, and she had to content herself with the fact that her barb concerning Angie's questionable paternity had wounded Mara. Dena smiled slightly at the thought. "All right, Mara, I'll wait until you get back. But if you step on my toes, you had better believe that I'll call my lawyer in an instant and contest Pete's will!" She snapped her long fingers to add emphasis to her warning.

"Oh, Dena," Mara sighed, suddenly weary. "Does it always have to be this way between us? Are you really threatening me?" Mara's large blue eyes looked beseechingly up at Dena's triumphant smile.

"Don't think of it as a threat, *dear*," Dena suggested with a voice that dripped venom and a self-satisfied smile lighting the green depths of her eyes. "Consider it a promise!" With her final words, Dena didn't wait for Mara's response. The redhead whirled on her high leather heels and clicked out of the room, following the path whereby the grandmother had escaped earlier with her grandchild.

As the porch doors banged shut, rattling the glass panes, Mara felt herself slump into the nearest chair. How was she going to cope with the Wilcox family? What could she possibly do about June's failing health and Dena's imperious demands? It was difficult enough making the adjustment into widowhood and single parenting, but to make matters worse, she had to fight Dena tooth and nail on every topic concerning the toy company. It crossed her mind that perhaps Mara should give in to Peter's older sister's demands. Then if Imagination continued to lose money, Dena would have no one to blame but herself. Maybe the best thing for all concerned would be for Mara to pack up Angie and leave her in-laws to squabble among themselves. But she wouldn't do it—couldn't. Too many other people depended upon her strength for her to just give up. Peter's mother, June, had been especially kind to her. And Mara was a fighter. It went against everything she believed in to give up without exhausting all possible alternatives. There had to be a reasonable solution to the problem with Dena.

The fatigue that had begun to creep up her spine finally overcame her and she shuddered. The last six months of watching Peter slowly wither away had been excruciating, and for the first time since his death Mara gave in to the bitter tears of exhaustion that burned at the back of her eyes.

The drive back to Atlanta was a blur in Shane's memory. So lost in thought was he that he didn't even notice when the sharp mountains melted into the plains and low hills of western Georgia. He was angry with himself for trying to see Mara and even angrier at the sophisticated gray-haired woman who had refused his admittance. It had crossed his mind to ignore the protests of the older woman and push past her to find Mara, but his common sense and decency had changed his mind. His timing was all wrong, along with everything else he had done since he had read Peter Wilcox's obituary two days earlier.

He would bide his time, at least for the present. He knew that he had to see Mara again, and soon, and he damned himself for his weakness. But certainly with a little imagination he would be able to find a way to get close to her...for just a little while.

Chapter Two

A week in the Florida sun had brightened Mara's disposition and outlook on life. She and Angie had spent the time playing on the beach, making sand castles and hunting for treasures cast upon the white sand by the relentless tide. They played keep-away from the waves and watched as tourists, dressed in gaudy colors, lapped up the sun's warm golden rays. It was a wonderful time for mother and daughter to become reacquainted, without the shroud of Peter's illness cloaking them in its black folds.

The sun had tanned their skins, and Mara looked robust and healthy once again. A sparkle had returned to her cornflower-blue eyes, and two rosy points of color enhanced the natural arch of her cheekbones. Angie's hair had bleached to a lighter hue, which seemed to imitate the long, golden tendrils of her mother, the brighter shade deepening the color of her near-black eyes. The little girl seemed healthy and happy, and it was with more than a trace of hesitation and dread that Mara returned home, back to the ancient clapboard-and-brick house that she and Peter had shared, and back to the offices over the manufacturing plant of Imagination Toys, located in the heart of the industrial section of Asheville.

Months had passed since the funeral, and the mountains surrounding Asheville had warmed with the summer sun. The white oak trees lining the drive displayed their lush, green leaves, and the air was laden with the scent of pine. Already the large dogwood tree in the backyard had lost its petals, and only a few remaining flaming azaleas and purple rhododendron blossoms lingered on the branches.

Summer had come, and for the first time in several years Mara felt free. Free from the disease that had ravaged Peter but had bound her to him, and free from the hypocrisy of a loveless marriage. The days were long and warm. Although Mara spent many hours working at the office, she always managed to put aside a special time of the day to spend alone with Angie. During the day, while Mara was working, Peter's mother, June, watched carefully over her three-year-old granddaughter, but in the late afternoon and evenings, when the soft breeze of twilight whispered through the pine boughs, Mara and Angie were inseparable. It was this time of day that Mara found the most precious. She loved being with her curly-haired, slightly precocious daughter and found Angie's bright smile and eager young mind a continued source of contentment. And Angie, for her part, seemed to thrive on the love she received from her mother and grandmother.

Mara's days at the plant were more difficult than her quiet evenings at home. There was an almost unbearable undercurrent of tension between Mara and her sister-in-law. After returning from her vacation, Mara had agreed to let Dena run the advertising department. Mara had hoped that the added responsibility would satisfy the fiery Dena. She reasoned that if she gave Dena a fair chance to show her talents, perhaps Dena would work harder and pull with Mara instead of always against her. In the beginning Dena had seemed content, but as time passed she began getting bored with the job, realizing that it was little more than an empty title—a placebo to satisfy her ego. All of the major decisions concerning Imagination Toys were still handled by Mara, the job she had taken over slowly, as Peter's illness had forced him into inactivity.

Also, despite Mara's efforts to the contrary, the company was still losing money. Several larger corporations had expressed interest in buying out the controlling interest in Imagination, but Mara had steadfastly refused their offers. The last thing she would allow to happen was to prove Dena correct and be forced to sell the family business. The toy company had been started by Peter's great-grandfather, and each successive generation of Wilcox family members had lived comfortably from the profits. That was, until the company had begun losing money under Peter's mismanagement. Now the recession was complicating the problem, but no matter what, Mara wouldn't let the company fail, or so she promised herself.

One larger corporation based in Atlanta, Delta Electronics, was persistent in offering to buy out Imagination. Mara had never spoken to the owners directly, but each week she had received several inquiries from Delta's attorneys. Just last week Mara had spoken to Mr. Henderson, counselor for Delta, and hoped that he had understood her position about the sale—that there would be none. Henderson wasn't easily put off—in fact, he was persistent to the point of being bothersome—but this week was the first in several that Mara hadn't opened a formal-looking envelope from Atlanta. Mara congratulated herself; it seemed as if Mr. Henderson had finally gotten the message.

She stretched in the chair. It was late Friday afternoon

and shadows had begun to lengthen across her tiny office. As she sat at her desk she cast a glance out the large window and at the sun lowering itself behind the wall of Appalachian mountains. Long, lavender shadows climbed over the colonial and modern rooftops of downtown Asheville. The familiar view of the skyline and the charcoal-blue mountains shrouded in wispy clouds was calming after what had been another hectic week at the office. Her eyes moved from the window to the interior of her office. She smiled lazily to herself and ignored the small pile of paperwork that sat unfinished on her desk. Slowly she let her hands reach behind her neck and lift the weight of her tawny hair from her shoulders. Still holding her hair away from her neck, she slowly rotated her head, hoping to relieve some of the tightness from her back and shoulders. It had been a long, tiring day, punctuated by arguments with Dena, but it would soon be over. The antique wooden clock on the wall indicated that it was nearly six o'clock, and Mara looked forward to going home and spending a long, quiet evening alone with Angie.

Mara let her eyes drop from the face of the clock to roam across the interior of the office. Although she was now legally president and general manager of Imagination Toys, the tiny room was somewhat austere. She had allowed it to be cut down in size from the immense room that it had been while Peter ran the company. The plant needed more work space and less administrative office, she had determined, and therefore allowed the room to be divided into workable office space. The same room that had housed only Peter before was now able to provide a work area for a secretary and two salespeople, and still allow Mara room to move. The only luxury that she insisted upon was that she keep the large window with the view of the mountains she loved.

Mara would have liked to have refurbished the office, but that was one extravagance that would have to wait, along with a list of more important and necessary items. As it was, the budget couldn't be stretched to cover the new three-needled sewing machines that were needed for the dolls, nor would it allow for a new shipment of higher grade plastic for colored building blocks...or fabric, or an upgraded puzzle saw—the list seemed to be endless. At the very bottom was interior design for Mara's office.

The velvety tones of her secretary's voice on the intercom scattered her thoughts. "Mrs. Wilcox?"

"Yes?" Mara inquired automatically, not letting her eyes waver from their silent appraisal of the office.

"There's a gentleman to see you... A Mr. Kennedy."

"But I don't have any appointments this afternoon." Mara began, before the weight of Lynda's surprise announcement settled upon her. In a voice that was barely audible, Mara spoke into the transmitter, her attention drawn to the little black box on the corner of her desk. "What did you say the gentleman's name was...Kennedy?" Mara's mind began to whirl backward in time. She sucked in her breath and then chided herself for her breathless anticipation. After four years of living with the truth, why did she still feel a rush of excitement run through her veins at the memory of Shane? A dryness settled in her throat.

Mara could hear a confused whisper of conversation coming from the other end of the intercom. Then Lynda's voice once again. "I'm sorry, Mrs. Wilcox, but Mr. Kennedy insists that he has an appointment with you. He's with...just a minute...Delta Electronics."

Kennedy...Kennedy...Kennedy, the name repeated itself in Mara's mind. It had been so long since she had allowed herself to remember Shane—his dark eyes, the deep resonate timbre of his laughter, the warmth of his touch...

"Mrs. Wilcox?" Lynda asked uneasily through the intercom. "He says it's urgent that he speak with you..." Lynda was becoming unnerved by Mara's hesitation and Mr. Kennedy's persistence. "Mrs. Wilcox?"

Mara tried to quiet her suddenly hammering heart and gather the air that had escaped from her lungs in a gust at the memory of Shane. "Delta Electronics?" Mara repeated. She didn't bother to mask the interest in her voice.

"That's correct," Lynda agreed quickly, relieved to hear the usual ring of authority back in Mara's voice.

"I've already responded to Delta's law office. Mr. Henderson understands exactly how I feel, but if it would make Mr. Kennedy feel any better, I'll be glad to see him. Please show him into my office." Mara's fine, dark, honey-colored brows drew together in concentration. Why was this Kennedy so insistent—hadn't Henderson conveyed her message properly? She tapped her fingernails nervously on her desk and then straightened the collar of her blouse.

The knowledge that one of the representatives for Delta Electronics was named Kennedy had shaken her poise. Not that Kennedy was an uncommon name, by any means. Yet each time she heard it, she became distracted by vivid visions of the past and long-dead emotions would try to recapture her.

Not knowing the reasons for her actions, Mara let her fingers sweep all traces of her personal life from her desk: the family portrait of Mara and Angie, a Lucite cube with snapshots of Angie as a baby, and a few scraps of construction paper that were Angie's first unsteady attempts at art. As Mara's nerves tightened, she pushed all the mementos of her life into her desk drawer and turned the lock, thinking at the time that her actions bordered on paranoia, all because of a common surname.

Satisfied that no tangible evidence of Angie was visible, she placed a friendly, though slightly strained, smile on her lips. She stood up to meet the man who had already shaken

her poise and felt a queasy uneasiness in the pit of her
stomach.

The door swung open and Mara managed to stifle the
scream that threatened to erupt from her throat. Her eyes
widened in disbelief, and she clasped an unsteady hand to
her breast as her knees began to give way.

"Oh, God," she whispered hoarsely. "Oh, dear God…"

She found it impossible to breathe as Shane Kennedy, the
man she thought dead, entered the room. In an instant, four
years of Mara's life dissolved into thin air. Her heart began
to clamor unreasonably in the confines of her rib cage, and
she knew that she desperately needed some fresh air. Her
eyelids fluttered closed for a woozy instant. Was it really
Shane, or merely a mirage that her willing mind had created—a trap of her subconscious? Her legs were still rub-
bery, and she braced herself on the edge of the desk, letting
the strong mahogany support her weight. Her face blanched
with the shock of seeing him again, and though she tried
heroically to pick up the pieces of her poise, she found it
impossible. Her fingers dug into the polished veneer of the
desk and her vision became distorted with tears that had
been hidden away for four years.

Time hadn't been particularly kind to him. Although his
strong masculine looks were still intact, he seemed hardened
and weathered. A touch of gray lightened his otherwise jet-
black hair, and there were deep lines of strain running across
his forehead. Though dressed impeccably in a lightweight
jute-colored business suit, the tanned texture of his skin suggested that he spent much of his time outdoors. His face
was angular, as it had always been, but it seemed more
proudly arrogant than she remembered. In that one breathless instant, when their eyes met, all time seemed to have
stopped. And though he didn't smile, a quiet surge of recognition and remembrance lighted his eyes. Mara swallowed
with difficulty and tried to quiet her thundering heart, hop-

ing to God that when he extended his hand to hers, he wouldn't notice that her palms were damp.

"Dear God, Shane," she murmured. "Is it really you?"

"Mara," he began, walking more closely to her desk. The voice was the same deep-timbred tone that had haunted her nights. "It's been a long time—too long!" He reached for her outstretched hand and closed his over it warmly. Mara felt as if she might faint. She looked into his eyes. They were as black as she remembered, but different, somehow, as if they had witnessed sights that no man should see. In their ebony depths she visualized pain and agony.

"Shane?" Mara whispered, weakly, and her voice cracked with the dry emotion of four dead years. "But...your father told me...I thought that..."

"You thought that I was dead," he finished for her, and his voice held no hint of emotion.

Her face became ghostly white from the shock of seeing him, and her weak knees gave way. Pulling her fingers from the strength of his grasp, she braced herself on the desk and lowered herself onto the chair. Shaking her head in disbelief, she lifted her face to meet the power of his gaze. Dresden eyes reached out for his. She wanted to run to him, to let him fold her into the security of his strong arms. She longed to touch every inch of him, to let her trembling fingers confirm what her eyes were seeing—that he was alive and not just a part of a distant memory. She felt compelled to tell him her most intimate secret and cry the tears of yesterday. But she couldn't. Her voice remained still as the severity of his gaze held her pinioned silently to her seat.

Mara let her head rest heavily on the palm of her hand, and her golden blond hair fell over one shoulder as she tried to calm herself and deal with the fact that he was here, with her, after all of this time. Shane was alive! She looked up at him again, letting her eyes travel upward to meet his.

Tears that had been pooling in her large eyes began to run unchecked down her cheeks.

An ache, deep and primitive, spread through Shane. What was it about Mara that made him want to cup her chin in his hand and whisper promises to her that he couldn't possibly keep? Why, still, did he feel an urge to protect her, even though she had wounded him once before?

"I didn't mean to startle you, Mara. As a matter of fact, I would have preferred that my attorney handle this entire affair," he said, knowing his words to be false. He avoided her probing gaze and straightened the cuff of his sleeve. A knife twisted in her heart as she realized that he hadn't even wanted to see her. He had only come because his attorney had been ineffective. "But you proved just as stubborn as I remembered," Shane continued. Then a quiet cough caught his attention, and he remembered the receptionist who had led him into Mara's office. The girl's face burned with embarrassment over witnessing the unusual and intimate reunion between the stranger and her employer.

Shane's chilling statement indicating that he would rather not have seen Mara personally helped her find a portion of her shattered composure. She managed to dismiss the receptionist, to the girl's obvious relief. "Thank you, Lynda, that will be all." Lynda nodded curtly and hurriedly left the room, carefully closing the door behind her.

Mara closed her eyes for a moment and tried to get a grip on her tattered emotions. He was here, after four long years. He'd been alive all the time, her mind reminded her, and a cool sense of betrayal mocked her. Where had he been these past four years? What had he done? Why had his father lied to her? And why had he supported that lie by not returning to her as he had promised? Why would he let her believe him dead, only to resurrect himself now?

The air in the small room was charged with electricity, and the unanswered questions loomed between them like an invisible barrier. For several seconds there was a heavy, uneasy silence, as if the questions about the past were insurmountable.

"Why?" she finally asked him, and somehow found the resolve to look directly into his frigid dark eyes. "Why did you let me think that you were dead...all of these years...all of these years?" her voice became a hoarse whisper. There was disbelief and anguish in her question, and she felt the strain of unwanted tears once again filling her eyes. Unashamed, she brushed the tears aside.

Her poignant question and tortured expression were too much for Shane to bear. Knowing it to be a mistake, he stalked over to the desk and leaned across it to bring his face only inches from hers. Without hesitation, he let his finger touch the curve of her cheek and cradled her delicate chin in his hand. She felt herself tremble at his familiar touch, and a tear slid down her cheek. His eyes were dark, cloudy, but when she looked more closely, she could swear that she noticed a tenderness and a yearning hidden in the ebony depths of his gaze. As he whispered her name, letting the warmth of his breath touch her face, she thought she could melt into him. "Mara...there's so much to say...so many questions that have to be answered"—a confused look stole across his features—"but I don't think that this is the right time, nor the right place. You and I...we need time, alone together, to sort things out."

His words were soothing to her raw nerves, and his caress was encitingly familiar. She closed her eyes, tender memories returning in full force.

As the words came out of his mouth Shane mentally cursed himself. He should never have come back again. Never! But as the months had passed he had found it more difficult day by day to stay away from her. And so he had come, with the flimsy excuse of purchasing her toy company for bait. He had come back, and now he found himself caught in the web of her charms once again. Even now she was so innocently alluring, so sensitive, so perfect. His hand slid easily against the silken texture of her neck. His thumb found the erratic pulse in the hollow of her throat and lingered, and with his free hand he pushed aside the golden curtain of her hair that had partially hidden her face. Although he paused long enough to look into her eyes, Mara knew that he wanted to kiss her, and the knowledge warmed her. Perhaps the last four years weren't wasted. Her pulse began to quicken, and when his eager lips found hers, she felt a ripple of desire shake her entire body. His lips, warm and inviting, seemed to touch her soul and set her body on fire, just as they had always done. She knew that he wanted her still, even after hiding for the last four years.

When he dragged his lips from hers, disappointment shadowed her features, but as her blue eyes found his she recognized a raw and naked passion smoldering in his gaze. And there was something else, an incredible anger—deep and ugly.

"Why are you here?" she asked. Her senses were dazed, numbed by his touch, but she had to understand the resentment and wariness that seemed to control him.

"I wish I knew," he answered quickly. And then, as if denying the naked truth in his voice, he suddenly stood up and tugged at the hem of his suit coat. "Didn't my attorney get in touch with you? I thought that he had made my position clear. I want to buy Imagination Toys!" The intimacy of the moment before was shattered.

"You?"

"Let me rephrase that; Delta Electronics is interested in your company." His voice was still husky with passion, and as if to cool the intensity of the moment, he walked over to the window and stared at the mountains. One of his hands was plunged deeply into his pants pocket, pulling the expensive weave of his tailored suit away from his body. As the coat stretched backward his shirt tightened against his flat, taut stomach. Even though he was fully dressed, Mara was reminded of his slim, well-muscled build. Four years hadn't changed the masculine strength of his physique, nor the stirrings in her own body at the sight of him.

"And you own Delta Electronics?" Mara guessed, trying to keep her mind on the conversation while her thirsty eyes drank in every inch of him.

A curt nod was the only response as Shane continued to stare at the distant mountains. When Mara didn't immediately continue her questions, he paced back to the desk. His austere gaze prompted her.

"Oh, Shane," she murmured, but his face remained tense. She swallowed with difficulty, and said, with as much professional aplomb as possible, "I'm sorry. But as I told your counsel, Mr. Henderson, the company is not for sale." She tried to quell the anger that was beginning to boil within her. Anger that he had left her, anger that he had come back into her life without so much as an explanation or an apology, anger that the only thing he wanted from her was the Wilcox family business, and anger with herself for still loving him. She had dreamed about him, relived the violent nightmare of his death, but never had she realized how desperately she still loved him...a love that was just as it had always been—unreturned. And now the cold betrayal. He had left her without so much as a second glance, until now, when he wanted something.

"Isn't the price high enough?" he asked, breaking into her thoughts.

She shook her blond head and lowered her gaze to meet his directly. "It has nothing to do with money. The company is not for sale. Period! Now, if there's nothing more..." She left the sentence dangling between them and without words invited him to leave. Her throat tightened at the thought that he would walk away from her, but she knew she had no choice, she was much too vulnerable to him. And, after all, what he wanted from her was business—pure and simple. She needed time to think things out and get her tangled thoughts in order. As much as she feared being separated from him, she knew it was the wisest course of action. She had to find the courage to tell him those things that he would need to know, now that she knew that he was alive.

His dark eyes narrowed, he rubbed the back of his neck thoughtfully, and he paced restlessly before her. "You'd like that, wouldn't you?"

"Like what?" she asked, perplexed.

"You'd like to be able to just turn me down and send me packing," he accused. "Well, it won't work." A smile tugged at the corner of his mouth. "I want this company, and I intend to have it!"

"Just like that?"

"Just like that!"

"But I'm not selling...remember?" Mara's temper was barely under control. "I don't see how you think you'll be able to persuade me to change my mind!" Despite her strong words, she felt herself beginning to tremble.

"Maybe I won't have to," Shane mused, pulling thoughtfully on his lower lip. "As I understand it, you didn't inherit all of the stock of the company. You don't even have controlling interest. Perhaps some of the other members of the Wilcox family would be interested in my proposition..." he suggested.

A picture of a triumphant Dena entered Mara's mind. Unconsciously she pursed her full lips, and her eyes held steadily to Shane's. "Am I to assume that you're threatening me?" she asked in a voice that she hoped showed no strain of emotion. His dark head cocked with interest. "I really don't know what it is that you expect of me," she accused, tossing up her hands in exasperation. "First, you come marching in here, right from the grave, I might add, and nearly shock me to death. And, secondly, you try to intimidate me into selling something to you that is definitely *not* for sale! I don't know how I can make my position any more clear! The company is not for sale.'' Her eyes had turned to chips of blue ice. ''I'm sorry if my response disappoints you!''

Shane laughed, and the familiar sound destroyed all of Mara's resolve. ''You haven't disappointed me, Mara. I thought that maybe you had changed, but I was wrong. Thank God!'' The severity of his gaze eroded, and for the first time that afternoon Mara saw kindness in his eyes— the kindness that she remembered.

He reached for her hand and held it lightly in his. ''It's good to see you again,'' he whispered honestly.

''But Shane...why?'' She tried to ignore the tingling of her fingertips where they touched his. ''Why?''

''Shh...'' He placed a sensitive finger over her lips to quiet the questions that were uppermost on her mind. ''Have you had dinner yet?'' Shane asked, still holding her fingers.

''At six o'clock in my office?'' Mara inquired, feeling the tension begin to leave her body. ''Not hardly.''

''Then let's have it together.''

''Now?''

''This evening.''

Mara began to shake her head. Everything was happening too quickly and she was beginning to feel claustrophobic, caught in the same emotions that had trapped her four years ago. He was pushing, and she needed time to think. It was too easy to fall under his magic all over again. She ached to fall into the seduction of his onyx eyes, but she couldn't allow it. It was too late.

''Why not?'' he asked smoothly. Too smoothly.

''I...I have plans tonight.'' It wasn't a lie. There was Angie to consider. Shane's hot hand closed more firmly over hers, and she felt as if she were beginning to melt. "And," she withdrew her hand shakily, "I don't think that it would be a very good idea…"

"Why not?" he interjected. His dark eyes deepened as they found the blue of hers.

"You sound like a broken record…"

"Well?"

"I'm…really…very busy," Mara stammered, and knew in an instant that it sounded very much like the lie it was.

"Trying to maintain the image of the suffering widow?" Mara's back stiffened, but a crooked smile slashed wickedly across Shane's tanned face. For a moment, Mara could see him as she remembered: younger, softer, and…warmer. That was it. Even when he grinned, she could sense a brooding coldness lying under the surface of his smile.

Unconsciously, Mara rubbed the warm spot in her palm that could still feel his touch. "It has nothing to do with images," she retorted. "I really am swamped."

"Oh?" his dark eyes moved over the top of her desk, which was barren except for a few shipping invoices.

"Yes," she replied hastily, feeling a compulsion to explain. "We're a little late with some of our shipments…"

"I know that!"

Mara's eyes met his in a clash of black and blue. Just how much did he know? She continued, a little breathlessly, "Then, of course, you understand that I've got a million and one things to do."

"Name one," he suggested laconically, and dropped himself into a chair opposite the desk. He propped his chin up with his folded hands and a slight glint of amusement touched his eyes.

Mara breathed deeply and wondered fleetingly why she was even participating in this absurd conversation. "Well, for one thing," she began, slightly goaded but refusing to back down on her lie, "it's almost the end of August, our busiest season. I've got Christmas orders that will have to be shipped, and very soon.''

"Isn't that what the shipping department is for?'' he suggested wryly.

"Everyone pitches in!''

"Including the president?'' A black eyebrow cocked suspiciously.

"Including the president!'' Mara's eyes snapped for an instant before she erected the cool facade on her face that suggested total authority. She straightened her shoulders and unconsciously inched the defiant tilt of her chin upward.

"Is that the way Peter ran the company?'' Before Mara could think of a suitable response, Shane continued. "And just how is it going?''

"How is what going?'' she asked, trying to keep up with his twists in the conversation. The scent of familiar cologne wafted toward her, tantalizing her. Pleasant memories came thundering back, unwanted.

"The business! Now that dear old Peter is gone—by the way, my condolences—how is the business managing?'' His tone was sarcastic, and once again angry fires blazed in his ebony gaze.

"Just fine!'' she lied again. Why did she feel that she had to lie to him, to defend her position? The thought continued to nag at her and she vainly tried to push it aside.

"Is that so?'' He looked at her skeptically as if to say "convince me.''

"Of course it is!'' Mara emphasized, a trifle irritably. Just who did he think he was, waltzing into the office without an appointment, shocking the living daylights out of her, dredging up old memories, and making her feel a burning need to explain her life to him? Shane's eyes dropped to her hands, and she realized that she was twisting the wedding ring that she still wore on her right hand. Scarlet crept

up her neck as she let her fingers drop beneath the desk top
and out of his line of vision. Once again, his gaze hardened.

"Well, then, if everything is going so smoothly, there's
no reason that you can't have dinner with me, is there?"

Trapped! He had tricked her, and they both knew it. She
had let him corner her all too easily. Mara breathed more
deeply and tried once again to dissuade him. Her most win-
ning smile neatly in place, she responded. "Look, Shane,
just because the company is doing well doesn't mean that
there isn't any work to be done. Quite the contrary. The
busier the toy company is, the busier I am." She stretched
her palms upward in a gesture that said more clearly than
words, "any fool can understand that simple logic." "Besides which, I told you that I'm busy tonight."

"And you can't fit me into your busy schedule?"

"Exactly."

Shane's eyes seemed to darken to the color of midnight.
"Then I take it you're not interested in my proposition?"

Mara pushed her hair away from her face and looked
away for a minute. What did he mean? "Proposition?" she
repeated. "What proposition? I already told you that the
company is not for sale!" She tried to keep the interest in
her voice at a minimum. She could sense that he had another
offer, and she hadn't spent the last three years learning the
business from the ground up to blow it at this point. Perhaps
he was willing to invest some capital in the company, for a
minority interest. In any event, she had to find out what his
proposition was. Obviously, Shane Kennedy wanted something from her, and very badly. Her heart stopped at the
thought that perhaps he wanted her, but she quickly ban-
ished the traitorous idea. She wasn't a fool, and she realized
that he hadn't waited four years to pick up what he had
once thrown away so ruthlessly. No, this was only business,
she reminded herself, but a part of her longed for more. She

would have to try and maintain her cool disinterest until she heard all of the facts.

In answer to her question he replied, "The proposition that I'm going to make to you over dinner." His voice had deepened an octave, and Mara had to stifle an urge to let herself remember a younger time when they had shared a smile, a kiss, a caress...

"I thought the question of dinner was settled," she heard herself retort.

"Not until you agree to have it with me."

Mara was becoming exasperated. Even though the man seated across from her was devastating her senses, she knew that she had enough complications in her life at the moment and that she didn't need to add Shane Kennedy to the list. It was he who had left her. Mara knew herself well, and she realized that she was still just as vulnerable as the day that they had said their farewells. Four years hadn't muted her senses or her imagination; her racing pulse gave witness to that fact. Several years may have come and gone, but no man had ever touched her the way that Shane Kennedy had. No man, including Peter. Mara turned crimson at the thought, feeling guilty and apprehensive. Why was Shane back? Did he know about Angie? The thought frightened her. Why did she feel that there was more than just his interest in the toy business that had prompted Shane to return to Asheville—and to the mountains where they had first made love?

As she looked pensively over to the man that had once been her closest friend and most intimate lover, she wondered if he could read her thoughts. Could he ever realize just how desperately she had loved him and how many nights she had found herself dreaming of him? Ever since Peter's death, Shane's image had become more clearly defined on her tired mind. Unconsciously, she wetted her suddenly dry lips with the tip of her tongue.

Shane maintained his composure, though Mara's unintentional provocation had bothered him. A thin smile played over his lips as he rose from the chair and took her hand in his. "Please have dinner with me, Mara," he whispered, and at the moment he breathed her name, she knew it was useless to argue. More than anything in the world at this moment, Mrs. Mara Jane Stevens Wilcox, recently widowed wife of Peter Wilcox, wanted to spend time with the only man she had ever truly loved: the father of her child.

"All right, Shane," she agreed, with the first sincere smile of the day. "I'd love to have dinner with you...and to listen to your proposal."

"Proposition," he corrected with a mirthless smile, and Mara found herself wondering if she had made a bitter mistake. *He's changed,* she decided. *He's changed very much.*

Chapter Three

The meeting with Shane had left Mara drained and bewildered. As she watched him leave her office she sat motionless; her eyes following the strong, swift strides of his straight-backed exit. He didn't turn around.

A part of Mara, still young and incurably romantic, urged her to run after him and hold onto him for fear that he would once again vanish in the night and this time be gone forever. She wanted and needed to throw her arms around him and cradle his head close to her breast. She could almost feel the pounding of his heartbeat echoing against hers.

She wanted to cry out *"I had your daughter—I couldn't give her up, she was my only link to you. I loved you; God, Shane, but I loved you and I love you still!"* But she remained at her desk, silent. Restraint and common sense held her tongue. His name, which had been forming in her throat, died before reaching her lips, and she watched quietly as the door closed behind him. He was gone.

Mara reached for the wheat-colored linen jacket that was draped over the back of her chair and paused for one last calming look through the window to the mountains. Dusk was painting a purple shadow against the gentle hills, and the line of the distant horizon was melting into darkness with the coming nightfall. As her fingers rubbed idly against the cool windowsill, Mara tried to think rationally about Shane and the past. An increasing anger burned quietly within her as the shock of seeing him ebbed and she came face to face with the fact that for four long years he had allowed himself to hide from her—hidden in a feigned death. Why? Her thoughts nagged her, and she idly rubbed her temple in concentration. *Why,* after all of those tender and loving months together, would he suddenly reject her and conceal himself in the lie of his death? Her thoughts were ragged and scattered, but no matter how much she tried to ignore the obvious, it remained as the only possible solution. Four years ago Shane hadn't wanted her. Had he found out about her pregnancy? Was the love she imagined that they had shared together only a simple girlish dream, dashed when he had somehow learned of her pregnancy?

Her honey-colored brows knit together in concentration as she tried to remember the past. The memory was elusive, kept in the corner of her mind that she had tried to ignore for years.

"Working late?" A cool female voice broke into Mara's thoughts, and she visibly shrank from the sound.

Recovering herself, she turned to face her sister-in-law, who was leaning casually in the doorway. Mara glanced quickly at the clock, and then back to Dena. "What are you doing here? It's after six!"

"Dedication to the job?" Dena asked coyly, and laughed at her own sarcastic sense of humor. Mara could feel the cold tightness of apprehension. There was a long, tense pause as her gaze locked with Dena's.

"Was there any reason in particular that you wanted to see me?" Mara asked while she fished in her purse for her keys.

"I thought that you wanted to go over the advertising budget," Dena explained.

"Oh, that's right!" Mara agreed, and shook her head as if to clear out the cobwebs. "I'm sorry, Dena. I forgot all about it."

"Your mind on other things?" Dena suggested, with a twisted smile curving her full, glossy lips and one gracious eyebrow cocked.

"I guess so..." Mara replied evasively as she walked back to her desk, flipped open her appointment book, and scribbled a note on one of the blank sheets. "There!" she said with finality. "I've jotted a reminder to myself to meet with you early Monday morning." Mara looked up from the desk and gave Dena a warm, ingratiating smile. She hoped that Dena would take the hint and leave, but she was mistaken.

The redhead remained in the doorway. It was obvious that something was on her mind.

"Isn't Monday all right with you?" Mara asked, and crossed to the front of the desk.

"Monday's fine," Dena agreed with an indifferent shrug.

"Good!" Mara exclaimed with more enthusiasm than she felt. "Then...I'd better be going. I'm late as it is. Was there anything else?"

"Not really," Dena returned while seeming to be distracted by a flaw in her cuticle. When she looked up from her fingernail, she smiled. "Who was the man that came to see you this afternoon?"

Mara wasn't surprised that Dena knew about Shane. No doubt Lynda, the receptionist, had mentioned the unusual reunion to Dena.

"Have you been lurking around here for the past forty

minutes just to find out about Shane?'' The thought amused Mara, and she couldn't hide the twinkle in her eyes.

"He's the same man that came to the house on the day of Peter's funeral," Dena announced, and let her eyes watch Mara's reaction. It was Dena's turn to be amused as she noticed the color draining from Mara's face and the look of surprise that was reflected in the cool, blue depths of her eyes.

"Shane? He was the stranger?"

"If Shane is the name of the man who came to see you this afternoon, then none other. I don't suppose that he told you about his confrontation with Mother?" Mara had difficulty in finding words, but Dena read her face. "I didn't think so," she said aloud, obviously pleased with herself.

"You know him?" Mara asked, still sifting through the information that Dena had given her. Shane had been to see her on the day of the funeral? Why? Surely not with his business proposal. He wouldn't bother the grieving family just for the sake of business—or would he? She couldn't help but remember the frigid look of Shane's black eyes. And, realistically, why else would he try and reach her? But then, what about the last ten months? Why had he waited?

"No, I don't know him," Dena replied, watching the play of emotions on Mara's face. "At least, not yet."

"But you intend to?" Mara guessed, and a sinking feeling swept over her.

"I didn't say that," Dena responded coyly. "But I would like to know what it is that makes him appear and disappear so suddenly. What did he want from you?"

Mara sighed and leaned heavily against her desk in pensive concentration. She wanted to tell Dena that it was none of her business and leave it at that, but she couldn't. Actually, Shane's purpose did include Dena, and every other member of the Wilcox family. And since Dena had already heard about the peculiar meeting this afternoon, it would be

better for all concerned for Mara to be honest with her sister-in-law. Mara crossed her ankles in front of her and let
her hands and hips support her weight against the desk top.

"Shane's an old friend of mine," Mara began, leaving
the intimacy of the relationship out of the discussion. "I
haven't seen him in quite some time. As a matter of fact, I
thought that he was dead." A gleam of interest sparked in
Dena's eyes, but faded when Mara continued in the same,
even, businesslike tone that had commanded the conversation. "I didn't know that he was alive, and so naturally it
came as quite a shock when he walked in here, robust and
as healthy as a horse. The reason that he came here is that
he's interested in purchasing Imagination Toys."

If she thought that she would shock Dena with her announcement that Shane was interested in purchasing the toy
company, Mara was disappointed. Dena listened to Mara
intently and pursed her lips thoughtfully.

"And you're considering his offer?" Dena surmised.

"No. I told him, from the beginning, that Imagination
wasn't for sale!"

"He doesn't look like a man who would be easily discouraged," Dena mused, and let her green eyes follow the
hallway to the outer office, where she had seen Shane pass
on his way out of the building. "Maybe you should hear
him out," she suggested, and tossed an errant copper lock
back into place behind her ear.

"About selling Imagination? You must be kidding!"

"Well," Dena began, shrugging her slim shoulders,
"why not? If the price is right..."

"Dena! Listen to you! Imagination was your great-grandfather's lifeblood. We can't just sell it to the first man who's
interested..."

"Of course we can. Stop living in the glory of the past
and face facts, Mara! The company's losing money, and it
has been for quite some time. Unless you can come up with

another inspiration like those ridiculous reincarnations of space creatures from the last hit space movie—''

"You mean the plastic action figures from *Interplanetary Connection?*"

"The same. Since we lost the contract for the movie's sequel and we haven't come up with any other blockbuster toys to fill the gap, Imagination's profits have plunged! A man like—''

"Shane Kennedy," Mara supplied, with a touch of reluctance. Aside from her personal feelings, Mara knew that Dena was close to the truth.

"He might just be the godsend that we're looking for!" Dena touched her lips absently and Mara could almost hear the wheels turning in her mind. To herself, Mara begrudgingly admitted that Dena was making a valid point. "Come on, Mara, what do you need this company for, anyway? You know as well as I do that you'd rather be spending more time with Angie—she needs you..." Dena's words hit a raw nerve with Mara, guilty that she left her daughter with June every day so that she could work full-time. Dena pressed her advantage. "And, after all, what do you know about running a toy company?"

Mara's back stiffened. "I think I know as much as Peter did. At least I should," she sighed. "My degree in business administration should count for something, don't you think? And I worked in several offices before I married Peter and came to work here..."

Dena didn't seem convinced, and Mara felt tired and drained from the ordeal of meeting Shane again. Suddenly she gave into the pressure. "All right, Dena, you know that I'm opposed to the idea, but if it makes you feel any better, I'll talk with him and try to keep an open mind. I'm supposed to meet with him tonight—to discuss an alternate proposition rather than a complete buy-out."

"Tonight?" A light of interest brightened Dena's face,

and then she quickly sobered. "Just give him a chance, Mara. Hear him out. What have you got to lose?"

"The company," Mara murmured, but wisely Dena didn't comment. With a flourish, Mara locked the door of her office and headed out of the building. She wondered about Dena's concern. It seemed almost too genuine. Wearily, Mara thought that perhaps she had judged Dena too harshly at times. And yet, whether it was intuition or mental wounds from past experience, Mara still didn't feel that she could completely trust the svelt-figured redhead. Was it possible that she was overly suspicious of Peter's older sister?

It was later than usual for Mara to leave the office. She pulled out of the parking lot under the building and carefully merged her car into the traffic of the business district of Asheville. The small sidestreets of town were relatively free from traffic at this time of evening. The air was thick and hazy as Mara drove through the colonial town with its splashes of modern architecture and onto the highway that would eventually take her to the countryside and the Wilcox estate. Fortunately the Friday night traffic had thinned to the point that allowed Mara to wheel her imported car home in record time. The lemon-colored Renault darted up the prestigious tree-lined drive and ground to a halt near the garage at the back of the house. Mara slipped from behind the wheel of the car and half ran up the brick walk. She was too preoccupied to notice the bloom of the late azaleas or the hint of honeysuckle that perfumed the air as she opened the kitchen door and called out her familiar greeting.

"Angie! June, I'm home..."

June appeared promptly from the den near the back of the house, and a wave of relief washed over her pinched features. "I was just about to call the office," the older woman chastised as she removed her reading glasses. "I was beginning to get worried about you. It's late..."

"Nothing to worry about," Mara replied with a wan

smile. June's piercing eyes looked questioningly at Mara. To avoid her direct gaze, Mara reached for a glass and turned on the faucet. The cool water slid deliciously down her parched throat. After a lengthy drink she dried her hands on a nearby dish towel and faced her mother-in-law. June's features were drawn, and Mara couldn't help but wonder about the older woman's health.

"I had an unexpected appointment at the last minute," Mara explained. "That's why I'm late." She gave her mother-in-law a warm smile and tried to brush June's fears aside, but the anxious expression on June's face indicated that Mara had failed to reassure her. "I'm sorry," Mara sighed with genuine affection. "I should have called."

"It's all right, dear. I suppose I worry too much," June acquiesced, and then with more vehemence than Mara thought possible, June continued. "It's just that you're so wrapped up with that damned toy company!" Mara stiffened at her mother-in-law's change in attitude, and June chuckled softly. "Forgive me, Mara, I shouldn't use such foul language."

Mara looked seriously at the little old woman. "Do you think that I'm neglecting Angie?" she asked, mentally bracing herself for June's reply. Once again the guilt for the hours away from her child weighed heavily on her conscience.

"Oh, goodness, no, Mara!" June murmured and touched a fond hand to Mara's shoulder. "Angie's just fine. If anything, I'd say that she's a little spoiled."

"Then?"

"I don't think that you take enough time for yourself. If you're neglecting anyone, it's *you*."

Mara let the pent-up air escape from her lungs, but June hadn't finished. "It's unnatural the way you spend all of your time at home or the office. You're young, you should be around young people..."

June's lecture was interrupted by the sound of the back screen door slamming and light, running footsteps hurrying to the kitchen. Angie let up a shriek of delight and gales of childish laughter when she caught sight of her mother. "Mommy! Mommy!" Angie shouted, and scurried over to Mara's outstretched arms.

Mara scooped her daughter up off the floor. "How's Momma's big girl?" she asked, and placed a kiss on Angie's smudgy cheek.

Angie giggled with joy and tightened her arms around Mara's neck. "Southpaw got kitties!" Angie declared, crossing her chubby arms importantly over her chest.

"She does?" Mara asked, and Angie wriggled out of her arms. Before the tiny feet hit the floor, they were in motion, and the little blond girl ran out the back door as quickly as she had entered. "Hurry, Mommy...I show you the kitties!" she called from somewhere in the vicinity of the back porch.

"So the big day has finally arrived?" Mara asked June.

"Oh, yes, I guess so. Angie's found the spot where Southpaw has hidden her kittens," June explained with a chuckle. "I haven't been able to pull her out from under that porch all afternoon!" Mara laughed aloud at the thought of her daughter and her fascination for Southpaw's proud new family.

Mara reached into the refrigerator and gathered some vegetables for Angie's dinner. She glanced at her mother-in-law and noticed that June seemed preoccupied while staring out the window at Angie. "June, are you feeling well?" Mara asked carefully.

"Of course, dear," June replied spritely, and Mara wondered if she had imagined the strain on the older woman's face.

"You're sure?" Mara prodded.

"Of course, Mara. Why do you ask?"

"Well, I was hoping that you would be able to stay with

Angie tonight," Mara mentioned, and hastily added, "but if you have other plans…or if you would like to rest…"

"Nonsense! I'd love it!"

"Good. I really do hate to bother you, but the man that came to see me late this afternoon insists that I hear him out—tonight!" Mara's thoughts lingered for a moment on Shane.

"That's perfect!" June responded, and her tired eyes brightened at the prospect of having Angie for the evening. It was a luxury that she hadn't experienced much. Since Peter's death, Mara hardly ever went out. "She can stay at my place with me! I've been meaning to take her on one of those miniature train rides in the park, but it's been impossible. The train only runs on the weekends."

"Great," Mara whispered.

June knew her daughter-in-law well, and she regarded Mara's oval face thoughtfully for a moment. There seemed to be a trace of disturbance in her wide-set blue eyes. "Mara…"

"Yes?" Mara looked up from the potato that she was peeling.

"Is everything all right?" Gentle concern forced June's graying eyebrows together.

"Sure." Mara laughed, but she heard the hollow sound of her voice. How could she explain to her mother-in-law, the woman who showered so much love on Angie, that Mara was going out with her old lover—the father of her child, the man that she would have married if it had been possible? How would June react to the knowledge that Angie wasn't Peter's daughter, and that the man who fathered the little girl whom June cherished was a total stranger to his child? How could Mara wash away the deception that she had committed for the last four years, under the false belief that Angie's father was dead?

"If you say so," June agreed, absently, as she studied

Mara. June had been raised with Southern manners, and she never was a woman to pry, not even into the private lives of her own family. She watched Mara's slim and graceful figure anxiously as Mara headed out to the back porch in search of Angie. In June's opinion, Mara took life much too seriously.

"Angie," Mara called as she opened the screen door and searched the back yard for her spritely young daughter. "Angie! Where are you?"

"Right here," was the muffled reply from somewhere nearby. Mara looked down the porch steps in the direction of the sound. Two dusty tennis shoes were the only evidence that Angie was close at hand. Mara hurried down the steps and balanced on one slender knee as she grabbed Angie's exposed ankles. A muted squeal of surprise and anticipation erupted from somewhere under the porch.

"Angie Wilcox! Just look at you!" Mara exclaimed, with a good-natured laugh. She extracted the little girl from beneath the lattice work that supported the back porch, and she brushed the cobwebs from Angie's golden curls. "You're a first-class mess!" Mara teased as she surveyed the dirty child.

"Kitties! Kitties! Southpaw got kitties in there!" Angie jabbered excitedly and pointed a knowing finger at the porch. Against Angie's better judgment, Mara picked up her daughter and carried her up the steps toward the house.

"Let's go up and have some dinner," Mara suggested, hoping to deter Angie's interest in the newborns. Angie looked longingly back to the porch until Mara whispered in her ear. "Guess what, dumpling?" Mara asked in a secretive voice.

Angie's eyes widened expectantly. "What?" the little girl whispered back, in a show of affectionate collusion with her mother.

"You get to stay overnight with Grammie tonight. What

do you think about that?'' Mara asked, and poked a loving finger at the exposed belly button in the gap between Angie's shirt and pants.

"Are you coming, too?" Angie asked eagerly, and Angie's cherubic face, aglow with anticipation, tugged at Mara's heartstrings.

"Not this time, sweetheart," Mara admitted, and Angie's animated face lost its smile. Mara hurried on. "But you'll have to tell me all about it tomorrow. Grammie's going to take you on a train ride in the park."

"A train with a whistle?"

"I think so…"

Once again Angie's impish face illuminated with expectation, and Mara gave the child a bear hug as she carried the little girl into the kitchen for dinner.

The grandfather clock in the living room chimed eight o'clock, and Mara could feel herself stiffen with each vibrating note. She thought about pouring herself a drink but discarded the idea, seeing it as a show of weakness. The big, old house was dark and cold ever since June had left with Angie, and the tightness in Mara's stomach seemed to knot and twist with each passing minute.

It had been impossible not to think about Shane in the last half hour, and each time his image assailed her, Mara sensed the same old feelings that he had aroused in her in the past: intrigue, joy, contentment, and finally despair. Now, new and ugly sensations marred the beauty of the past as she felt the chill of betrayal and the heat of anger.

It had been over four years since Mara had called Shane's father on the telephone and learned the devastating news that Shane had been killed in a terrorists' attack in Northern Ireland. Mara had realized that as a television camera man, Shane's occupation could at times be dangerous. She knew that this particular assignment in Belfast would be difficult and risky. But when confronted with Mara's fears for his safety, Shane had waved them off, emphasizing that the film, a frank documentary on the political battle in Northern Ireland, was important, not only for his personal career advancement but also for public awareness. It was his hope that the film would demonstrate the political unrest of a society torn by religious and economic strife.

Shane had downplayed the hazards and dangers of the assignment, and Mara had reluctantly accepted his careful explanations and ultimate decision to make the trip to the tiny island. Later she realized that it had been her own foolish attempt to hide behind a curtain of half-truths, because the knowledge of the bloodshed and risks that Shane might have had to encounter were too much for her to bear.

Mara hadn't known that she was pregnant when Shane had left her alone in the airport terminal. Perhaps if she had realized that she was carrying a child, she could have convinced him to stay with her and the baby, and they could have been married, as she had hoped. But as it was, she never saw him again—until he walked into her office over four and a half years later.

It was in the telephone call to Shane's father that Mara had hoped to get in touch with the father of her child and let him in on the glad news. Shane had been gone for over six weeks, and in that long, lonely time, she had received only one badly connected telephone call and a hastily written card. Then, abruptly, nothing.

But the raspy voice of Shane's father, and the heavy pause as she asked about Shane, heightened the dread that had been mounting. Before the old man could whisper the news to her, she understood that Shane was gone—forever. She managed to quell the scream of disbelief and bereavement in her throat and murmur her sympathies to the stranger on the other end of the line. She tried to hang up the phone, but didn't, and the receiver dangled awkwardly in midair for the rest of the evening as she sat in stunned silence. She cried herself to sleep that night, and when slumber did finally come, it was fitful and shattered by the truth: Shane was dead.

For the rest of the week she cried intermittently, unable to piece together the fragments of her broken life. Her appetite disappeared with fatigue and nausea. When Peter Wilcox, an old high school friend, had dropped by to visit her, he had found Mara lying on the couch, disheveled, crying bitter tears and battling unsuccessfully with morning sickness. He had helped her to the bathroom, and the sight of her thin body, torn with uncontrollable retching as she hung her head over the basin, didn't stop him from attempting to comfort and console her.

With strong and commanding movements, he had helped her get dressed and had listened compassionately when she had explained, through convulsive sobs, about Shane. And the child.

Peter had the strength to make the decisions that Mara couldn't. He understood her grief for Shane, and then forced her admission into a local hospital insisting that it was necessary for her health and that of the baby. The one consoling thought throughout Mara's turbulent period of anguish was the knowledge that she was carrying Shane's child.

Slowly she regained her strength, and though never nonexistent, the pain of her grief eased. Peter helped her through her deepest depression. His words were comforting, his arms were strong, and above all else, he was kind to Mara rather than critical or judgmental. It was as if he had taken it upon himself to see that she was cared for. And as the days passed, Mara could sense that Peter was falling in love with her. Although she never returned the depth of his feelings, it seemed only reasonable that she should marry him. She had a child to care for and Shane was dead—or so she believed.

The first arguments in the marriage didn't begin until after Angie was born. It seemed to Mara that once the baby arrived, and the physical evidence of Mara's passion for another man existed, Peter and she became alienated. Although Angie bore the Wilcox name and the secret of her parentage was never discussed, all of the attention that Mara lavished upon the child seemed to annoy Peter and add to his resentment of the blond little girl.

Mara and Peter would quarrel, bitterly at times. Then he would leave her, sometimes for days. She had heard the gossip about his supposed affairs, but she ignored it and refused to forget the kindness he had shown her when she needed it most. And then came the sudden shock of his illness and the steady deterioration of a young and once healthy man.

The grandfather clock struck the quarter hour, and Mara was jarred back to reality. Headlights flashed through the windows and a car engine died in the driveway. It had to be Shane. Mara felt a shiver of anticipation—or was it dread—as the doorbell announced Shane's arrival.

When Mara opened the door, she braced herself and tried to cool the race of her pulse that gave evidence to her tangled emotions. But as the doorway widened and the warm interior lights spilled into the night, Mara suddenly realized how vain her attempts at composure were. Shane was too much the same as he was when she had been so mindlessly in love with him. She could sense the return of familiar seductive feelings, and she wanted to be propelled backward in time to a familiar setting that was carefree and loving.

A smile touched the corners of the hard line of Shane's mouth, and his eyes seemed to come alive as he looked down at her. His gaze poured over her, and even fully dressed in a rose-colored crepe gown, she felt naked. Shane loosened his tie and raked his fingers through his ebony hair in a gesture of indecision. "You...look...gorgeous," he murmured with a frown, as if the thought were a traitorous admission. "But then, you always manage to look elegant, don't you?"

His voice was a seductive potion to her, and she felt a need to break his disarming spell. "Shane...I—"

He interrupted. "Aren't you going to invite me into your home?" A black, somewhat disdainful eyebrow cocked.

"I thought we were going out."

"We are. But we have to talk a few things over first. Don't you agree?" There was an urgency to his words, as if four years was too long a time to bridge the widening abyss that separated them.

Mara drew in a long, unsteady breath as she realized that she hadn't moved out of the doorway, as if her small body would somehow discourage him from entering her home. She didn't know quite why, but she understood that she couldn't let him into the house, into her privacy, into her heart. Not again.

"Can't we talk in the restaurant?" she asked, still forming a weak barrier to her home.

"Would you feel safer in a crowd?"

"No...yes...oh, Shane so much has happened in the last four years. Perhaps we're making a big mistake. I'm not really sure that I want to—"

"Of course you do," he coaxed. "As much as I do." His dark eyes held hers for an instant, and without consciously thinking about it she stepped away from the door. By her movements she invited him inside.

In a scarcely audible voice she managed to pull together her poise and her graciousness. "Excuse my manners, please come in," she whispered. "Could I get you a drink?"

The tightness of his jawline seemed to slacken a little. "Yes—thanks. Bourbon, if you have it."

"I remember," Mara murmured, and led him through the tiled foyer and into the drawing room. As she walked she sensed his eyes roving over the interior of the house, probing into the most intimate reaches of her life. Although he said nothing, there was an air of disapproval in his stance. His dark eyes skimmed the elegant drawing room with its expensive furnishings. He missed nothing: the gracious mint-green brocade of the draperies, the peach-colored linen and velvet that highlighted the Chippendale chairs, the ornate and lavish antique tables that had been part of the Wilcox home for generations, the walls covered in linen and proudly displaying past members of the Wilcox family, even the plush pile of the authentic Persian carpet. Nothing escaped his gaze, from the French doors near the garden to the hand-sculpted Italian marble fireplace. Shane stood with one hand in the pocket of his chocolate-colored slacks, his tweed jacket pushed away from his body, and Mara could tell that he was tense, tightly coiled. When she handed him his drink, she was careful not to let her fingers brush against his, for fear that the passion that had smoldered within her for so long would suddenly be ignited.

Shane's studious gaze traveled to the fireplace, and Mara froze. The glass of wine that she held in her hand remained motionless in the air, suspended halfway to her lips. Upon the Italian marble of the mantel stood a picture of Angie as an innocent two-year-old. The portrait captured Shane's attention, and he strode meaningfully over to the fireplace for a closer look at the child. Mara's breath constricted in her throat as she watched him. Dear God, would he know? Could he guess? Should she tell him—could she? *"She's your daughter, Shane! Your own flesh and blood."* Mara wanted to shout the words but was unable. She raised the trembling glass of wine to her lips and let the cool liquid slide down her suddenly parched throat.

"Is this your little girl?" Shane asked, studying the portrait carefully.

"Yes...yes it is. It...I mean, the picture was taken almost

two years ago..." Mara whispered. Again she swallowed the wine. *Tell him! Tell him!* her insistent mind commanded. *No matter what has happened in the past, he has the right to know about his child! No pain or anguish that you have suffered at his hand gives you the right to withhold the fact that he fathered Angie. It's his right! Tell him the truth! Tell him NOW!*

"She's very pretty," Shane observed, "just like her mother." He fingered the portrait as if drawn to the beguiling child's face, and Mara knew that if she didn't steady herself, she would faint. If only she had the courage to tell him the truth. A faint shadow hardened Shane's features. *He must know,* Mara thought.

"Are you all right? Mara?" Shane asked the question, suddenly aware that Mara's face had blanched. His voice seemed distant. "Is something wrong?" Concern flooded his features, and he let his hand drop from the picture frame as he half-ran across the room to Mara's side. His arm captured her waist just as she felt her knees give way and the glass in her fingers slid to the carpet.

"There's so much to explain," she whispered against his jacket.

"I know, I know, baby," he murmured, and kissed the top of her head as he persuaded her to sit on the stiff Victorian sofa. "Don't try to explain anything now. Are you all right, or do you need a doctor? Where are the servants tonight?" His dark eyes darted to the hallway. He started to get up, but Mara placed a staying hand on his sleeve.

"I don't have any servants," she said softly. The faint feeling had passed and color returned to her cheeks.

"No servants? In a house this size?"

"No live-ins. I...do have a woman who comes in once a week to help me with the cleaning. The same for the gardener. But that's it. I cook my own meals, and June watches over Angie."

"June? A governess? Where is she?"

Mara's throat tightened again. "No, June's not a governess. Actually, she's Angie's gr-...Peter's mother. Angie's with her this evening."

"I see," he retorted, and took a long swallow of his drink. He pulled uncomfortably at his tie and gave Mara a reassessing look. "She must have been the woman who threw me out of here on the day of the funeral!"

"So you were the stranger! Dena guessed as much!" Mara gasped. "Why were you here that day?" Her large, liquid eyes looked directly at him, and he remembered a younger, more innocent time. He found it impossible to fight the urge any longer. An unsteady finger reached out and traced the delicate outline of Mara's refined jaw. Tenderly he persuaded a wisp of tawny hair back into place behind her ear. She felt herself shudder at his touch. He sighed deeply and shook his head.

"I was there that day simply because I couldn't stay away from you any longer. Peter's death was an easy excuse; I wanted to see you. But for some reason your mother-in-law balked, wouldn't let me near you. It was as if she suspected me of something...sinister. I could read it in her eyes. I explained that I was an old friend, gave her my card, but she absolutely refused..." His voice trailed off, and Mara could sense the restraint that he forced upon himself. The finger stopped its seductive motion. With a scowl he pulled his hand away from her face.

"Then it wasn't business," she whispered.

"Not at all." He walked away from her and buried his fists into his pockets. Satisfied that the distance between them was sufficient, he leaned against the fireplace and surveyed her. Involuntarily, his jaw tightened.

"And now, Shane?" she demanded, hoping that her voice wouldn't give her ragged emotions away. "What about now? Is it business that brings you back here?"

"Yes and no." The expression on his face was as enigmatic as his words. There was a kindness in his features, and yet a different, steely hardness stormed in his eyes. For a moment he hesitated, and Mara was aware of a breakdown in his reserve, but it was quickly reconstructed.

"Did you say that you gave June your card?" Mara inquired, puzzled.

"Yes—but she wouldn't have anything to do with me. Did she give it to you?" he asked, and read the negative answer in her eyes. "I didn't think so. I know it sounds absurd, but that woman holds something against me."

"That's impossible. She doesn't even know you."

Shane shrugged his broad shoulders. "That's the impression that she left with me. But it really doesn't matter."

"She was just upset—it was the day of Peter's funeral, you know."

"Like I said, it doesn't matter. I think we should get going," he suggested, curtly. "We're already late for our reservation."

"I thought you wanted to talk..."

"I do and we will. But you look like you could use a good meal, and so could I. We have lots of catching up to do."

Mara regarded him with interest. "What about the proposition about Imagination?"

"That, too."

The evening was dark and still, and the silence was a thick, heavy cloud that separated Mara from Shane as they rode together in the sports car. Neither spoke, afraid to shatter the tranquility of the evening. Each was surrounded by the cloak of his own private thoughts. As Mara cast a surreptitious glance at Shane, she noted the thick black hair blowing softly in the wind, the slightly arrogant straight nose, and the deep-set darkness of his eyes. In the car, with only inches separating their bodies, she was acutely aware of him and his brooding masculinity, just as she had been on the first night that they had met. It had been nearly five years ago, but she could remember that night as clearly as if it were yesterday.

Mara hadn't wanted to attend the surprise birthday party that one of the girls in the office was throwing for the boss. But the hostess had been insistent, and Mara succumbed to the pressure. She didn't want to be the only employee who couldn't make it to Mr. Black's fiftieth birthday party. Against her better judgment she agreed to attend.

That night Mara toyed with the drink in her hand, already forming a plausible excuse to leave the festivities early. The music was loud, the guests even louder, and she seemed distinctly out of place. She looked around the room to find Sandy, the hostess, in order to excuse herself and make a hasty exit.

The dark-eyed stranger must have arrived late because Mara hadn't noticed him earlier. But when she finally did see him, she found him staring intently at her from across the room. His black eyes were friendly, beguiling, and although there must have been over twenty people in the room, in the one suspended instant, when her eyes touched his, Mara felt that she was alone with him. Her breath caught in her throat as he advanced toward her, but she was unable to tear her eyes away from his face.

His was an interesting profile, contoured in smooth angles and planes. His eyes were deepset and very black, the color of midnight. His jaw was strong and square, with the slight trace of a dimple cleaving it, and his nose was extra straight. There was the beginning of laugh lines around his eyes and lips, and an amused twinkle in his eye sparkled as he sauntered over to Mara.

For a hushed moment there was an awkward silence between them, and finally, out of embarrassment, Mara dragged her eyes away from his. She swirled the untouched drink in her hand and gazed at the small whirlpool she created, hoping that she didn't appear as nervous and out of place as she felt.

The man leaned against the counter that separated kitchen from family room and startled Mara by uttering a curse under his breath. "God, I hate these kinds of parties, don't you?" he asked, studying her and taking a long swallow from his drink.

"Birthday parties?" she repeated, thinking the question strange. She shrugged dismissively. "No...they're all right, I guess."

His lips formed a grim sort of smile and his eyes reached out for hers. "No, you don't understand. I don't have anything against a birthday celebration—usually."

Mara was clearly confused, and her bewilderment showed on her delicate face. She shook her head negatively, and her blond hair brushed against her neck. "You're right, I don't understand."

"You really don't, do you?" he inquired, obviously amazed. Her subtle innocence intrigued him.

"If you would just tell me what you're talking about," she suggested, a bit sarcastically, and feeling as if he was playing some sort of private game with her.

"Don't you get it? Look around you. Do you notice anything different about us?" He waved his hand expansively, including the rest of the guests in the room.

"About *us?*" she echoed as her eyes glanced toward the other people in the room. Suddenly it dawned on her, and she felt herself blush. "Oh, I see," she mumbled, and discovered that she couldn't meet his dark, probing gaze.

"Damn that Bob Brandon and his wife! They're always trying to get me matched up with somebody!" His jaw clenched and Mara felt an uncontrollable urge to run. She could see as plainly as he that she had been set up as the only single woman to naturally balance the one odd man out. That explained why Sandra Brandon had been so insistent that she attend the party. When Mara had attempted to make excuses yesterday at the office, Sandra had become positively demanding that Mara attend. It was evident now why Sandra had been so insistent. Sandra liked everything in life even, and in her mind there was no such thing as an unattached male.

Shane finished his drink with a flourish and placed the empty glass on the counter. Mara could see that he was trying to control his irritation with the uncomfortable situation. At first she imagined that he was disappointed that she was his date, but his next statement changed her opinion.

"Well, if Bob and Sandy think that I need their assistance in my love life, who am I to argue?" He smiled mockingly. "How about a dance?"

Mara was embarrassed, uncomfortable, and angry with Sandra. She didn't need any man thinking that he *had* to keep her entertained for the evening. She tried vainly to get out of the dance. "You don't have to...I mean I..."

"You mean 'yes,' don't you?" His dark eyes brooked no argument and he pushed her carefully into the center of the room. The music was soft, barely discernable over the din of the party, and Mara felt stupidly self-conscious, as if she were trying to draw attention to herself. But the moment that the tall man with the strangely appealing eyes wrapped his arms over her and held her intimately against him, she forgot the rest of the guests. It was as if all of her senses were immediately electrified, and the soft, sultry music filtered over the slightly boisterous noise of the crowd to encompass her and the powerful man who held her.

At first her movements were stiff, but as Shane pressed more closely to her, she felt herself begin to relax and mold to the warmth of his long, lean body. His hand at the small of her back guided her. Her head rested lightly against the soft fabric of his shirt, and she closed her eyes to listen to the beating of his heart. She heard a controlled, rhythmic beat, unlike the pulsating drumming in her rib cage.

When her eyes fluttered open for an instant, she noticed Sandy Brandon smiling smugly at the sight of her wrapped in Shane's strong arms. Color darkened Mara's cheeks, but she couldn't help but feel totally at ease with the stranger. They danced together, their bodies swaying with the music, for what seemed both an instant and an eternity. When the tempo of the songs quickened, Shane pulled Mara by the wrist toward the door.

"Let's find a spot that's not so crowded," he decided with a husky voice.

"What do you mean?" she inquired cautiously, and her breath seemed too tight for her throat.

A smile blazed across his tanned face. "I'm suggesting that we leave."

"Together?" she blurted incredulously.

"Of course together," he whispered. "Otherwise our plan wouldn't work, would it?"

"What plan?"

"Well," he drawled, eyeing the crowd with apparent disdain, "I don't know about you, but I'm tired of Sandy Brandon playing the role of matchmaker in my life."

"I don't see how you can hope to change her. She's an incurable romantic who adores fixing people up."

"Doesn't she, though," he observed dryly. "Maybe we can change all that, at least in our case."

"How?" Mara asked, bewildered.

"You'll see," he stated enigmatically. "Do you have a coat?"

Mara couldn't resist the intrigue of the moment. And the look on Sandy Brandon's surprised face as she spied Mara leaving with Shane was worth the gamble of leaving with a complete stranger.

Shane and Mara left together in the flash and roar of his sports car. At the time Mara told herself that she was being careless and throwing caution to the wind—acting completely out of her usually shy and reserved character. All for the sake of a practical joke, or so she tried to convince herself. If she had been honest with herself, she would have had to confess to falling prey to an attraction that she had never before experienced. The dark-eyed stranger was bewitching.

They drove for over an hour in the convertible, at first quietly, as if each might have suddenly regretted the impulsive dash away from the party. But as the black night sped by, and the minutes ticked forward, Shane began to talk and draw Mara out of her silence. Mara was entranced by the romance of it all—riding into the night with a virile, handsome stranger and casting aside all consideration for time or reality. She felt as free as the wind that caught her honeyed hair and brushed it in tangled waves away from her face. His words were serious and kind, and when he favored her with a smile that touched his eyes, the sound of her laughter was caught in the night wind and left in the darkness.

It was nearly midnight when Shane stopped the car. They were far from the city—light-years away from the real world—parked in the solitude by a wooded river. The moon cast a rippling slash of silver on the water and the stars dotted the sky. A light, midsummer breeze played with her hair and the faint fragrance of honeysuckle hung in the air.

Shane held her hand as they walked along the shore of the river. She leaned on him often as the heel of her sandals would slip against the rocks at the river's edge. They spoke hesitantly and softly, as if the silence of the night were a fragile spell that they dare not break. He paused underneath the protective, needled limbs of a large pine tree, and in the darkness his hand pulled her more intimately to him. In the night, with eyes wide and searching, Mara read the silent passion in Shane's features. His lips found hers in a tentative, gentle kiss, and she felt herself respond to the warm, enticing pressure of his mouth. The faint taste of brandy wet her lips, and she let herself lean against him as the hot burst of womanhood exploded in her body. The kiss, which started so tenderly, deepened in passion, and a dizzying, unreal sensation swept over her. Mara sighed deeply against Shane's lips, yielding to the warm, liquid mouth that was enveloping her.

Suddenly he froze, and as he dragged his lips from her, he swore at himself under his breath. He rotated his head from hers, as if by gazing out into the distance, he could assuage the hunger of desire that ripped through his body.

Mara listened to her own ragged breathing, and she could almost see his body stiffen as she noted with a welling sense of disappointment that he was trying to escape from her and the yearnings of his body by putting a distance between them.

"Oh, God," Shane groaned to himself and looked heavenward. "What am I doing?"

He glanced at her with eyes full of smoldering passion and put a protective arm across her slim shoulders. Tenderly he led her to the base of the pine tree, on a bed of soft boughs, and helped her into a sitting position against the trunk. He sat with his back braced by the tree. She sat, half-laid, in the warm cradle of his strong arms. Her pulse was running wild with surging heat through her body, and she leaned against him. Her heart pounded loudly in the silent, starry evening, destroying the peace of the night.

Time and rational thought had ceased. Mara was mesmerized by the soft night and the warm touch of the man who held her so intimately. His breath fanned her hair, and a musky scent invaded her nostrils. The whisper-soft kisses that he rained against the back of her neck teased her skin and heated her blood. Her pulse, already on fire, blazed through her veins.

"Mara," his throaty voice murmured against her hair. "I want you..." It was an unnecessary admission, a fact as true as the night itself.

"I know" was the only response that would pass her lips. His hands on her shoulders were enticing, inviting. The evening was warm and seductive, and the pine tree hung over them, guarding them in its heavy, needled branches. Only a slight breeze disturbed the serenity of the nightfall by mildly moving the boughs.

"You're beautiful," Shane coaxed, and his fingers tickled her neck. "I know this is crazy—I don't know how to describe it—but I need you, Mara. Not because you're a woman, but because you're unique...special...captivating. You're you, and I want the most intimate part of you."

"You don't even know me," she protested feebly, knowing that she was succumbing to the magic of the seductive night.

"But I do," he whispered hoarsely, and she believed him. She believed the persuasive touch of his fingers against her skin. She believed the warm enticement of the night. And she believed the ragged sound of longing in his voice as it was torn from his throat in an admission of surrender.

His fingers found the buttons of her blouse, and she didn't stop the tender exploration of his lips against her burning skin. She knew only that she wanted him and needed him, and she let him guide her into a new feeling of awareness. He taught her of a need so great that it was a consuming, unquenched ache that burned within her. They discovered each other, and Mara found for the first time in her twenty-four years the bittersweet yearnings and fulfillment of love. She found a satisfaction so strong that it dissolved the pain and replaced the ache with rapture. It was a night lost in the stars. The quiet lights of Asheville winked in the far-off distance while Mara experienced a night ridden with flaming desire and warm, molten surrender.

Dawn awakened her with its rosy warming rays, and Mara realized in the filtered sunlight that she could never love another man. Shane Kennedy, a virtual stranger, but most intimate lover, possessed her body and soul. The memory of the passion that they shared beneath the pine tree overpowered her with its intensity.

When she stirred, Shane opened a lazy eye and squinted against the filtered glare of the morning as it passed through the soft curtain of pine needles. A pleasant, enticing grin stole over his features as he watched with unashamed interest when Mara tried to conceal and cover her nudity. Embarrassment welled within her and she held the scanty protection of her blue chiffon blouse over her exposed breasts.

His dark eyes became serious. "Don't!" he commanded.

"Don't what?" she asked, feigning innocence.

"Don't ever hide from me." He tugged at the blouse and slowly pulled it out of her fingers. His eyes slid restlessly over her breasts and the directness of his gaze mingled with the cool morning air forced her nipples to harden into taut rosy buttons.

"I'm not…trying to hide," she murmured, but her voice cracked with emotion and she lowered her head, letting the gilded curtain of her hair shelter her face.

With a groan, he hauled himself up to sit beside her. His face was close to hers, and his fingers cupped her chin in order that she meet his inquiring gaze. "What's wrong?" he asked and she could feel his black probing eyes.

"I'm not used…to being…naked with a man," she admitted huskily before closing her eyes and letting the flush of scarlet that burned on her cheeks speak for her.

"Well," he mused, encircling her with his arms and giving her a bear hug. "I think that you should get used to it..."

She shook her head and feared that the tears gathering in her eyes would spill. "I can't," she whispered.

"Sure you can. You have a beautiful body, and you should be proud of it. You're not ashamed, are you?"

She answered mutely with only her eyes, and bit her lip in order to choke back the sobs that were threatening to explode within her. Her head was rested on her knees for support, as she tried to fight back the storm of tears that threatened to overcome her.

"Mara." His voice was firm. "Please look at me. Don't push me away from you. Not now. Not ever! You mean too much to me."

"You...don't have to say..."

"Shh. I'm only saying what I mean," he admitted solemnly.

Her eyes found his and she could feel herself begin to drown in the warmth and kindness that she saw in his face, a face that was virile and masculine yet softened with the innocence of recent sleep. His words were spoken slowly and deliberately, as if he had weighed their importance all night.

"I want you to come and live with me."

Mara felt a frown distort her features, and the tears that were promising to fall began to slide unchecked down her cheeks. "Live with you?" she repeated hoarsely, and turned her face away from him. "I...I don't know if I can live with you—or any man for that matter, without being married."

"Don't you think that we should get to know each other a little better before we talk about marriage?" he asked realistically, and gave her an affectionate shake.

"I don't know what to think," she admitted.

"Then just trust me, Mara. Trust me..."

And she did.

Chapter Four

That period in her life, when she lived so naively and happily with Shane, was long over, she reminded herself as the sleek silver car raced through the busy streets of Asheville. The sports car ground to a halt before an expensive restaurant and inn. The large, three-storied structure stood out in gleaming relief against the darkness of the night. Established just after the Civil War, the inn was painted white, with traditional green shutters on each of the bay windows. Shimmering lanterns, reflecting against the paned windows, poured out a Southern welcome to Mara, beckoning her to enter the well-known establishment.

Mara was propelled unwillingly back to the present and the betraying fact that Shane had a purpose in seeing her. She moistened her lips and couldn't help but wonder if he, too, had been absorbed in memories of the past that they had shared together. The thought was intriguing, but traitorous. If he had wanted to see her, if he had needed her as desperately as she had needed him, he would never have left her to think that he was dead for all of these years.

The shimmering lanterns and the warmth of the night reminded her of the romance and passion that she had shared with Shane. How many times in the past four years had she fantasized about just such an evening with the only man she had ever truly loved? And how many times had she ruthlessly destroyed those conjured imaginings because of what she had thought was the truth—that Shane was dead, gone forever?

Once again the creeping sense of betrayal cooled her blood. Shane must have felt the change in her mood, because as he helped her from the car, he trapped her with a dark, questioning look.

She walked gracefully toward the colonial restaurant, Shane's commanding fingers guiding her with a light but persuasive pressure on her elbow. She tried to ignore the enticement of his touch and concentrate on the elaborate restaurant. The cheerful decor of gleaming wainscoting and blue, floral-print wallpaper helped to lighten her mood. And the staff of the inn, dressed in colonial attire, made her forget momentarily her dilemma with the man she still so feverishly loved.

Shane declined the waiter's invitation that he and Mara join some of the other guests along a long, linen-clad table for family-style dining, where the "down-home" feeling grows as you sit down at the large table with the other patrons and pass the chef's specialties around the table. He preferred more intimate dining arrangements, and the amiable waiter led them to a corner of the inn near a large window, where they could enjoy privacy and a view of a private duck pond. Amber-colored lamps reflected on the water, and a few water birds skimmed quietly on the surface of the pond near the shoreline.

The waiter began to hold Mara's chair for her, but Shane

smiled at the man and assisted Mara into her seat himself. Once she was comfortable, he took his place directly across from her and stared deeply into her eyes, as if trying to delve into the farthest reaches of her mind. Without asking her indulgence, he ordered for the both of them, and for the moment Mara forgot the nagging feeling of deception that had converged upon her. A smile teased her lips, lessening the crackle of the tension in the air, as she noticed that still, after all of the years apart from him, Shane remembered all of her favorite dishes, even down to pecan pie.

After a vintage bottle of Cabernet Sauvignon had been poured and Shane had tasted the wine, he broke through the pretense of small talk that had enveloped them since entering the restaurant. His dark brows drew together and he rubbed the back of his neck with his fingers. Mara sipped her wine patiently, waiting to hear explanations, reasons, alibis, excuses, ANYTHING that would help her understand why he had lied to her four years ago and what he wanted from her now.

"I told you that I was interested in purchasing Imagination Toys," he stated, and watched for her reaction.

Mara nodded slightly and ran a polished fingernail over the rim of her wine glass. "And I told you that Imagination wasn't for sale." A muscle worked in his jaw and a scowl creased his forehead. His entire body became rigid.

"That you did. But I was hoping that you might have altered your position."

In answer she puckered her lips thoughtfully, but shook her head. To Shane, her pensive motion and concentrated brow were the most alluring provocations that he could imagine. Her tawny hair moved wistfully against her cheek as she thought.

"I'm sorry, but I can't sell. It's not that your offer isn't tempting..." Her deep blue eyes met his in total honesty.

"It's just that I feel...responsible...not only for the company, but also to Peter's family."

Something akin to anger swept his face, and his eyes, once darkly enticing, became stony. "Responsible to the Wilcox family?" he echoed, incredulous. "Your loyalty surprises me!"

"*My* loyalty surprises *you?*" she repeated in disbelief.

"That's right," he snapped. "I really don't think that devotion is your long suit!"

"Why not? I've always been faithful to..." she tried to explain, but the last word, which should have been Shane's name, stuck in her throat. It was the truth. In her mind she had never loved another man, and she had remained faithful to Shane until she had thought him dead and Peter had convinced her to marry him. But even during the marriage, she had never loved her husband—not with the same burning intensity that she had tasted with the man who was seated angrily opposite her in the quaint Southern restaurant. She tried tactfully to change the subject. After clearing her throat, she spoke in a voice that was devoid of the feelings that were raging within her.

"You said earlier that you had an alternative proposition? I'd like to hear it. I'd also like to know why you're so interested in Imagination. There must be a dozen toy companies that would do just as well."

"You're probably right. But I chose Imagination because of you. No other reason."

"Not exactly sound business practice," she deduced, but she couldn't help but lift her eyebrows to indicate that she hadn't missed his comment or any of its poignant implications. Her heart turned over, and for a moment she thought that he might elaborate, but the waiter came to remove the dishes and serve the dessert. Shane's intimate mood seemed to have vanished.

When he spoke again, it was in a tightly controlled, businesslike voice. "Do you know anything about Delta Electronics?" he asked.

"Your company?" She shrugged her slim shoulders and touched her napkin to her lips. "Not much, other than the fact that you manufacture computers—"

"Micro-computers," he corrected. Her brows pulled together, and he sighed. "I guess I'd better start at the beginning."

"It might help!" She leaned back against the chair in a totally attentive pose.

"When I got back from Northern Ireland," he began, but her face froze in disbelief at his words, and all of the tension of the last few hours destroyed her facade of Southern civility.

"When you got back from Northern Ireland?" she whispered with a distinct catch in her voice. "Just like that?" She snapped her fingers. "You haven't even explained to me what happened to you in that horrible war, and why you let me think that you were dead!" Her eyes showed the anguish that she had lived four years ago and her breath was ragged and torn from her throat. "You were just going to start a lecture on micro-computers with a phrase like 'when I got back from Northern Ireland'? For God's sake, Shane, what happened over there? Why did your father tell me that you were dead? For so many years you let me think…" Her voice broke with emotion and tears began running down her face and onto the table. She reached for her napkin to cover her eyes, but her small clenched fist continued to pound against the table, rattling the silver and the wine glasses. "Why? Why?" she murmured, only vaguely aware that people at nearby tables were beginning to stare at the spectacle she was creating. Her shoulders drooped, and she couldn't stem the uneven drops that ran in darkened smudges from her eyes.

Shane listened to her tirade, his large hand half covering

his face, as if to shield him from her torment. He couldn't bear to see her so ravaged, and yet he knew that he was the source of her anguish. Aware that he had to get her out of the restaurant, he fumbled in his pocket for some bills and stuffed them into the open palm of the waiter as he helped Mara to her feet and ushered her out of the building past the disapproving eyes and gaping mouths of several of the well-to-do patrons.

The drive home was silent, and with extreme difficulty Mara regained her poise. She stared into the night and felt the brooding silence of the man seated so closely to her. Mara was drained and exhausted, and Shane was driving the small car as if the devil himself were chasing them. The tires screeched against the pavement, the gears were ripped savagely, and Mara wondered vaguely if Shane was going to kill them both. It didn't matter, she thought wearily, but an image of Angie's laughing face broke into her lonely thoughts, and she realized that everything mattered. It mattered very much. Her life, Shane's life, and most especially their daughter's welfare.

When the headlights flashed against the oak trees that guarded the circular drive and the large front porch of the house loomed into Mara's view, she felt a wave of relief wash over her. The strain of the day had taken its toll on her, and she was thankful to be home.

Shane walked her to the door, and she didn't object when he asked to come in. She fumbled with the key, and he helped her unlock the door. Their hands touched in the darkness, and a warm possessive heat leaped in Mara's veins. She tried to calm herself and tell herself that all of her reminiscent memories were to blame for her reaction to him, but she couldn't ignore the pounding of her heart at his touch. Shane pushed open the door, and once inside, locked it. Mara didn't protest—it was impossible to do so, because it felt so natural that he was home with her again after nearly five long, lonely, years.

Still silent, he poured himself a drink from the decanter at the bar. He lifted the glass to her in a silent offering, but she shook her head negatively. The last thing she wanted was a drink to cloud her tired mind.

After slumping onto the couch, Mara kicked off her shoes and tucked her feet beneath her on the soft cushions. She waited. Shane finished his quick drink and poured himself another. She watched. Was it her imagination, or did Shane's hands tremble slightly as he poured the drink? He poured yet another glass of brandy and handed it to her over her whispered protests.

"You want to know about what happened in Belfast, don't you?" he asked curtly.

She took a deep breath and nodded. Her blue eyes reached out for his as she nodded her head.

"All right, but here." He gave her the brandy.

"I didn't want a drink, remember."

"You might change your mind," he responded gravely, and without further question she accepted the drink.

Shane sat beside her, but didn't look at her. Instead, he concentrated on the clear amber fluid in his snifter and pulled at his tie, which he finally discarded angrily. When he began to speak, his voice was hushed, disturbingly distant.

"You know that several of us went over there?" She nodded. "Well, everything was going just fine—most of the work had been completed. The rest of the crew had already taken off back for the States, leaving just Frank and me to finish the last few finishing touches. There wasn't much work left—Frank and I just had to retake a couple of feet of film that hadn't worked out quite right the first time. If everything had gone as planned, we would have been home within the week.

"It was uncanny how well everything went together."
He paused for a long drink, and his eyes darkened in memory. Mara felt her stomach tighten. "The last day that we
were shooting, it wasn't even anything controversial, just a
shot of parents and kids in the park, that sort of stuff. There
was this cathedral, a huge stone building, and the parishioners were just arriving for services. It was an absolutely gorgeous Sunday morning…"

"And?" Mara prodded, as his voice trailed off.

"And…Frank and I stopped for a quick shot. We left
everything in the van, other than the shoulder camera and
the portable microphone.

"There were a lot of people there, all ages. Parents, children, babies, grandmas, all talking and climbing the steps.
The children were playing, laughing, but suddenly I—" he
searched for the right words, and his voice was tight, as if
it was an effort to speak "—sensed…felt that something
wasn't right. I had been filming the gardens, near the steps
of the church, but I pulled my camera away from the church
just as a horrible noise came from a parked car. The car
exploded, metal flew everywhere, people screamed and
ran, the timbers of the church rocked, the stone steps
cracked…there was blood, bodies…cars smashed into
parked vehicles to avoid running over the people who had
been knocked into the street by the explosion. And then I
felt something painful on the side of my head—I heard a
baby cry just as I passed out. When I came to, I was in a
hospital bed, and a nurse was shining a light into my eye.
Two weeks had passed." Shane's voice sounded as dead as
Mara felt. Tears glistened in her eyes and she took a sip of
the brandy.

"And the children that you saw playing?"

Shane drew a whispering breath and shook his head.
"That's the worst of it. Several entire families were killed.
All of them." Shane turned to face Mara and she saw the

rage and guilt that contorted his features. "Those people died because of me, Mara."

"What? How can you blame yourself? That's crazy…"

"Why do you think that particular church was bombed—at that time? It was common knowledge that we were filming a piece on terrorism at the time—"

"No!"

"It wouldn't be too difficult to have figured out the general area where we would be—"

"I don't believe it. How could they have known?" His eyes held the sincerity and the pain of the guilt that he had borne for nearly five years. "You can't be sure…" she whispered, but knew that her protests were only the ghost of hope that he would absolve himself of his blame.

Pain twisted his features. "I know, damn it! I know. It was our story that brought attention to that area of the city. We'd been friendly with several of the local residents, and they must have been on the opposing side, you see, and somehow, we weren't careful enough. The word got out, and we created an opportunity for the terrorists to strike again!"

Mara closed her eyes, as if by force she could destroy the painful picture that Shane was painting.

"You can't blame yourself!"

"Then who is to blame Mara? Who?"

"The system…the economics of the country…the Protestants…the Catholics…I don't know."

"Well, I do!" With his final damning admission, Shane swallowed the remainder of his drink. He looked to the bar, as if he intended to pour himself another, but put the empty snifter down in disgust. "Don't you think that I've tried to convince myself that there was nothing I could have done to prevent this—that we were all just victims of fate? But late at night, when I have to face myself alone, I see those young eager faces, and I know that somehow I was a part of that tragedy!''

"Oh, Shane," Mara murmured, hoping to somehow heal the wounds that had been festering within him. She reached out her hand and gently stroked his chin. Her fingers became moist from the tiny beads of sweat that had accumulated over his upper lip. He swallowed before continuing.

"And so...there was a mix-up of some sort. Everyone at the hospital thought I was Frank—and that Frank was me." His voice was low. "We didn't carry our identification on us— it was locked in the van, and the van was totaled as a truck braked to avoid colliding with some of the injured on the street. Our I.D., camera gear...film...clothing...everything was in the van. And somehow, at least for a while, in all of the confusion and aftermath of the explosion, the mix-up in our identities remained."

Mara guessed the rest of the grisly story. "And Frank was killed?"

"He died before the ambulance could get him to the hospital."

"Oh, God," Mara breathed, and felt a nauseous rumbling in her stomach.

"That's right, Mara. Dad didn't lie to you. He actually thought that I was dead."

"Oh, no..." Mara murmured, her fingers still caressing the firm line of his jaw. "So much has happened to us..."

"I know, Mara, I know." His lips touched hers and she felt a yearning that she hadn't known for years. His tongue outlined her lips and tasted the salt of her tears that had passed over her mouth. With a shudder, he groaned as he pulled her more closely to him. When he parted her lips and their tongues met, she felt a rush of molten desire well up from the deepest part of her and spread through her blood in thundering currents of fiery passion. His hands touched her hair, at first tentatively, and finally in heated desire as he wound the blond curls through his fingers and let his face nuzzle the length of her neck, exploring her throat, the shell of her ear, the supple muscles of her shoulders.

His fingers moved from her hair and down her neck in down-soft touches of intimate persuasion. She gasped for air as his thumb found the pulse at the base of her throat and outlined the delicate bone structure in warm circles of desire. The seductive movements created a whirlpool of heat, to churn desperately within her. She sighed against him and felt his own labored moan as he searched for and discovered the top button of her dress. He took the pearl button in his mouth and with ease forced it through the buttonhole. As he did so, his tongue touched deliciously against the rounded swell of her bosom, and her breast ached with need. His head dipped lower—to the next button. Once again the warm, wet tongue lapped enticingly at her breast, only to draw away in agonizing suspense. His fingers slowly opened the dress, parting it only enough to let him caress the ivory cleavage with his face.

"Oh, Shane," Mara sighed, the warmth of ecstasy overtaking her. A nagging thought told her that she should stop him, but she found it impossible to deny that which she had wanted for four years. She wanted to enjoy the sweet surrender of her body to his, and forget, at least for the next few hours, all of the sadness and sorrow that had separated them over the past four years. She wanted to reach out to him and help salve some of the guilt that he had borne.

He sighed against her and pushed the clean angles of his face into the folds of her skirt. The same words that she remembered from their first night together echoed in her ears. "Mara, God, but I want you. I've ached for you for over four years," he admitted in hot breaths that scorched through the silk fabric of her dress and caressed her legs in hot whispers. "Let me love you again."

His hand reached under the hem of her skirt to embrace her thigh, and she groaned softly as her legs parted. "Let me love you, Mara," he pleaded, and her answer was a breathless moan of yearning hunger. He stroked her thigh, and involuntarily she arched. He pulled at her panty hose and discarded them into a heap on the floor. And then, ever so gently, he petted her—letting his warm fingers brush against the length of her calves and thighs. "I want you, Mara, I want you as no man has ever wanted a woman."

"Oh, God…Shane, I want you, too."

With her soul shaking admission, he scooped her into his arms and lithely carried her out of the drawing room and up the expansive sweep of the staircase. She clung to him and placed liquid kisses against his neck, but at the top of the stairs he hesitated, and she nodded in the direction of her room. He carried her into the expansive bedroom and stopped near the door. He eyed the darkened room speculatively, and for an indeterminate minute he hesitated.

"Is this the bed you shared with Peter?" he asked harshly.

Her eyes, glazed with drugged passion, instantly cleared. "No," she whispered. "I moved into this room…before he got sick."

"Humph!" His dark eyes found hers, and after a flicker of doubt he carried her over to the bed. The down comforter sagged beneath their combined weight, and the cool satin felt smooth and welcome against her bare legs.

"You don't know how much I've missed you," Shane conceded, his breath dew-soft against her earlobe.

Her own breath, a prisoner in her lungs, escaped with the question that had been searing her mind for the past twelve hours. "Then why, Shane? Why didn't you come back to me?"

Her blue eyes pleaded with him, and the picture she made—a lovely full-grown woman, still innocent in her own blushing manner—was too much for him to bear. The golden hair, tousled carelessly against the cool blue comforter, the flush of pink under the surface of her creamy complexion, and those eyes—blue as the morning sky and innocently mature. "It doesn't matter—not anymore—I'm here now," he whispered before pressing his lips, moist with hunger, against hers.

She let her lashes fall over her eyes, and let her body react to the exquisite rapture that he was evoking within her. Too many years had passed, and too many unanswered questions still lingered. An ugly corner of her mind nagged at her, but she ignored the thought and abandoned herself to him. Her hands caught in the thick black silkiness of his hair, and her fingers moved against his scalp, as if by their touch she could erase the pain of four desolate years.

His hands slid beneath the dress and let it slip silently to the floor. Warm palms pressed urgently against the contour of her spine and the supple roundness of her hips. He pulled her urgently to him, and she could feel his virile need and hunger burning in his loins. "Oh, Mara," he whispered as he unclasped her bra and let her breasts, snowy white, fall unbound against him. "You're more beautiful than I remembered." Tentatively, he reached forward and circled one rounded swell with his finger, enticing a sweet ache in Mara that aroused her to even higher pinnacles of yearning.

His tongue, warm and soft, touched delicately against her breast and teased her nipple until she felt a swelling ache of torment. His hands and fingers massaged her, and finally, just as she thought she could endure no more of his teasing, the warm, moist cavern of his mouth closed over her waiting taut nipple, and a bursting wave of desire engulfed her. She shuddered with the force of her emotions.

Quickly, he discarded what was left of their clothing, destroying the flimsy barriers that kept her from him. She sucked in her breath as she looked upon him, long and lean and virile—exactly as she had remembered him and precisely as she had fantasized about him a hundred times over in her mind. Her fingers outlined the strong muscles of his back and abdomen which glistened with a salty film of perspiration.

His voice broke through the night, in pure animal pleasure. "Oh, God, Mara...I can't wait any longer..."

His head lowered and he kissed her abdomen and belly button, letting his tongue slide urgently over her skin. His hands pulled against her hips, until his face was covered with the warm creamy complexion of her abdomen. Soft purring noises escaped from her throat as he murmured her name over and over against her warm flesh.

Just as she thought she could endure no more of the tormented ecstasy, he pushed her legs apart with his knees and settled comfortably in the saddle of her soft hips. "I'm sorry, Mara, but I can't wait any longer," he groaned, as his face came up to hers and his lips sought the warmth of her mouth.

"Neither can I," she whispered, and in one hushed instant, he came to her, moving against her with the desire that had tortured him for years. She felt molten hot explosions ripping through her body, his cataclysmic, shuddering surrender, and a burst of passion as their bodies came hungrily together in complete, rekindled union.

Shane cradled her against him, and she felt younger than she had in years. She gave into the yearnings of her body, and fell asleep nestled in the warm strength of his arms. She knew that she had to tell him about Angie, and she wanted desperately to understand everything that he had experienced in Northern Ireland, but she couldn't bring herself to shatter the peace that they had found and shared together.

Late in the night, when Shane awakened her with his own returning passion, she thought about the absurdity of the situation, but kept her thoughts to herself. In the morning, she promised a guilty corner of her mind—I'll get everything straight with him...in the morning.

Chapter Five

When morning dawned, sending forth warm rays of summer sunshine, and Mara awakened sleepily, she felt a tranquility and a peace that she hadn't experienced in years. Curled up comfortably against Shane's strong body in a dreamless sleep, had created a warm, delicious, feeling that wrapped her in a rosy cloak of good humor as she stretched languidly on the bed.

She watched Shane, still sleeping soundly next to her. The lavender sheet, which she clutched to her naked breast, was draped casually over his dark-skinned body. All tension seemed to be drained away from him, and the rock-hard muscles were relaxed in slumber. Even with the evidence of a beard against his chin, he looked younger and softer than he had the night before. He lay on his side, an arm stretched over his head, his bronzed skin deepened by the pale color of the bedding.

The morning sun was to Mara's back, and through the

window it cast warm rays past the thin slats of the blinds, causing an uneven striping of shadows over his body. He stirred after a few moments, the sun in his eyes and Mara's intense gaze awakening him.

A sleepy eye cracked open and a smile, crooked but becoming, spread across his features as he let his eyes wander caressingly over her body. He stretched, and in one lithe movement pulled the sheet away from her breasts. His dark eyes reached for her, and she could sense the flames of passion sparking in their ebony-colored depths.

"Do you know," he inquired lazily, as a finger came up to outline the swell of her breast, "that you're more beautiful in the morning than I had remembered?" His finger stopped its warm, seductive movement. "I didn't think that was possible."

She reached for his finger and halted its further exploration by holding it to her lips. "And do you know," she countered, suggestively, "that you and I have an incredible mountain of things that have to be sorted out today?"

"But we've got all morning," he assured her, and brushed a golden curl away from her face.

"No...no, Shane, we don't."

The firm quality of her answer surprised him. "What do you mean?" he asked, and suddenly became serious. Noting the pained look that had crossed her face, he pulled away from her, but couldn't help but touch her forehead, as if to wipe away the lines of concentration that furrowed her brow.

"There are things that we have to discuss..."

"Nothing so earth shattering that it won't wait," he argued seductively, and pulled her down to lie next to him before covering her lips with his. The weight of his chest, crushing against her breasts, made her heart race in anticipation. His magic was working on her again.

Reluctantly, she pulled her mouth from his, determined

to explain about Angie. "Shane…there's so much to say," she began, trying to ignore the passion that was heating within her. "Some things have to be discussed."

"So…let's discuss them right now," he suggested. His smile was satisfied, almost evil, as he let his fingers circle her lips in rapturous swirls.

"Shane! Be serious…*please,*" she implored breathlessly.

His weight shifted and he eyed her studiously. Something was weighing heavily on her mind—that much was obvious. "All right," he agreed, pulling apart from her. The few inches on the bed that separated them seemed an incredible distance to Mara. He levered himself on one elbow, partially supported by a pillow, and watched her, waiting to hear whatever confession she thought was necessary. He thought fleetingly of Peter Wilcox, and a sour, uneasy feeling formed in the pit of his stomach.

His stare was intense, and his partially covered body compelling. Mara had trouble finding the words that should have come easily to her—how could she begin?

"Let's go downstairs," she suggested, biting her lip.

"I thought you wanted to talk."

"I do. But I would rather do it…somewhere else…where I can think more clearly…"

His dark eyebrow quirked in interest and he shrugged his shoulders. "If it would be easier for you." He reached for his clothing, cast in a wrinkled pile on the floor, and wondered about the upcoming discussion. There was a confrontation in the air—he could almost taste it.

Knowing that if she didn't explain to Shane about Angie as soon as possible, she would lose her frail nerve, she wondered how he would take the news that he had a nearly four-year-old daughter. Would he believe it? How would he react? Mara slid off of the bed and walked quickly to the closet to grab her apricot-colored terry robe that was hanging on a peg. She didn't turn around, but she could feel

Shane's dark eyes roving over her naked backside as she shrugged into the robe. "A pity," she heard him mutter to himself, but she didn't respond to the passion she visualized was on his face. She knotted the belt of the robe angrily, forcing herself to keep the promise of the night before—that she would tell him about Angie. It was his right! She meant to keep that promise to herself, no matter how difficult it proved to be. Also, before anything else happened, she *had* to know why he had waited so long to come back to her, and the reason for his sudden desire for her after four quiet, lonely years.

The seductive mood of the bedroom was broken by the airy cheerfulness of the kitchen. The clean hard surfaces of bright rust-colored tile and warm butcher-block countertops brought Mara back to reality. As she sat across from Shane at the small breakfast table, Mara wondered if she had the nerve to ask all of the questions that plagued her. She swirled cream into her coffee and watched her cup studiously as the dark brown liquid absorbed the milky cream.

Steeling herself, she raised her eyes to meet his. The pungent aroma of coffee filled her nostrils as she looked deeply into his black gaze. As if anticipating the worth of her question, Shane's face became completely sober, his stare penetrating. Mara felt as if he was looking into the deepest corners of her mind.

"You wanted to talk," he coaxed gently.

She licked her lips, a movement he found devastatingly distracting. Her voice was low and direct. "That's right," she agreed hesitantly. Oh, God, why was this so difficult? "There are things that we have to discuss. Things I need to know…things that you *have* to know."

A dark eyebrow cocked. "Go on…"

Mara sighed deeply, took an experimental sip of the scalding brew, and glanced out the windows, past the broad expanse of green lawn, past the now empty stables to the backdrop of the imperial mountains. How could she begin? How could she explain that he had a daughter? Turning back to face him, the silence beginning to gnaw at her, she found Shane still glaring at her, and this time she found the strength to meet his unwavering black gaze. Her voice, though breathless, was firm, and she controlled her hands that had begun to tremble by gripping the coffee cup tightly.

"Shane, I need to know why you didn't come back to me. I just don't understand why it took you four years to show up."

A flicker of doubt and confusion flashed over his face. He seemed almost suspicious, and his voice was harsh, brittle. "I thought that I explained all of that last night."

Mara closed her eyes and bit her lower lip. This was going to be more difficult than she had imagined. "I understand about the hospital and the identity mix-up. And I realize that your father didn't lie to me—he thought you were dead at the time that I spoke with him." She gulped a drink of hot coffee to steady herself and strengthen her determination. "But," she continued, "what I don't understand is why, when you finally got out of the hospital...why you didn't...you wouldn't..." her voice trailed off.

"I didn't come back for you," he finished for her. "You don't understand that?" he snapped, fury and incredulity twisting his features. A storm of emotion passed over his face, and his eyes had turned to stone. His voice was vehement with the anger that he had repressed for the last four years. "I *did* come back for you, Mara, after spending nearly two months in a London hospital! And when I got back here, what did I find? Were you waiting for me as I had expected you to be? No! Of course not—that was much too much to ask, wasn't it?" he challenged from across the table.

The words that were forming in Mara's throat died as he blasted on.

"You know, I wondered why you never answered my letters. And I thought it strange that your phone had been disconnected, with no forwarding number. But I found out, didn't I? The hard way. I found that the woman I loved and who I thought loved me was married to another man. Within three months, Mara…three lousy months!" His lips curled in contempt as he looked at her and the fury that he had hidden away surfaced.

A feeble protest formed in her mouth, but he continued to speak harshly, as if the dam of silence that had held his torment at bay was suddenly washed away. All Mara could do was listen, unbelieving.

"Not only that, Mara dear," he sneered, "but you were pregnant, weren't you? I wonder just how long you had planned to keep me on the string? My trip to Northern Ireland was very convenient for you, wasn't it?" he blasted.

She shook her head in confusion and frustration, tears sprouted in her eyes and blurred her vision, but still he continued. His tirade wasn't over.

"I don't know how I could have been so blind," he admitted, his voice heavy with self-contempt. "You must have been seeing Wilcox while I was still here—or very soon after. All the time that I was away, I thought—no, make that I *expected*—you to be faithful, but I guess that was too much to ask, wasn't it? The minute my airplane took off, you conveniently found yourself another lover, didn't you? Tell me—" his voice broke with the emotion that he had hoped to keep hidden within him "—just how long did you think you could keep up the charade with me? Were you seeing Wilcox while I was still in Asheville? What was it—his money that attracted you to him?" Bright fires of anger and disgust burned in his eyes.

"No!" she screamed, finding her voice. He grabbed her wrist menacingly.

"Liar!"

"No, no!" She shook her head in shame and disbelief. Was this the same man who had been so gentle, so thoughtful in bed only minutes before? "Peter was never my lover!"

Shane yanked on her wrist, and she was forced closer to him, leaning across the table. The coffee cup clattered to the floor, breaking and splashing the murky liquid against her robe. Shane's tormented face was only inches from hers, and his hot, angry breath scorched her cheeks.

"Don't lie to me!" he commanded.

Blue eyes snapped in indignation. Without thinking, she felt her free hand arc and she slapped him with all of the force that she could find, while she pulled her head regally high, over the taunts of his degrading insults.

"You bastard! How dare you accuse me of being unfaithful!" she shot back at him. "I never looked at another man, much less slept with one!"

"How can you expect me to believe that?"

"It's the truth!" Her lips thinned, and her eyes glittered like ice. "If you would let go of me and just listen for a minute, you could stop these ridiculous insinuations."

Shane's eyes narrowed. He knew that he should be suspicious, but the honesty of her eyes and the haughty disdain with which she looked upon him shook his resolve. His grip on her wrist slackened. She withdrew her hand and rubbed the wrist, never letting her eyes leave his face.

"Then...what about Wilcox?" he accused, harshly. "Why did you marry him?"

"I thought you were dead, for God's sake!" She slumped back into her chair and rubbed her tired eyes. "Shane, if you would just calm down and listen, I'll try to explain." A tremor in her voice belied her commanding words.

Shane crossed the kitchen and raked his long fingers through his black hair. Leaning against the cherrywood cupboards, he folded his arms over his chest and eyed her warily. His muscles were tight, tense, as he watched her. She wasn't lying, he knew that much instinctively, and the sting of her contempt still burned against his cheek. "All right," he conceded impatiently, his voice barely audible. "I'm listening."

"It's true," she began, her blue eyes never leaving his. "I was pregnant when I got married."

His lips thinned menacingly, but he remained silent, his stony gaze daring her to continue.

"But...it's not what you think. You see...I...I was pregnant when you left—only I hadn't realized it at the time. And then—" her voice trembled and she began shredding a paper napkin from the table "—and...then, when you didn't call...or write, I became worried. I called your father, because I needed to get in touch with you, and that's when I found out that you were dead..."

"You wanted to get in touch with me?" Shane was incredulous and darkly angry. "Why? Did you want my address in order to send me a wedding invitation?" he asked, his lips curling with sarcasm. "Why, damn it!" A fist crashed against the countertop.

"You're not listening—I wanted to get in touch with you—needed to tell you about the baby..."

"As if I would want to know!"

"...our baby, Shane—don't you understand? I was pregnant with *your* child!"

"Oh, God," he groaned, and shook his head. "No...it's too farfetched..." he began, but the anger in his eyes died as he came to terms with the truth. A quiet uncertainty lingered in his gaze, and his tanned face drained of color. "What are you trying to say, Mara?" he demanded, his lips barely moving and a look of incredulous disbelief crossing his face. His fingers gripped the edge of the counter as if for support.

"For God's sake, Shane," Mara cried, her breath torn

from her lungs. "I'm trying to explain to you that Angie's your daughter, that I only married Peter because it was the best thing that I could do for *our* child!"

"You can't expect me to believe...all of this," he retorted, but his midnight gaze wavered.

"It's true," Mara breathed. "Why would I lie?"

"I don't know..."

"Then why can't you believe me?"

Shane pushed a wayward lock of hair angrily aside, and Mara noticed that his hands trembled. "You can't really expect me to believe that you were pregnant with my child, and yet the minute you thought I was dead, you were able to find a replacement father. It's all too incredible."

"Incredible or not—that's the way it happened, all because I thought that you were dead!" Her blue eyes, clouded with disappointment at his reaction, pierced his. "Angie is your daughter!"

"Why...why didn't you tell all of this to me last night?"

A grim smile captured her lips. "Yesterday was confusing and shocking—I hadn't expected to ever see you again. And when I did, I wanted to be sure that the timing was right, I guess." Her honeyed brows drew together thoughtfully. "I needed time to work things out..."

"You mean, that it occurred to you not to tell me," he accused.

"Never!"

"Oh, God," Shane moaned in painful prayer as the realization of the worth of her words caught hold of him. Mara wasn't lying. As incredible as it seemed, Angie was his daughter. Knowing what he did now, the resemblance in the portrait he had fingered just last night startled him. Peter Wilcox had raised his child in the four years that he had been away. "And how," he asked raggedly, stunned by the weight of her announcement, "did you think that marrying someone else would be good for her?'' His question slashed through the air like a gilded saber.

"What else could I do?" she implored, her eyes filling with tears of despair as she witnessed an impenetrable mask closing over his angled features.

"You could have been honest and strong enough to have kept the baby yourself and not be pressured by Asheville society's morals. You could have given *my* child *my* name, if indeed she is mine!"

"You saw the picture on the mantle—she's your daughter, Shane, whether you want to believe it or not! And I won't stand for your giving me the advantage of your hindsight and telling me what I should have done with my life!" She stood up and faced him with an arctic gaze. "I thought you were dead, Shane—DEAD! Not missing. Not even hiding from me, but dead! I *never* expected to see you again. You could have prevented that, you know, by coming home to me. I don't think I owe you any apologies, none whatsoever. Peter wanted to marry me, and I agreed. I wanted our child to grow up in a normal lifestyle, with loving parents. Everything that I did was with Angie's welfare uppermost in my mind! Can't you see that?"

"What I see is that you schemed for Wilcox to marry you, and I call that tantamount to prostitution—passing off another man's child as his!"

Mara slapped the table in frustration with her small, curled fist. "Don't even suggest anything so absolutely preposterous!" she warned him. "I didn't pass Angie off as anything but your child—to Peter. And he had the kindness and the decency to marry me and accept Angie, nonetheless. He knew that she was your child, but for the sake of practicality we let everyone else think that she was his."

For a moment there was a long silence. Shane looked out the window, seemingly mesmerized by the view of the gracious lawn, the gleaming white fence, the empty paddock.

He rubbed the back of his neck furiously with his hand as if trying to wipe away some of the anger that was raging within him, before turning once again to face Mara.

"Shane," she said evenly, "if I had had even the slightest idea that you were alive—"

"What about my letters?" he demanded.

"I never got any letters from you...and the mail from my old apartment was forwarded here..."

"Well, someone got them, you can be sure of that. They were never returned to me!" He paused for a moment, his black gaze clouded as he thought. "And what would you have done, Mara, if you had known that I was alive? Would you have waited for me? Is that what you were beginning to say?"

"Of course."

He waved his hand angrily in the air and cut her off in mid-sentence. Closing his eyes and shaking his head, he walked past her and out the kitchen door. As the screen door banged shut Mara sighed deeply. Her own anger and indignation burned within her, and she knew it was best to let him be, give him time alone to accept the fact that he had a child. What had she expected anyway? That he would be thrilled with the fact...that he would love the child instantly...that he would fall in love with her all over again?

As she reached down and began to pick up the pieces of the shattered coffee cup, she wondered to herself, what was it that they always said—you can never go back? Well, they were right.

Mara took the time to wipe up the floor and straighten the kitchen before following Shane outside. Once again in control of her ragged emotions, she knew that she had to finish the discussion about Angie. Whether Shane liked the fact or not, he had a daughter to consider.

Her resolve wobbled a little as she saw him sitting, his head in his hands, on the top step of the long, shaded back porch. The morning sun was high in the sky, and only a few wisps of white clouds lingered near the mountain peaks. The air was flavored with the scent of pine and honeysuckle, and aside from the deep anger that kept Shane and Mara apart, the day promised to be perfect.

If Shane had noticed her entrance into his privacy, he didn't acknowledge her presence. He continued to hold his head in his hands and stare, almost unseeing, at the glorious Carolina day.

Mara dusted a spot on the steps and sat next to him. "Perhaps I shouldn't have told you," she whispered, half to herself as she smoothed the apricot robe over her legs.

"Don't be ridiculous. I wanted to know," he muttered in a voice devoid of emotion. "Besides which, you can't run from the truth, Mara, as you did when you married Wilcox."

Mara sighed heavily. "I told you that I married Peter for Angie's sake."

"Is that right?" he shot back vehemently. "And what about you? Didn't you do it for yourself?" His dark eyes swept over the large colonial house, the expansive back porch, the elegant gardens, and the rest of the well-tended grounds. "This isn't such a bad way to live, is it? Lots easier than raising a child on your own. I don't suppose that it took you very long to get accustomed to this kind of life-style, now, did it?"

"You don't understand..."

"You bet I don't! How could you marry another man, Mara, knowing that you were carrying my child? And what about all the nights after you were married? Do you expect me to believe that you and Wilcox never made love? You can't possibly take me for such a fool!"

The tears that she had pressed back began to tumble unwanted down her cheeks, but she managed to level her gaze at Shane. "No, Shane, I don't expect for you to believe anything of the kind. If I did, it would be a lie. I did make love to Peter, over and over again in the three years that we were married." Shane winced at the words, his dark eyes glowering in bitterness. "But you have to remember," she cautioned, noting the twisted look of rage on his face, "that I believed you were dead. Otherwise, I swear that I would never have let Peter, or for that matter any other man, lay a finger on me! You have to believe that!"

Shane's face was rigid, his severe jawline clenched as he watched her. The clear honesty in her eyes, the regal tilt of her defiant chin, the stain of tears that ran down her cheeks, everything about her posture convinced him that she was baring her soul to him.

He groaned to himself and then reached for her hand, which he pressed to his lips. "Oh, baby," he sighed, letting his broad shoulders droop. "What's happened to us? Why can't we trust each other?" He pulled her gently onto his lap and buried his face against her breasts. "I believe you, Mara—I believe you."

Mara shuddered in relief and clutched him as if she thought he might disappear. Her choked words came out between breathless sobs. "I can't pretend that Peter and I didn't sleep together...nor do I expect that you have remained faithful to me..." He began to interrupt but she quieted him with a finger to his lips. "Let's just not talk about it...or think about it. I don't want to hear about any of the women in your life, and Peter is dead. It's just us now—the past doesn't matter."

"And Angie," he reminded her as he crushed her to his body. She could hear the pounding of his heart echoing deep within the cavern of his chest. Tears slid silently down her cheeks in long-denied happiness.

"Come on, Mara...let's go upstairs and get dressed. There's a young lady I can't wait to meet, and you and I have a lot to do."

"Such as?" she asked quietly.

He regarded her silently for a moment, and then a sad smile crept over his face. "Such as pick up our daughter and get married as quickly as possible."

Against all of the urges of her body, she slowly extracted herself from his embrace. "It's just not that easy, Shane," she whispered. "We can't get married."

His hand, which still caught hers, tightened around her fingers and the muscles in his face hardened. "Of course it's that easy, Mara. We can get married immediately. What's to stop us?"

"There are things…"

"What things?" he demanded, deep furrows edging over his brow.

Her voice was soft and low, but decisive. "It's not just us, you know. We have other people and their feelings to consider."

"What kind of a game are you playing, Mara? I don't give a damn about other people!" He stood up, and pulled her up beside him—forcing her to gaze into his eyes. His hands clutched the terry robe at her shoulders, and his strong arms held her away from him. His fingers, once gentle, held her tightly, roughly pinching her arms, and his face was twisted in suspicion. "For God's sake, Mara," he implored. "What do we care about other people. We have a daughter to think of—don't we?" Doubt was beginning to creep into his eyes.

"Of course we do, Shane, but you can't expect a three-year-old child to just accept you as the natural father that she didn't know existed. She thought that Peter was her dad—and he was! Angie needs time to adjust—and…and so do I!" Her admission was torn from her, and the words surprised even herself, but the firm resolve in her cold, blue eyes never slackened for a moment.

"What are you suggesting?"

"Give it time, Shane…"

"You've had time."

"Angie hasn't! Think of her!"

"I am thinking of her, damn it, but I don't know if, after all of these years, I can wait any longer…knowing that she's mine."

"You have to! We all need a little breathing room— we've all had some rather extensive shocks, wouldn't you say? You and I…we have both come over some incredible, almost insurmountable hurdles in finding each other again. And time has a way of sorting out all of the unnecessary things in life and healing old wounds. We need time, and we need it now."

"You're stalling!"

"I'm not! Just think about it, Shane."

Shane reluctantly released Mara, and she stepped backward. His eyes, two black diamonds, glittered with mistrust and confusion. "All of this is hard for me to accept," he admitted. "First you tell me that I have a three-year-old daughter that I've never met, and then you tell me that I can't have her with me."

"This isn't any more difficult for you than it is for me," Mara reminded him. "Less than twenty-four hours ago, I still thought that you were dead, and now I find out that for four years you deliberately hid away from me. Four years!"

"Not intentionally," he clarified, again taking solace in the view of the mountains from the back porch. "Remember, I thought that you had betrayed me."

"There's just so much that we have to work out, don't you see?" Mara asked, reaching out and touching his cheek.

"I don't know if I can wait," he admitted moodily, and rubbed his forearms in frustration. "I want to see Angie now, this very minute, and I want to change her name to Kennedy. If I have a child, I want that child to bear my name and live with me. Enough of this pretense about her being Wilcox's child!''

Mara let her hand slide from his cheek to his shoulder, but if he noticed her gesture of consolation, he didn't respond. ''I'm not asking for you to give up anything that is rightfully yours. I wouldn't. I'm only asking for a little bit of patience. Maybe after you meet with Angie, actually see her, touch her, talk to her, you'll understand. She's a little precocious—perhaps spoiled, and she's only three. She needs to get to know you before we try and explain that you're her 'real' father.''

Shane's face was captured in a storm of emotions. He wanted desperately to believe and trust Mara, and he couldn't fault her reasoning. But there was a deep, primeval urge that controlled him and argued that he should immediately claim what was rightfully his.

''There are other people to consider, too,'' Mara suggested.

''Who?'' Anger and frustration were boiling just beneath the surface of his visibly calm exterior.

''June, for one, and—''

Shane interrupted viciously. ''June?'' he sneered in contempt. ''Peter's mother? You're concerned about her welfare?''

''Of course I am. She's not particularly well, and the shock of finding out that Angie isn't her grandchild...well, I don't think that it would be particularly good for her health. I don't want to do anything that might worsen her condition.''

''Condition? Are we talking about the same woman who wouldn't let me in to see you on the day of the funeral?'' he demanded in disgust. ''You're concerned about her welfare, when she has had every opportunity to know and love my daughter as her own grandchild? Stop the theatrics,

Mara—June Wilcox has already gotten more than she deserves!''

"She's not well,'' Mara attempted to explain, but Shane silenced her with a rueful stare.

"Neither is my father,'' he said through clenched teeth. "As a matter of fact, he's in a nursing home, and he hasn't even suspected that he has a granddaughter, much less one that is going on four years old. Would you deny him the joy of knowing Angie in order to promote the charade of your life as the faithful wife of Peter Wilcox?''

"No...but...'' Shane was seething. He dusted off his hands and leaned against one of the heavy white posts that supported the porch roof. He crossed his arms over his chest and watched Mara, mutely inviting her to continue her denial and explanation. She could tell that he was tired of the conversation, and that his anger was simmering just under the surface of his self-control. Barely concealed rage fired his ebony eyes, and Mara found herself desperately attempting to control the conversation that was rapidly deteriorating into another battle.

"But what?'' Shane prodded as her voice trailed off. He came up with his own assumptions. "But Peter's mother's state of mind is more important than Angie's real grandfather? The man that's lying in an Atlanta nursing home, barely able to feed himself. The man that doesn't even *know* about his grandchild. Is that what you were beginning to say?''

Mara shook her head violently, and the golden curls of her hair moved in soft waves against the light peach color of her robe. "Of course your father has to know,'' she said quietly.

"When, Mara? Today? Next week? Six months from now? Ever? When will you think the time is right?'' Shane asked, his fists clenching and relaxing against his body.

"Just how long would you be willing to wait, gambling on my father's health?"

Suddenly Shane looked old. His hastily donned clothing was wrinkled, and the shadow of a beard that darkened the lower half of his face seemed to age him. The barely controlled fury that had taken hold of him when he understood Mara's position, emphasized the deep lines that etched his arrogant forehead. His eyes, dark and distrustful, never left Mara's face. They silently challenged her, dared her to deny him.

Mara couldn't answer. Her emotions had tangled up within her to the point that she couldn't speak. How could she expect him to understand? How could she ask him to wait? And yet, what else could she do? It had taken four years to get where they were today; could it all be undone in just a few minutes?

Shane's voice challenged her pensive thoughts. "Are you sure that your only concern is for Angie, and for Peter's mother?"

"You have to understand that—"

"What, Mara?" he demanded. "That you're afraid to give up what little hold and control you have on the Wilcox estate? The role of Peter's widow gives you control of the corporation, doesn't it?"

"Peter's will has nothing to do with us!"

"Doesn't it?"

"Of course not! If I were concerned about my ownership of the stock, I wouldn't be foolish enough to tell you about Angie, would I?" she tossed angrily to him. "Honestly, Shane, I don't think I know you anymore. How could you think so little of me—after all we shared together?"

"Then why the wait?" he demanded. "I've met June Wilcox, and I doubt that she really is sick. And as for Angie, I think she probably will adjust to me without too much trouble. This entire argument is about the Wilcox fortune, unless I miss my guess. Aren't you afraid that when Angie's true identity is announced, the rest of Peter's family will contest his will and try and take back whatever inheritance Peter left you and Angie? After all, how does anyone know that Peter knew the secret of Angie's paternity—they have only your word, don't they? And that won't count for much, believe me. As far as the Wilcox family is concerned, June included, you're a traitor, Mara, and I doubt that they would tolerate you running Imagination Toys...or—'' his gaze swept the vast estate, bathed in early morning sunlight ''—allow you to be mistress of this house...''

"No!" Mara cried, leaning against the polished white railing for support. "It wouldn't be like that!"

"Prove it!"

"What? I...I don't understand."

"Sure you do." His rough voice was flavored with honey. "All you have to do is give me the right to claim my child!"

"I will, you know that," she said, letting her forehead drop to her hands. "I just need a little time..."

"You've had four years!" he snapped.

"And you gave them to me, didn't you?" His arms, crossed rigidly over his chest, as if to ward off her words, dropped to his sides. His gaze softened slightly, and he pinched his lower lip between his fingers as he regarded her thoughtfully.

"All right, Mara. You win. I'll give you a little more time to let everyone adjust to me...but not much!"

"I...we...don't need much..."

"Good. How about one week, is that enough?"

"Two would be better..."

"Fine! Two it is." His smile was nearly genuine. "But that's it—no more stalling!" His dark eyes gleamed with satisfaction, as if a particularly savory thought had occurred to him. "Now," he suggested, "why don't you get dressed and we'll get going. I'd like to meet Angie as soon as possible.''

The elation that Mara should have felt escaped her. There was something almost too pleasant about Shane's change of mood—something too practiced and smooth, and it continued to bother her as she hastily took a shower and pulled on her clothes.

Chapter Six

The drive toward Asheville was quiet and fast. Shane seemed to concentrate on his driving, his brooding thoughts keeping him silent, while Mara feigned interest in the view from the car as it sped through the mountains and toward the city. The countryside of deep rolling hills, ancient wooden fences, and bright splashes of wildflowers passed quickly out of Mara's range of vision as the sleek sports car hurried northward on Interstate 26, across the clear waters of the French Broad River and into the city limits of Asheville.

Mara felt the usual rush of pride that always captured her as she entered the city. Nestled in the heart of a million acres of natural mountain wilderness and the tallest mountains in the eastern United States, the Asheville plateau and the city that bore its name seemed to reach out to her. Tall, stately modern office complexes stood proudly against older, more finely detailed turn-of-the-century buildings,

and the entire city was graced with tall mountain trees—
pine, oak, chestnut...Mara took in the familiar scenery that
never failed to awe her. The clear mountain air and the
bright morning sunlight only added a deepening intensity to
the grandeur of the busy town.

Shane pulled the car into the parking lot of one of the
older, nineteenth century inns near the center of the city and
helped Mara out of the car. With his arm hooking persua-
sively under her elbow, he gently pushed her into the elevator and tapped impatiently on the paneled walls as it as-
cended to the fourth floor. Mara sat mutely, somewhat
amused, as Shane raced around his hotel room, changed,
and shaved, as if every second was being wasted. Secretly
she was pleased with his anxiety and nervousness at the
prospect of meeting Angie, and yet, she still couldn't shake
a feeling of wariness and tension about the meeting. How
would Angie react to Shane? And what about June? Why
did Mara feel that there were serious undercurrents of tension that seemed to take hold of Shane at the mention of
her mother-in-law's name? Was it jealousy of the woman's
relationship with his child, or was it deeper than that?

"Come on. Let's go," Shane called to her, interrupting
her thoughts. He was racing to the door, fumbling with his
tie, and reaching for his keys all in one movement.

"Slow down," Mara cautioned good-naturedly. She got
up from the bed, where she had been sitting, and reached
up to help him with the knot on his tie. "We've got the rest
of the morning..."

"Can't you see that I'm in a hurry, damn it!" Shane
muttered, jerking on the tie impatiently.

"Too much of one," she said chuckling and touched his
cheek, where he had obviously nicked himself with the ra-
zor.

A crooked, lazy smile stole over his lips as he noticed
the amused twinkle in her eye. "You're enjoying all of this

aren't you? You're actually taking pleasure in watching me fall all over myself as I try to hurry to meet my daughter.''

Mara couldn't help but blush. ''I guess you're right,'' she conceded, avoiding his gaze. ''It's heartwarming to see your more human side surfacing. And—'' her eyes locked with his ''—it's an incredible relief to realize how important Angie is to you.'' Her voice caught for a moment. ''I...I was afraid that maybe, when you found out about her, you wouldn't want her...''

A pained expression crossed his features. ''How could you think anything of the kind?''

''It's been a long time, Shane.''

''Too long,'' he agreed and wrapped his arms around her. He brushed a kiss across the top of her forehead. ''You know that I'd love to stay here and make love to you all morning,'' he murmured, his eyes sweeping over to the large, comfortable wooden-framed bed, ''but I really do want to meet my child. I've waited much too long, already.''

No one answered Shane's impatient knock, and so after several awkward moments, Mara let herself into June's apartment with her own key. She called out to her daughter and mother-in-law, but there was no answer, only a dull echo from the empty rooms.

Shane followed Mara through the entry and into the living quarters of the tidy, modern apartment. Other than a few pieces of Angie's clothing draped unceremoniously over the back of a floral couch, there was no sign that the child was about. Without Angie or June inhabiting it, the apartment seemed cold and sterile, the cool blue tones of the carpet and furniture austerely precise and impractical.

Shane eyed the living room with obvious contempt, his dark eyes only softening when he observed Angie's tattered blanket tossed carelessly on the floor. He stooped to pick it up, and smiled to himself as the worn pink blanket unfolded to reveal a nearly naked and slightly dirty doll. "Can't you afford something a little bit...cleaner?" he asked, eyeing the doll's tousled frizzy hair and lazy blue eye.

"I've tried, believe me," Mara laughed. "But she prefers Lolly."

"Lolly?" Shane repeated uncomfortably. "But...you manufacture toys. Isn't there something you could find to replace...Lolly?"

Mara's lips curled into a grim smile. "I would hope so," she muttered, shaking her head pensively, "but it seems that our Angie, like the rest of the toddlers in America, prefer the products of the competition."

"Lolly isn't manufactured by Imagination?"

Mara shook her head again. "Ironic, isn't it?"

Shane looked upon the doll quizzically. "A damned shame," he whispered, straightening himself to his full height. Still holding the doll tentatively, his eyes swept the apartment to rest on the wall behind the couch. His frown deepened as he recognized portrait after portrait of Angie and Peter adorning the smooth white surface. "Your husband?" he guessed, with a bitter edge to his voice.

Ignoring the sarcasm, Mara walked to the wall laden with family portraits. She rested with one knee on the couch and pointed to several of the pictures, her voice taking on the quality of a teacher. "Yes, this is Peter—with Angie, when she was about six months old. And this one, next to it, is a picture of June, her husband, Peter, and his older sister, Dena. The next picture is of Peter, Angie and me...Angie was about two at the time; it was just before we learned of his illness—June insisted that we have it taken. And this large portrait, here on the left, is of the entire family, including the cousins and aunts of Peter and his family. The lower, smaller shot is..."

Mara had been pointing to each of the photographs in turn. The fact that Shane was obviously angry spurred her onward. No matter what else happened, Shane would have to learn to accept the fact that she had been married to Peter. Nothing could change the past.

"That's enough," Shane nearly shouted, reaching out and capturing Mara's arm. "I've seen enough of the Wilcox family history for one morning. Let's go and find Angie. Where do you think she would be?"

Mara retrieved her hand from Shane's grasp. "June mentioned something about taking her to the park for a miniature train ride. It's just across the street…"

"Good. Let's go."

"Don't you think we should wait? June was really looking forward to spending the morning with her."

"We're going, Mara, and now. You really can't expect me to sit here—in this shrine to your husband—and wait for his mother to bring back my child, can you?"

"No, I suppose not…"

"Then stop dragging your feet, and let's go."

Shane grabbed the few belongings that he recognized as being Angie's and followed Mara out of the apartment and across the street to one of the well-manicured parks of Asheville. It was nearly noon, and although the day was warm the mountain breezes that cooled the city made the late August morning feel crisp and invigorating. The trains were on the far side of the park, near a small depot, and although the track wound through the lush vegetation all along the perimeter of the gardens, Mara reasoned that the most likely spot to find June and Angie was near the miniature station.

Mara heard her daughter before she actually caught a glimpse of her. Over the clacking of the wheels on the small track and the occasional blow of a whistle, Mara could hear Angie's laughter and shouts. Both Shane and Mara stopped in their tracks when they rounded a bend in the path and could view grandmother and child. Angie was digging in a sandbox of sorts, and June was watching her over the top of a magazine as she sat on a bench in the sunshine. Angie was obviously having the time of her life, and June seemed to be enjoying the peaceful, warm morning. Mara smiled, but couldn't help but feel a lingering sadness steal over her as she thought about June and her frail health. June so obviously enjoyed and loved Angie, and Shane didn't hide his dislike for Peter's mother. Mara felt her heart go out to the elderly woman who had been so kind to her. With Shane's preoccupation with his child, and insistence that Angie become his legal daughter, June would lose that fragile link that she felt she had to her dead son. She had always thought that Angie was Peter's daughter, and Mara knew that when the truth came out, June would be devastated to learn that Angie was Shane's child. Would she feel betrayed, lied to? Suddenly Mara's life seemed a complicated labyrinth of deception.

Shane's hand tightened over hers, and after a momentary pause he walked directly toward the unsuspecting grandmother and child. Mara found her throat tightening with each step she took. After all the years of yearning for the chance to be with Shane again, she found herself dreading what she had dreamed about. When it came time for Shane to claim Angie, how would it affect June…Dena…and Angie herself? How could Mara anticipate that final confrontation with such sublime happiness and increasing dread?

June looked up from her magazine and then used it as a shield over her eyes to ward off the late summer glare from the sun. She watched Mara and Shane approach her bench, and the broad smile that had lighted her face when she recognized Mara faded as she identified the strange man walking briskly and determinedly toward her.

"Good morning, Mara," June beckoned, noticing the lines of worry crowding Mara's normally clear forehead.

At the mention of her mother's name, Angie looked up from her digging and squealed with delight at the sight of

Mara. "Mommy!" she chirped, running over to Mara and leaping into her arms. She clung, monkeylike, to her mother and began chattering wildly. "Grammie take me on train rides—just like the big ones in the book, and they have whistles and real smoke and…" her voice trailed off as she observed Shane for the first time. Her black eyes collided with her father's and although Shane smiled, there was distrust in Angie's stare. "Who he?" she asked pointedly, sticking out her lower lip. "Why he got Lolly and my blankie?"

One chubby arm held onto Mara's neck, while the other reached out impatiently to claim her things. Shane handed the doll, draped in the tattered blanket, to his daughter. Importantly, Angie clutched them to her chest, all the while eyeing Shane with suspicion.

Mara had trouble finding her voice but finally managed the introduction. "Angie…June…this is Shane Kennedy, a friend of mine, and someone who's interested in the toy company."

"We've met," June replied, taking Shane's proffered hand with obvious disinterest.

"That we did—on the day of the funeral," Shane agreed amiably. June's blue eyes narrowed icily.

"I don't like you," Angie said, glaring at her father.

Mara gasped and turned several shades of crimson. "Angie! That's not nice! We don't say things like that. You apologize to Mr. Kennedy."

The child folded her arms defiantly over her chest and stared up at Shane with obvious mistrust. "No!"

"Angie," Mara cajoled, her patience beginning to thin. She set the girl down on the bench next to her grandmother. "Now you be nice. Mr. Kennedy is Momma's friend…"

Silence. Awkward, warm, embarrassing, uncomfortable silence. Angie turned her head so as to avoid direct eye contact with her mother, and a small smile tugged at the corners of June's mouth. She seemed to be extracting a small sense of satisfaction at Angie's behavior and ill manners.

Shane ignored Angie's rejection altogether. "There's no need for an apology, Angie," he said, and Mara shot him an uncompromising glance. "I've met a lot of people that I didn't like in my life; I just wasn't honest enough to admit it."

"But she shouldn't—" Mara began, but Shane waved off her arguments.

"You're right, she probably shouldn't be so...forthright. But it doesn't matter—not with me."

Angie looked as if she didn't quite know what to make of the conversation. Fully expecting further protests from her mother, she was surprised when none came about. After casting a confused and furtive glance at her mother's friend, she sat down on the bench and began playing with the doll and blanket, telling Lolly about her morning in the park on the trains.

"Excuse me, Mr. Kennedy," June said, meeting Shane's dark gaze. "Did Mara say that you were interested in purchasing Imagination?"

"That's correct."

"Well, I hope she explained to you that the company is absolutely, without condition, not for sale!" June retorted. Mara was surprised. June never took an interest in the family business, much less interjected an opinion of company policy.

"That she did," Shane agreed, leaning against an oak tree and watching Angie play with her doll.

"Then...I guess...I don't understand why you're still here..." June evaded.

"As Mara stated earlier, she and I are old friends," Shane replied smoothly, almost intimately. Mara felt a wave of color once again stain her cheeks.

"Oh, then you're here in Asheville for the weekend?"

"At least," he drawled, a slow smile spreading over his arrogant features.

June's lips pursed slightly. "I see you were at the apartment. Did you get all of Angie's things? Her nightgown was in the spare bedroom."

"No, we only picked up the blanket and the doll. But I thought you could bring her other things over when you come to stay with her on Monday."

"Well," June began crisply, a hint of exasperation flavoring her words. "In that case, I'll be running along." She picked up her magazine, tossed it into her basket, and rose from the bench. At the effort, her skin seemed to pale.

"Wouldn't you like to spend the rest of the afternoon with us—perhaps go to lunch?" Mara offered.

"I don't think so" was the stiff reply, aimed directly at Shane. "Dena's coming over later in the day—for the life of me I don't know why—I can't remember the last time she came to visit me."

"Thanks so much for looking after Angie," Mara whispered, giving June a kiss on the cheek. "I'm sure she had a wonderful time."

June's face relaxed a bit as she looked at Angie, busy again in the sandbox. "Yes, I think she did. It was my pleasure." June's long, bony hand clasped firmly over Mara's. "I'll see you Monday morning."

"All right."

"Good-bye, Angie," June called out to the little girl, who looked up from her play long enough to flash June her most ebullient smile and wave her hand and blanket at her grandmother.

When June was out of earshot, Shane turned his attention back to Mara. "I'd say she doesn't like me much, wouldn't you?" He cocked his head in the direction that June had taken.

"She probably just didn't like the fact that you attempted to see me on the day of Peter's funeral. She was pretty upset. Peter was her only son."

Shane shrugged indifferently, but Mara couldn't help but think about her mother-in-law. The chilling undercurrent of tension that had developed when Mara had introduced Shane to June couldn't be ignored, and the withering look of haughty disdain in the older woman's eyes—a look so atypical of June—spoke of a deep-seated mistrust or hatred. Why did June instantly dislike Shane? Was it, as Mara had suggested, because he had broken through unspoken bonds of civility and tried to see Mara on the day of the funeral? Did June overreact because she was emotionally drained at the time, or could there be another, deeper, angrier cause for June's personality reversal?

"I think your suggestion earlier was great," Shane said, breaking into Mara's distracted thoughts.

"What...what was that?"

"Lunch. I'm starved. One cup of coffee wasn't quite enough this morning." Shane dropped a protective arm over Mara's slim shoulders. "Quit worrying about June. It's her right not to like me."

"It's just that I don't understand it. It's all so out of character for her. She's usually a warm, open person."

"Somehow I find that hard to believe."

Further conjecture was cut short as Angie came up dragging her blanket behind her. Mara smiled at her child. "Are you hungry, Angie? How about some lunch?"

"Hot dogs?" Angie asked, her eyes lighting.

"Hot dogs?" Mara repeated. "Is that what you want?"

Angie shook her blond curls vigorously and pointed in the direction of a local vendor pushing a metal cart with large bicycle wheels and a bright green umbrella.

"Hot dogs it is," Shane agreed with an amused smile.

"Are you sure?" Mara asked, eyeing the mustached vendor and his steaming wares dubiously.

"Whatever the young lady wants," Shane laughed, and Angie began running off in the direction of the vendor.

"Don't you think you're pouring it on a little strong?" Mara asked. "Angie's already spoiled. The last thing she needs is an overindulgent father."

"We'll see," Shane said enigmatically, his dark eyes following the path of the escaping child.

The rest of the afternoon was spent in the park with Angie. Though shy at first, Angie finally accepted Shane and even let him have the privilege of holding her blanket as they walked through the city. The Summerfest Art and Craft Show was being held at the Civic Center, and Shane insisted upon looking over the various arts and crafts made by local mountain craftsmen and the Cherokee Indians. At the show, Shane purchased Angie a beaded bracelet, which she proudly wore around her wrist. By the time the afternoon shadows had lengthened, Shane carried a tired Angie against his shoulder, back to the car parked near June's apartment.

The drive back to the house was as quiet as the drive into the city. Dusk was beginning to take hold of the countryside and a deep red sunset formed a backdrop for the purple-hued mountains. Angie slept quietly in the back seat, with only a deep, contented sigh escaping from her lips disturbing the quiet hum of the sports car. Shane was thoughtfully, broodingly silent during the journey home, and Mara could almost feel his dark thoughts begin to take hold of him. They were almost back at the Wilcox estate before he broke the silence that had captured them.

"I don't know if I can hold up my end of the bargain," he admitted.

"The bargain? What bargain?"

"Our deal, that I give you two weeks to sort things out before we tell Angie that I'm her father."

"You promised," she reminded him, gently touching his coat sleeve.

"I know…I know. But—" he paused, trying to find the right words as he shifted down and turned up the long, circular drive "—that was before I knew her. She needs me."

"And?"

A sarcastic grin curved his lips. "You were waiting for this one, weren't you? Well, you're right. I need her. That's what you've been waiting to hear, isn't it?"

Tears began to pool in Mara's eyes, and her voice deepened. "I'd be a liar to deny it. You see, well…Peter and Angie never did get along…"

"What do you mean?"

Shane stopped the car, and pulled the key from the ignition. Angie stirred but settled back into a comfortable sleep.

"Peter resented Angie."

Shane touched Mara's shoulder, and she could feel the heat of his fingertips through the light cotton of the blouse she was wearing. "He resented her?" Shane whispered. "But I thought that you married him in order to have a normal family life. Isn't that what you told me?"

Mara nodded mutely. "I did, and I thought it would work. But I was wrong. After she was born, everything changed. And he was never close to her. Not as a baby or a toddler…"

Shane rested one arm on the steering wheel, and supported his head with his hand. His voice was level, and quiet, but filled with rage. "He didn't do anything to her, did he?"

Mara gasped. "Oh, no. Peter was never violent or cruel. "No…no…but he was impatient with her, or he would ignore her altogether. He wanted more children…his children. But after seeing his lack of interest in Angie…" She shrugged her shoulders.

"So that was your 'perfect marriage,' was it?"

"I didn't say it was perfect. I don't think that there is such a thing."

"No?"

She stuck her chin out determinedly and looked him in the eye. "No."

"You've changed a lot in the last four years, Mara."

"I don't think so. I've just become more realistic. Life has a way of forcing you to give up your dreams."

"Don't ever give up your dreams, Mara."

"Haven't you?"

He cupped her chin in his hand and watched while his finger outlined the soft hill of her cheek. "Never," he whispered and let his lips touch hers.

"Are we home?" Angie asked from the back seat, rubbing her eyes and only catching a glimpse of the intimate kiss.

"Yes, honey," Mara said, hurriedly opening the car door and reaching for Angie. "Come on in the house and I'll fix us a quick dinner."

"Can I play with the kitties—Southpaw's kitties?" Angie asked, her gaze running around the foundation of the house, looking for the mother cat.

"For a few minutes, honey. Until dinner is ready."

A smile spread over Angie's face, and she immediately took off in the direction of the back porch.

It was nearly nine o'clock by the time dinner was over, Angie was bathed, the dishes were done, and the little girl was asleep in her bed. She had found the kittens and talked Shane into crawling under the back porch to get them. Against Southpaw's soft protests, Shane extracted the kittens and helped Angie make a bed for them in the screened-in portion of the porch. Southpaw didn't seem too pleased with the new arrangement, but Angie was delighted with a bird's-eye view of the four chubby gray-and-white cats. "You can help me name them," she had announced to Shane, who was more than thrilled at the prospect, supplying names of his favorite football players.

"I don't think O.J. is a very good name for a kitty," Angie confided in Mara as she was being tucked into bed.

"Neither do I," Mara laughed. "But if Shane likes it, maybe we had better use it."

"Don't like it," Angie repeated with a yawn, and Mara kissed her lightly on the forehead. Angie snuggled against the pillow, and before Mara could turn out the light, the little girl was breathing deeply and evenly. Shane stood in the doorway, watching the intimate scene between mother and daughter, and wondered how he had found himself so tangled up with Mara all over again. It wasn't what he had planned, and he mentally chastised himself for his weakness where Mara was concerned. All the years of bitterness and deception were beginning to wash away, and he knew that if he allowed himself, he could fall in love with her, just as easily as he had the first time, nearly five years ago. An uneasy feeling that he had never really stopped loving her crept over him, and he wondered if there was ever a time when he hadn't cared for her, as he had forced himself to believe. But now, as she bent down to kiss his child, and the moonglow caught the golden highlights of her hair, a warm feeling of protectiveness stole over him. Was it Mara that he cared for, or was he just succumbing to latent feelings of fatherhood for the child he had never met until late this morning? Now that he knew about Angie, was he mixing up his feelings for Mara with his newfound emotions for the little blond girl with the slightly upturned nose and the mischievous twinkle in her dark eyes?

"She doesn't think much of the names that you gave the kittens," Mara whispered as she closed the door quietly and started down the long carpeted hallway toward the stairs.

"I heard," Shane chuckled, walking at Mara's side.

"Can you blame her? Who ever heard of naming newborn kittens after football heroes? No wonder she thinks the names are ill-fitting."

"'Crummy,' I think, was the word she used," Shane replied, and noticed Mara's wistful smile. "She's not exactly afraid to speak her mind, is she?"

"Not that one," Mara agreed.

Shane apparently found the thought amusing and chuckled at the image of the outspoken child.

"Oh, you think it's funny, do you?" Mara baited. "Well, just you wait. You'll get yours. Let me tell you, her outbursts can be embarrassing—damned embarrassing!"

Shane touched Mara's arm just as they stepped off the staircase and headed toward the back of the house. "You know what they say, 'From the mouths of babes—'"

"I know," Mara agreed, waving off the rest of his quote and snapping on the kitchen lights. "And I suppose you're right," she admitted reluctantly. "Anyway, I wouldn't change one thing about her."

"I would," Shane countered, and clicked the light back off. Once again, the kitchen was dark, except for the pale, filtered moonglow.

"What?" Mara asked, breathlessly. The light mood and banter of a moment before had changed when darkness had covered the room. It was as if she could *feel* Shane standing next to her, not touching her, and yet reaching out to her. "What would you change about Angie?" Mara was slightly taken aback. All afternoon she had been led to believe that Shane was absolutely enchanted with his headstrong young daughter.

"I want them back, Mara," Shane whispered, and his fingers brushed invitingly against her upper arm. "The three years that I haven't known her…haven't been around her…I want them back."

She paused a moment before answering. The silence was burdensome and painful, and it was with difficulty that she found her voice. Her fingers touched his and pressed his hand more tightly against her arm. "Those years are gone, Shane…if they were so important to you, you should have taken them when you had the chance."

"Damn it, Mara! I didn't have a chance!"

"Oh, Shane," Mara sighed, rotating to face him and looking deeply into his eyes that were almost ebony in the darkness of the room. "We can't change the past. It's difficult, I know—and we've both made mistakes. But we have no choice but to live with them."

"I suppose you're right," he admitted thoughtfully, though the tone of his voice lacked conviction. His fingertip reached up and touched her eyelid, and the thick brush of her eyelashes.

Mara closed her eyes and leaned against him. "For the rest of the weekend, let's try to forget all of our problems and the past. Can't we just concentrate on the present and the future?" she asked, leaning against his chest.

He hesitated, and reached for her right hand. After taking in a long breath and letting his fingers entwine through hers, he continued: "That depends."

"On what?"

"A couple of things. The first being that you tell me just how you think another two weeks will give you the courage you need to face June Wilcox and tell her that Angie is my child." His fingers tightened over her hand.

"I told you before, June's not well." Mara's eyes flew open, and even in the shadowy night, she could tell that Shane was becoming angry again. But why? His grip on her fingers was severe, nearly crushing, and her eyes flew down to their hands, suspended and tangled between them in the darkness.

"The second thing I would like to know is why you still

insist on wearing your wedding ring, even though your husband is dead? Does it hold some special significance? Or is it just that you don't want to give up that last little piece of evidence that you were married to Peter Wilcox? Was your love that lingering that you can't bear the thought of taking off his ring?'' Shane's words were ice cold and they shattered the intimacy of the moment. Mara fought to withdraw her hand, which he reluctantly released.

For a moment she was unsure, and then slowly, with careful and theatrical precision, she slid the wide gold band off of her finger and placed it on the windowsill, where it winked in the moonlight.

''Satisfied?'' she asked him, and once again snapped on the lights. Instantly the room transformed into the warm kitchen with rust accents. ''Why do you constantly want to battle with me, Shane? Why is it, just when I think we're making some concrete headway toward working things out, you find another excuse to bring up the past?'' Her eyes glittered with the provocation she felt. ''The reason that I wear the ring is obvious, at least to most people. It discourages unwanted male attention.'' She turned and placed the teapot on the stove to heat some water. She was angry and was having trouble reining in her temper. Why did she still love him so desperately? He was so unpredictable, so moody, so prone to swings in temperament, and still she loved him.

The whistle on the teapot caught her attention, and she carefully poured two cups of scalding water, before steeping in them a rare blend of pekoe. With barely controlled indignation, she handed Shane a mug of the hot liquid.

''You have a lot of admirers, do you, now that dear old Peter is gone?'' He observed her over the rim of his cup, and his black eyebrows quirked in dubious interest.

''That's not the point...''

''Then, please—'' he turned up a disbelieving palm, encouraging her to continue her explanation "—enlighten me."

Mara nervously tapped her fingers on the edge of her cup, feeling somehow as if she was being cornered and manipulated. Still, she couldn't help but take the well-placed morsel of bait, although she eyed Shane suspiciously before accepting his suggestion. She sighed wearily into the tea leaves. "I suppose that it's no secret that since Peter's death, when I became the woman in charge of Imagination, there have been a few persistent gentlemen—and I use the term loosely—who seem to think, in their lofty opinions of themselves, that I, a mere woman in charge of a large corporation, need their expert advice—or at the very least, their bodies—to help me deal with my loss of Peter and the awesome responsibility of running the company. It's apparent that most men can't understand how I can cope without a husband and father for my child, not to mention managing the business, to boot." As Mara began talking, warming to her subject, all of her secret thoughts came tumbling out. "I've become some sort of target, Shane, and I don't like it." Her proud chin inched upward in defiance. "I'm not the kind of woman who *needs* just any man who happens along." Her cheeks had become flushed, and she paused for a moment, to stop the angry quivering of her lips. "I don't understand why some of the men around here don't think a woman can run Imagination Toys..."

"Perhaps they've read the financial statements and realize that the company has been losing money ever since you took over the reins."

"Not fair, Shane," Mara admonished, suddenly willing to do verbal battle with him. "The company has been losing money for quite some time, long before I took over. It all started sometime before Peter's illness was diagnosed, and although I haven't been able yet to turn things around and operate in the black again, I refuse to take full responsibility. I'm not accepting the blame for the recession!''

"You're hedging! The recession is just a convenient excuse! You can look over the earnings reports of most of the companies in this region—and they're still making it. Why is it that Imagination can't face up to the competition, anyway?''

"We've had a few bad breaks…''

"It comes with the territory, Mara. Every company has 'bad breaks,' but some seem to rise above them and find a way to make a profit.''

"I guess I don't really understand where this conversation is heading," Mara snapped, and put her teacup down with a clatter against the butcher-block countertop. "Are you criticizing the way I'm handling the company?''

"Not yet.''

"But you intend to?'' she asked indignantly.

"Perhaps, if it's necessary," he promised.

"Then, why, now, all of the arguments?''

"I only asked you about your wedding ring.''

"And I was only trying to explain to you that the only reason that I wear the ring is to discourage certain businessmen from coming on too strong with me. Is that so hard to understand?'' Blue fire danced in Mara's eyes as she stood before him, silently challenging him to pursue the argument. When he didn't immediately accept the dare, she prodded him. "And really, admit it, isn't that what you thought, along with everyone else, that there was no way that I would be able to run the toy company effectively?''

An unsuppressed smile lighted his near-black eyes.

"I thought so!'' she stated, shaking her head and pursing her lips until they whitened. Blond curls rubbed angrily against her shoulders. "Well, just because I'm a woman doesn't mean that I can't handle the job. Nor does it mean that I need *any* male help!''

Shane's lips thinned, and he set his cup down next to hers on the counter. "I think that we should get something straight between us, once and for all," he replied with quiet determination. "I didn't come up here to Asheville with any intention of helping you."

"But I thought…"

"It doesn't matter what you thought. I came here with the express purpose of buying out the company. You know that. Because you refused to sell, I've had to alter my position."

"What are you getting at?"

"I just want you to know that my personal life, including the fact that I've found out that I'm Angie's father, doesn't necessarily alter my position with regard to Imagination. If anything, it probably strengthens it!"

"I don't understand," she admitted flatly.

"Don't you? Come on, Mara, you're a bright woman. Don't play games with me."

"I'm not playing games with you, Shane. I'm only trying to understand you."

"Then understand this—I don't like the idea that you and I made love in this house last night."

"What?" Mara was stunned. "What are you talking about?" she asked, clearly perplexed by the twists in the conversation and wounded that he hadn't shared the same supreme ecstasy and bliss that she had experienced during their lovemaking.

"I'm talking about playing second best to the memory of a dead husband," Shane ground out, his eyes darkening. "Do you know how hard it was for me to make love to you last night, in his house, his bed, his sheets? Everything around me, including you, was owned by Peter Wilcox! Do you have any idea how I feel each time that I hear his name or see his picture? Don't you realize that every time I see Angie, I wonder just how much influence Peter had over her? How did she feel about him? Did she love him? Was he kind to her? Did he hurt her, or mentally abuse her?'' He paused for a moment, but before Mara could find her tongue and refute his insinuations, he continued with his tirade. ''And the same goes for the toy company. I don't want to live, or work, in the shadow of another man's memory. I can't accept that.''

''For God's sake, Shane, can't you, for just a moment, forget about Peter?''

''How?'' He grabbed her by her thin shoulders and with a shake, forced her to look squarely into his tortured eyes. ''How, Mara?'' he repeated, through clenched teeth. ''Everything that I should have had, he took...''

''He didn't take anything that you weren't willing to give, Shane. And besides, what's the point? Peter's dead!''

''But he was alive once, wasn't he?'' Again the involuntary shake. ''And he made love to you, didn't he? How many times was he invited into your bedroom, like I was last night? How many times did you moan your surrender to him, just as you did to me?'' Shane asked, his grim face showing the strain of his pent-up emotion. His rage was so out of control that Mara could feel his hands trembling where they gripped her upper arms.

''I...I thought that we had decided to put all of that...behind us,'' she said, reaching up and smoothing a lock of black hair away from his forehead.

''It's difficult,'' Shane admitted, his grip relaxing slightly. ''And...I'm not really sure that I even want to try to forget. Not as long as we're trapped in this house—*his* house.''

There was a silence, long and charged with electricity that hung between them. Finally, Shane's arms dropped to his sides and he cleared his throat. Still visible, his anger was a tangible force.

''I'm going back to the hotel, Mara,'' he stated thoughtfully. ''I'll call you in the morning.''

"But you could stay here tonight," she invited, suddenly afraid that he might leave and, once again, be lost to her.

"No, I couldn't."

"But last night..."

"Last night was different. There's too much here to remind me of the things that I would rather not remember." His black eyes traveled over her body, and she could see the sparks of passion rekindling in their ebony depths. "I want you, Mara, as much as I ever have," he admitted, his dark eyes reflecting the intensity of his words. "But I want you on my terms—not yours, nor Peter Wilcox's. So I'll wait—as you've suggested for two weeks—to claim what is rightfully mine. But, then," he warned quietly, "things will be my way!"

As he turned to leave, Mara found her voice and called out to him. "But what about Angie? Are you just going to walk out of her life for the next two weeks?" she cried. What was he doing? Why, dear God, was he leaving, just as he had once before?

"Of course not. Don't you know that I'll be back?" The fear in her eyes was unmasked, and he felt an uncompromising urge to run to her, to wrap his arms around her thin shoulders, to whisper promises to her that he couldn't possibly keep. But somehow he found the strength to stand his ground. "I'll see you in the morning," he promised. "And we'll go out, just the three of us. But," his voice deepened again, "I don't want to spend any more time than I have to being reminded of your husband."

Mara took a step toward him and opened her mouth to protest, but his next words halted her.

"Remember, Mara, this was all your idea. You're the one that needed the extra time to adjust. For the next two weeks, we're playing by your rules!"

Mara followed him to the door, intent on changing his mind, but somehow lacking the resolve to argue with him.

She stood in the doorway as he stepped into his Audi, flicked on the ignition, and roared down the driveway. The headlights faded into the darkness, and the silver car and the man she loved were swallowed in the night.

Shane never looked over his shoulder, but Mara's image, a dark silhouette backed by the warm lights of the house, lingered in the rear-view mirror and burned in Shane's tormented memory.

Chapter Seven

The weekend passed quickly for Mara...too quickly. Sunday had dawned hot and humid, and Mara had packed a picnic basket filled with fruit, wine, cheese, sourdough rolls, and ham. Shane had arrived promptly at ten and, after a friendly reunion with Angie and the four kittens, hurried Mara out the door and into the car. They had driven to Chimney Rock Park, southeast of Asheville, where they had hiked along the terraced trails to view Hickory Nut Gorge and Hickory Nut Falls, one of the highest waterfalls in eastern America. The clean, cascading water, the steep cliffs, and the lush, dense foliage seemed to take the heat off of the above average temperature. Although Shane had to carry Angie part of the way up to Chimney Rock, he hadn't complained, and the awe on the little girl's face as she gazed thousands of feet down the hazy, spectacular, seventy-five-mile view of the canyon and Lake Lure was worth the hot climb.

But when dusk had stolen over the Blue Ridge, Shane had taken Mara and Angie back home, and once again left for his hotel. After a long, hot day of enjoying his company, Mara felt strangely empty inside as she watched his car disappear down the driveway. Would it ever be possible for Shane to love her? Would they ever have a chance to build a normal family life, or would there always be a reminder of the past to haunt them and keep them apart? Was the love of a child great enough to conquer the barriers that had separated them? Where would they go from here? The questions, nagging and whirling in her weary mind, kept her awake for most of the night. When June came to the house the next morning to watch Angie, Mara could almost feel the cold, piercing blue gaze of her mother-in-law knife through her thin layer of makeup and fresh blue, jersey print dress to see the effects of Mara's turbulent emotions for Shane.

"Hi, Grammie," Angie called from the kitchen table, where she was studiously attacking a stack of three pancakes and unknown gallons of blackberry syrup.

June's drawn face broke into a smile at the sight of the little girl, who was nearly covered head to toe in purple smudges of syrup. "Goodness, Angie! Look at you. You'll certainly need a bath this morning—" the older woman chuckled "—unless, of course, you plan on hiding under the porch all day with those kittens."

Angie set her fork down and looked quizzically at her grandmother. The syrup on her face and hair made her look almost comical. "Oh, no. The kitties is not under the porch anymore," she tried to explain. "Come on, Grammie. I show you." Angie bounced out of her chair and hurried out the back door, which slammed behind her.

Mara cringed at the sound. "Just a minute," she called to her daughter through the screen. "Why don't you finish your breakfast, and then Grammie can go with you to see Southpaw?''

"I all done!" Angie asserted, her voice sounding more distant than just the back porch. She was obviously too distracted with the kittens to eat any more breakfast.

"Are you sure?" Mara asked, almost to herself, as she surveyed the barely touched breakfast. "You haven't eaten much…"

Angie poked her head through the narrow opening of the screen door and hurried back into the kitchen. "I said I all done!" she reasserted.

"But you barely touched the pancakes."

Angie puckered her lips in thought and then decided to ignore her mother. She took a swipe at her mouth with her napkin, as if, once and for all, to close the subject on breakfast, and then raced out the back door, leaving the half-eaten stack of pancakes to soak up the remainder of the syrup.

Mara didn't feel up to battling with Angie so early in the morning after a restless night. Knowing that she was probably making a maternal error, she ignored Angie's disobedience and ill manners and tried to still the throbbing near her temples. Her early morning headache seemed to be pounding more harshly against her skull.

"Would you like a cup of coffee?" Mara asked stiffly, seeing the worried expression in June's eyes. Mara held the coffeepot in midair and avoided June's direct gaze. Was it Mara's imagination, or did June seem older and appear more troubled today than usual?

"I'll get some later," the older woman replied, and cast a furtive glance to the back porch. Angie was quiet, and June decided that the little girl was unlikely to interrupt, at least not during the next few minutes. She touched her neck hesitantly and nervously before she broke the silence that had been building between herself and her daughter-in-law.

"I saw Dena Saturday afternoon. She came and visited me," June began, gauging Mara's reaction.

"And how was she?" Mara asked, sipping her coffee and reaching for Angie's dirty dishes.

"Concerned."

Mara's throat tightened convulsively, and she unconsciously bit at her lower lip as she deposited the dishes into the sink and turned on the water. "Concerned? About what?"

"You for one," June replied, cautiously.

"Anything else?"

"The company." June's graying eyebrows drew together, and she hesitated for a moment, as if what she was about to say might be unpleasant. "She seems to think that you're being bullheaded about selling Imagination Toys."

Mara smiled grimly to herself as she placed the few dishes into the dishwasher. "I know that," she admitted, drying her hands on a nearby cotton towel and turning to face her mother-in-law. "But you have to understand that I want the company to make it, and I think that it can. Selling now would be a mistake, I'm sure of it," she stated, with more conviction than she actually felt. "Right now, with the company losing money, we couldn't get a decent price for Imagination, even if we did want to sell. But if we could just turn the company around, to at the very least a break-even point, the price we could ask would be substantially higher."

June seemed to relax a little as she pulled her ivory knit sweater more closely over her thin shoulders. "Chilly in here, isn't it?" she observed in a distracted voice, and then, as if suddenly remembering the train of the conversation, she snapped back to the subject at hand. "Well, Mara, I'm glad to hear that you're not anxious to sell Imagination," she offered. "I know it's a big job, running an unprofitable business in the middle of a recession, and sometimes I worry that you're working too hard, but the toy company is part of the Wilcox heritage. From my husband Curtis's grandfather down to Angie…'' Mara felt her heart stop at the mention of Angie's link in Peter's family. June hesitated only slightly. ''I know that Dena would like to sell the company lock, stock, and barrel,'' June stated through thinned lips.

After readjusting her sweater, the older woman sat down at the table and didn't argue when Mara placed a cup of black coffee and the sugar bowl on the table within arm's reach. After taking an experimental sip of the scalding brew, June smiled faintly and continued.

''It's really not Dena's fault, you know?''

''What isn't?''

''Her attitude toward you.''

Mara tried to shrug off the insinuations, but June would have none of it.

''Don't try to hide it from me, Mara. I know my own daughter, and I realize that she has never been fond of you…not since the beginning.'' Mara drew in a steadying breath. The subject of the bitterness that existed between herself and Dena had never been brought out into the open. It was as if under the cover of Southern civility, the unacknowledged problem would somehow disappear. As close as Mara was to June, she never expected that June would ever admit she knew of the animosity that existed between Peter's sister and his wife.

''She's always felt a little inferior, you know,'' June conceded, ''and I suppose she has every right to feel that way. Curtis made no bones about the fact that he wanted a son to carry on the family business, and Curtis could never quite hide his disappointment that Dena wasn't a boy. Not that he didn't love her, you understand. But, well, it's different between a father and daughter than it is with a son.'' June smiled sadly into her coffee cup. When she lifted her faded blue eyes to meet Mara's interested gaze, Mara noticed a genuine pain and empathy in the older woman's eyes.

"I guess that I should have tried to patch things up between father and daughter, but I thought that as Dena grew up the situation might change. I should have known better, you know. Curtis and Dena were so much alike, from their red hair to their hot tempers! Anyway, when Peter came along, five years later, Curtis was delirious that he finally had his 'son.' Dena couldn't help but feel left out, and slighted." June sighed. "I realize that now, with women's liberation and everything else, things have changed, and that today it's not so important to have that first-born son. But then, Curtis never really accepted his daughter as anything but the second child, although she was his first. And even if she did have the temperament to manage the business, he would never have given her the chance!"

June seemed tired and weary. "You don't have to explain all of this to me," Mara whispered, touching the frail woman's shoulder.

"Oh, but I do!" June responded viciously, and inadvertently spilled some of the coffee, sloshing it onto the saucer. "I know that Dena, well, she comes across a little catty sometimes, but I want you to know that it's really not a personal vendetta against you."

"I know that," Mara admitted. "Don't worry about it."

"I can't help it. She's caused a lot of trouble for you in the past, but I think it's because she's felt left out. First from her father's attention, and now from what she sees as her rightful inheritance. It didn't help, you know, when Bruce broke off the engagement after learning that she wouldn't inherit the bulk of Imagination Toys."

Mara felt herself cringe as she remembered how upset Dena had been when her flaky lawyer fiancé had jilted her only months before the wedding had been planned.

"What do you think I should do about Dena?" Mara

asked, feeling that June had recounted the painful memories with a purpose in mind.

"I don't know. I've never really understood Dena, or her reasons. But she seems to think that it would be best for all concerned to sell Imagination to that Kennedy man." Mara noticed June's jawline tighten at the mention of Shane.

"And you?" Mara asked quietly. "What do you want?"

June hesitated a minute. "This was the Wilcox family's lifeblood. Their way of life and their heritage. I...I would hate to see it sold to a stranger." June's voice had taken a firm, almost hateful tone that surprised Mara.

"Any decisions regarding the sale of Imagination will be put to the stockholders in the company, all of the members of the family. You know that, don't you? Just because Angie and I own the largest block of stock doesn't mean..."

The screen door banged shut, announcing Angie's return to the kitchen. "Mommy! Grammie! Namath's eyes are open!" the little girl squealed breathlessly. "Come see! Hurry!"

Mara laughed nervously as she dried her hands on a nearby towel. She was relieved to have a break in the intense conversation with her mother-in-law. She followed Angie and June out the door and onto the screened-in back porch that housed the more delicate hanging plants. It was already warm in the small enclosure, and aside from a slight breeze off of the mountains, the morning promised another hot day, despite June's comments to the contrary. Just as Angie had announced, the largest of the gray kittens' eyes were beginning to crack open.

"See, I told you," Angie whispered in obvious delight as she held up the fat fluff of fur.

"That you did," June agreed with a smile. "Now, tell me, what was that kitten's name?"

"Namath," Angie responded with a frown. "Mr. Kennedy gave him *that* name."

At the mention of Shane's name, June visibly paled. For a moment Mara wondered if the older woman would collapse, but just as Mara placed a supporting hand under June's elbow, the color came back into her cheeks.

"He...named the cats after football players?" June guessed with obvious distaste.

Mara nodded mutely while Angie chattered on about the kittens, pointing out O.J., Franco, and Bradshaw in turn. June was appalled, but didn't attempt to cool Angie's enthusiasm.

"Do you like O.J.?" Angie asked innocently.

"It's...fine," June managed, feebly, and Angie appeared satisfied with her grandmother's approval.

"I liked Whiskers better," the child mused, and June nodded her silent agreement.

"I have to get going to work now, honey...you be a good girl for Grammie, won't you?"

Angie turned her attention away from the kittens long enough to give her mother a kiss on her cheek. Mara's eyes caught June's distracted gaze. "Are you up to handling her today?"

"Of course."

"You're sure?"

"Don't worry," June said with a sad smile. "We'll get along just fine." A genuine fondness lighted her tired, blue eyes.

The sadness that had stolen over her mother-in-law hung with Mara during the drive into Asheville, and although she mentally tried to shake off the depression, she failed. The warm morning sunshine, the smell of wildflowers, the pastoral view of horses grazing on the high plateau, nothing discouraged the feeling of melancholy that converged upon her. The only thoughts that touched her were worries about June's health, Shane's impatience, and Angie's welfare.

How in the world was she going to solve her dilemma and tell June that Shane was Angie's father? And how would the little girl take the news? Would she understand? Could she?

The day was just beginning, and Mara found herself sighing as she opened the door to her office.

"Mrs. Wilcox!" a young female voice declared as Lynda came running up behind her. "I'm sorry, but I couldn't stop him!"

"What? Lynda, what are you talking about?"

"Mr. Kennedy—the man who was in here Friday night..." The receptionist blushed with the memory of Friday afternoon and the reunion of her employer and the stranger.

Mara smiled with only a trace of impatience. "Yes?"

"He...well, he absolutely insisted..."

"Insisted upon what?"

"I told him it was irregular, that no one was allowed in your office—other than you—but he just started ordering me around, and...well..."

Mara pushed open the door to her office and saw the object of Lynda's dismay seated regally behind Mara's desk, pen in hand, running through a stack of ledgers.

"It's all right," Mara stated stiffly to the confused receptionist. "Mr. Kennedy has my permission to be in my office...and...er...see any documents that he wishes."

Relief flooded the girl's features. "Thank goodness," she murmured as she hustled down the hallway back to her desk.

Mara felt her temper heating and braced herself against the closed door to the office before she confronted Shane.

"Just what do you think you're doing?" she inquired, eyeing him suspiciously. "You have Lynda half out of her mind with worry that she's done something wrong."

Shane tossed the ledger he had been studying onto

the desk top. "What?" His attention was finally focused on Mara.

"I said that Lynda has strict orders not to allow anyone in here without my permission. I'm surprised that you got away with it—much less bribed the accounting department out of the bookkeeping ledgers."

"I like to get to work early. I didn't know when you would get in, and I didn't want to wait." Once again he looked down at the stack of manila-colored ledger cards. A scowl creased his dark brows.

"So you just decided to take over my office..."

"For the time being."

Mara was becoming exasperated and found it difficult to hide the fact. She crossed the room, tossed her purse into a nearby closet, and marched over to the desk. "Why don't you tell me what you're doing," Mara suggested, and stood near him.

Perhaps it was her condescending tone of voice that galled him, but whatever it was, he picked up a stack of ledgers and waved them in the air arrogantly. "How can you possibly expect to run a company this way?" he charged, his black eyes igniting.

"What do you mean—what are you talking about?" Mara asked, stunned.

"I mean that I don't know how you can expect to compete effectively in the marketplace when you're working under such burdensome and antiquated systems in the office. It's no wonder that Imagination is in the red!"

"I guess I'm just a little overwhelmed by all of this," Mara stated, motioning to the stacks of records that covered her desk, "but I don't understand a word you're saying." She couldn't hide the hint of sarcasm and anger that tinged her words.

"What I'm saying is that you're trying to dig a well with a teaspoon..." The confusion and smoldering indignation in her gaze begged him to continue. "What I'm trying to say is this—Toys are a big business, and in a recessive economy any toy company, Imagination included, has to be not only innovative but also technologically advanced. You can't be so bogged down with paperwork that you're ineffective."

"You're saying that Imagination needs to modernize?" she guessed.

"Right."

"And...I suppose you think that the first step would be to purchase a computer?"

"You need the accuracy and speed that only a computer will give you..."

"What I don't need is someone, especially an owner of a computer company, to tell me how to spend money that I don't have!"

"You can't afford not to invest."

"Spoken like a true salesman," she quipped curtly.

"I'm serious, Mara. How many people do you have working in your accounting department, aside from Hammel?"

"Three."

"And the combined salaries and benefits total over thirty thousand dollars annually?" he guessed.

Mara nodded thoughtfully.

"A good microcomputer would cost you less than a third of that and would supply you with reports on inventory, financial statements, product costs..."

"Save your breath." She fell into a nearby chair. "I've heard it all before. It's just that I haven't had the time or money to convert to a computer. No matter what you say, it's an expensive investment."

"I don't see that you have much of a choice."

"Why not?"

"Because if you want my assistance, I'm going to insist upon it. There's no way that I'll invest in a company that doesn't have an effective way of keeping track of inventory and product costs or effectiveness of advertising and sales promotion. This is the age of computer technology, Mara, and you can't expect to run a competitive company the way it was run ninety years ago—''

"Wait a minute," Mara said, interrupting him. She held her palms outward, as if to push aside any more of his arguments. "You're getting the cart before the horse. Before you make any further decisions about the company, don't you think it would be a good idea to tell me exactly what you have in mind, in terms of investing in Imagination?"

A grim smile cracked his features. "Fair enough."

"Well?" she asked anxiously, and pushed aside the impulse to bite at her lower lip. Instead she studied the sharp planes of his rugged face, his thick black eyebrows, his brooding lower lip that protruded slightly, and the thin shadow of a beard that appeared even in the morning. In a dark blue business suit, striking burgundy tie, and crisp, white shirt, he bore an arrogant but somehow intriguingly masculine presence. He tapped his lips thoughtfully with a pencil as he spoke.

"I told you before, that I had no intention of giving Imagination the benefit of my assistance without something in return. And since you refuse to sell out to me, I'm willing to invest in the company."

"How?"

"I've done some research. You don't own a majority interest."

Mara's stomach tightened. "That's true," she admitted.

"However, I know that it's impossible to buy up enough shares of the company to take over. For one reason, June Wilcox would never sell her interest to me."

"That's probably true, too."

"So I've decided to buy up as many shares as the family is willing to sell to me—and then I'll offer to loan the toy company some money, at prime interest rates, for the purchase of some necessary pieces of equipment.''

"Such as a computer from Delta Electronics?''

"For starters, yes.'' Mara stiffened. "Along with some equipment to start converting the factory.''

"Into what?''

"An assembly line for computer components. The reason I want a part of Imagination so badly is that I want to start a new line of video games that would, for the most part, be built in Atlanta. The components, partially assembled, would be sent up here to be used for the inner workings of video games and small learning devices for educational toys.''

"Can't you do all of that from Atlanta?'' Mara asked, wondering aloud. "Do you really need Imagination?''

"Let's face it. Other than what I've read, I know very little about toy manufacturing and sales. On the other hand, Imagination has a sizable list of sales outlets, has, for the most part, a reputation for making durable, reliable products and a fair amount of name recognition. Besides which,'' he added in a more ominous tone of voice, "you need me more than I need you.''

"You're that sure of yourself?''

Shane leaned back in the desk chair and cradled his head in his palms, rumpling his black hair. "I know that you've had your share of bad luck, whether it was deserved or not.''

"Deserved?''

"Face it, Mara. Much of Imagination's problems stem from the fact that for the past ten years, ever since Peter took over the company, profits have plummeted—aside from the one shining spot in the past few years—those funny-looking plastic dolls from that hit space movie.''

"*Interplanetary Connection,*'' Mara said with a sigh, knowing that although she hated to admit it, Shane was right.

Shane seemed to sense her change in mood, and the look of defeat that paled her intense blue eyes made him feel inwardly guilty, as if he had been the cause of all of her problems.

"I understand that the movie production company has decided upon another manufacturer to handle the toy products for the movie sequel."

"That's right," Mara said, avoiding his gaze and looking out the large window at the towering Blue Ridge mountains in the distance.

"Why?"

Mara tightened her lips and swiveled to meet his inquiring gaze. "Several reasons," she began. "First of all, the production company didn't like the packaging, which I told them we would change, at our expense. Then they were unhappy with the advertising campaign, and I agreed that we would use an independent firm of their choosing."

"Then what was the problem?"

"It has something to do with a few of the more exotic extraterrestrial beings from the sequel. It seems they're much more intricate than the aliens in *Interplanetary Connection,* and the production company feels that a more malleable plastic for the action figures would make them appear more lifelike."

"And you disagree?"

Mara shook her head and pursed her lips pensively as her dark, honey colored brows drew inward over her eyes. Thoughtfully, she clasped her hands together and tapped her chin. "No, I'm willing to go along with just about anything Solar Productions wants, but unfortunately the competition seems to have cornered the market on soft plastic; at least they can produce the action figures much more cheaply than we can."

"And just who is the competition?"

"It's all confidential, of course, and Solar Productions

won't tell us, but my guess is it's San Franciscan Toys, a rather new company from California. They seem to have a budget that NASA would envy, and the right marketing skills to sell even the cheapest, most shoddily made toys, such as…that Lolly doll that Angie is so fond of.''

Shane's face relaxed at the mention of his child. ''And how is she this morning?''

''Just fine and still enthralled with the kittens.''

There was a pause in the conversation, and the smile left Shane's eyes. ''Did you see June this morning?'' he asked, almost under his breath.

''Yes.''

''And were you able to tell her that I'm Angie's real father?''

''I thought about it,'' Mara admitted, ''but I just couldn't. She looked so…tired this morning, I didn't want to risk it.''

''If the woman is so damned unwell, why do you let her stay with Angie? There could be an accident of some kind. Aren't you afraid for her?''

Mara rubbed her temples furiously. ''Of course I'm concerned,'' she snapped back.

''Well?''

''Have you considered the alternatives? With my irregular hours, a preschool is out of the question. And as for a private sitter, I've never been able to find one that would give Angie the same care and love that June gives her. There are no alternatives. June is the best choice. Besides which, being with Angie is good for her.''

As Shane rolled his dark eyes expressively toward the ceiling, the door to the office swung open and Dena slid into the room. She began talking before noticing Shane behind the desk. ''I waited for ten minutes, and then I realized that you had probably forgotten our…'' she stopped in midsentence, her green eyes taking in the tall man sitting behind Mara's desk and the crackle of tension in the air. It didn't take a genius to guess that she had walked smack-dab into the middle of an argument...and from the looks of it, a personal one. Dena stopped short of the desk and adjusted the bulging folder under her left arm.

"Oh, Dena," Mara cried, slapping her palm against her forehead. "I forgot all about our meeting..." And then, shaking her head at her own stupidity, she added, "Excuse me...I don't believe you've met Shane Kennedy," Mara apologized as Shane rose from his chair and offered his hand to Dena.

"Pleased to meet you," Dena drawled in her sweetest southern accent, placing her small palm in Shane's.

"The pleasure is all mine," Shane countered, his dark eyes twinkling to add reinforcement to his words.

Mara watched the exchange between Shane and Dena with curiosity. What kind of game were they playing with each other? Dena smiled demurely, and let her hand slide out of Shane's grasp.

"Would you like to postpone our meeting again?" Dena asked Mara. The smile never left her voice, nor her glittering green eyes. Her burnished hair was coiffed attractively to fall in curly tangles to her shoulders and her sleek Halston original knit suit hugged her body possessively. Dena looked every bit the professional advertising executive.

"What meeting?" Shane asked. "I hope I didn't interrupt any of your plans..." The phrase sounded innocent and natural enough, but Mara found it hard to ignore the intensity of his words or his gaze.

"Mara and I were supposed to go over the advertising budget," Dena quipped, sitting down on the couch opposite the large, glass window and crossing her slim legs with practiced elegance.

"Perhaps we should talk about the budget later..." Mara proposed anxiously. Why did she feel it much better to keep

Dena and Shane apart? The two of them together, for some unfathomable reason, seemed entirely too threatening.

Dena ignored Mara. "Shane Kennedy," she mused aloud, pursing her petulant wet lips. "You're the man interested in purchasing the toy company?"

"I was."

"No longer?" Dena pouted, tossing Mara a barely concealed look of disappointment.

Shane slid down in his chair and settled on his lower spine. "Mrs. Wilcox refuses to sell."

Dena's eyes narrowed just a fraction, and for a moment, her well-placed smile faltered. But gathering all of her professional aplomb, she begrudgingly said nothing about Mara's decision.

Shane answered the questions in Dena's eyes. "Mara has persuaded me to take an alternative position with the company…that is, if the board of directors approves."

"Alternative position?" Dena repeated innocently. Only Mara noticed the hardening of her sister-in-law's determined chin.

"I'm considering purchasing shares of the company and making a loan that would enable Imagination to continue its operation."

"Kind of you," Dena murmured, a bit sarcastically. She was reappraising Shane—sizing him up. There was something about him that was more disturbing than his evident male virility…an uneasy haunting familiarity…that kept nagging at her. What was it about him that bothered her so? Nervously she toyed with her pen as she watched him. "What's in this for you, Mr. Kennedy?" she asked, and Mara felt herself stiffen. Up until this point, Dena had held onto the pretense of being a competent, interested shareholder. But there was a relentless persistence in the redhead's eyes that unnerved Mara.

"Call me Shane," he responded with a pleasant smile.

"Don't worry…Dena—" he used her first name cautiously, but she nodded politely as he did so "—this isn't a one-sided endeavor. Delta Electronics will profit admirably from the venture."

"Hmm…" was her unsure response.

"Now, if you'll excuse me, I've got to get busy," Shane admitted. "Mara, first I'll need an office with a telephone. Then, I want all of these ledgers transferred to that office. Oh, and I'll need space for the terminal…" He ran his finger thoughtfully along his jawline.

"Anything else?" Mara asked sarcastically.

"Yes." His fingers snapped decisively. "Arrange for a board meeting sometime this week, if possible, and I'll have a written proposal for all of the members of the board."

Mara felt the muscles in her back stiffen. He was so efficient, so damned efficient. There was an unquestionable air of authority and businesslike demand to all of his movements.

"You can use Stewart Callison's office," Mara stated, reaching for a stack of the ledgers and holding the door open with her foot. "He's on vacation and won't be back until the middle of September. If you're still here when he returns, we'll rearrange everything, I suppose."

Shane reached for a pile of his paperwork and his briefcase, and followed Mara down a long, white hallway to the small cubicle that was Stewart's office. If he thought the accommodations confining, he didn't complain, but stacked his work neatly on a corner of the desk.

It took several trips to carry all of the ledgers to Shane's office. When at last Mara's office was once again her own, she was surprised to find Dena still sitting, half-draped across the small leather divan.

"Let's go over the budget right now," Mara suggested, finally dropping into her rightful chair behind the desk. She pulled a file from her drawer and spread it on the desktop.

"Can it wait?" Dena asked, distractedly.

"But I thought…"

Dena made a dismissive gesture. "The budget can wait. What I want to know is why you insist on being bullheaded about Kennedy's offer to buy out Imagination?"

"I explained all of that before."

"Wasn't his offer high enough?"

"We never even got down to dollar signs."

"Then you didn't give the man a chance!" Dena accused viciously.

"Listen, Dena. I told you before, I'm not interested in selling. At least, not now. Shane's made a very interesting counterproposal which he intends to present to the shareholders. If the majority accepts his terms, then perhaps Imagination will still be able to pull out of this slump."

"And if not? What then, Mara?" Dena cut in, her temper rising angrily. "Then we'll be in debt to Kennedy, along with a list of other creditors as long as my arm. What good will he have done us?"

Mara listened patiently, the only evidence of her anger being the silent drumming of her fingers against the empty coffee cup on her desk.

"Why don't you just give up, for God's sake? You were never cut out to run this company, and by now, even you should be able to see it. Ever since you took over, the losses have increased to the point of no return. Take your chance while it's offered; sell the whole damned company and be rid of it! Parceling off a few shares to Kennedy and having him loan us some more funds is only forestalling the inevitable."

"You're suggesting that I take the money and run?"

"In so many words, I guess so."

"Why? Why are you so anxious to get out of the company? If you don't like being a part of it, why don't you just sell your shares to Shane and be done with it?"

"You'd like that, wouldn't you?" Dena countered.

"What do you mean?"

"You'd like to be rid of me. I know that I've been a thorn in your side, and really, I haven't meant to be," Dena persisted. "But it galls me to no end that you…someone who really isn't related to anyone in the family…is running Imagination."

"Dena," Mara began, choosing her words carefully. "I understand why you resent me. And I know that you feel that you should have inherited the bulk of the company stock, as you were your father's first born, but—"

"Stop the theatrics, Mara," Dena commanded, rising from her insolent position on the couch. "And don't bother to try and convince me that you're doing the 'right thing' for either me, my mother, or your kid by carrying out Peter's wishes. The whole thing doesn't wash with me, not one little bit," Dena announced, bitterly.

"Dena—"

"Don't start with me, Mara," Dena persisted, rising up from the couch to look down her nose at her sister-in-law. "As far as I'm concerned, it's all or nothing with this company."

She turned on her heel to go, but Mara's voice arrested her. "Just give it a chance," Mara suggested wearily.

"Not on your life!" With her final retort, Dena marched regally out of the office and quietly closed the door behind her.

Mara gritted her teeth and quietly attempted to calm herself. The next two weeks were not going to be easy by any means.

Chapter Eight

The first week of Shane's visit flew by at an exhausting pace. Personnel were shuffled, the microcomputer, "Delta's finest," was shipped and assembled, and truckloads of information, anything from payroll records to scrapped ideas about products were fed into the large keyboard with the video screen. Shane insisted that everyone in the office be able to run the machine, at least to some degree. The more private files concerning personnel or secret new designs were specially coded so that only a few of the more trusted employees had access to them.

Mara was reluctant to sit at the keyboard and hesitant to work with the imposing piece of new machinery, but she couldn't hide the smile of satisfaction when she had mastered a few of the more basic programs. Within weeks, Shane assured her, she would be an expert concerning the Delta 830-G.

At home, where Mara should have had time to relax and

unwind, the situation remained tense. June's health was a very real concern for Mara, as the older woman seemed far too distracted at times, and the grayish pallor of June's face couldn't be hidden by even the most expensive cosmetics. Angie was as exuberant as ever, and Mara wondered if the vivacious child was too much of a burden on June. But every time that Mara broached the subject of June's health, the older woman found a way of avoiding the issue. Mara even suggested that June make an appointment with Dr. Bernard, but the advice was conveniently ignored.

Angie was busy discovering the world. The four plump kittens were one of her most time-consuming infatuations, and her idolization of Shane was apparent to everyone, including June. Several times in the past few days, June had made excuses to stay late with Angie, at least until Shane's sleek silver Audi pulled into the driveway. Mara caught June observing Shane and Angie, and the older woman's mouth drew into a fine line of pain when she noticed the easy familiarity that Shane lavished upon the child. And Angie's innocent and loving response wasn't lost on June. Whatever love that Angie harbored for Peter was forgotten when the child was with Shane; that much was certain.

Mara was torn. She cared for her mother-in-law, she cherished her child, and she loved Shane with a passion that at times burned wildly through her body. The past week of watching him at work, while he was absorbed in some minor problem, made her body ache with longing for him. He hadn't stayed with her since the first night together, and somehow she felt betrayed. She knew that it was his own way of saying that until she told June about Angie, he wouldn't have any physical contact with her.

Mara was wise enough to realize that he still wanted her, perhaps more desperately than ever. She would catch him gazing at her, his eyes touching her, caressing her, and she knew in the black intensity of his gaze that he was burning for her. And yet he controlled himself, silently waiting for her to tell the world about Angie. Mara flirted with the idea of attempting to seduce him, hoping to break down his iron-willed control, but she hesitated, foreseeing more problems than the three of them already faced.

It was the day of the board meeting that the simmering tension between them snapped.

It didn't help that the day dawned hot, and that the cool mountain breezes that usually favored the high plateau of Asheville hadn't appeared. Instead, the dull, sultry heat was unnervingly oppressive, even in the early morning. The dust and bothersome insects that Mara rarely noticed seemed to be everywhere, inside the house as well as out. And Angie, usually happy to spend the day at home, clung fitfully to Mara's legs, whining and crying, begging Mara to stay with her.

Mara was standing at the mirror, trying to apply a light sheen of plum lipstick to her lips while Angie complained loudly beside her. Angie's face was red from the heat and passion of her outburst. Mara dropped the lipstick tube on the counter and bent on one knee so that she could face her child on her level. As she did so, she felt the tickle of a run climb up her knee in her panty hose. Ignoring the fact that she was already late, and that she doubted that she had another clean pair of panty hose in the house, she cradled Angie's curly head in her hands.

"What's wrong, Angie?" Mara asked, wiping a tear from the child's flushed cheek and reaching for a tissue to wipe Angie's nose.

"I don't want you to go," Angie sobbed.

"But, honey, you know Momma has to go to work..."

"No!"

"Tell me what's bothering you," Mara suggested. "I can't make things any better unless you tell me what's troubling you. Don't cry, just talk to me."

"I...I don't want to stay with Mrs. Reardon...I want Grammie!" Angie demanded, stamping her bare foot imperiously.

"But, honey, Grammie will be here later. You know that she has to be at the board meeting today."

"No, she don't!"

"Angie," Mara said authoritatively. "Mrs. Reardon is a very nice lady. She comes here every Friday to help Momma..."

"But she don't play with me."

"Honey, she's very busy. She has to clean the house, but I just bet, if you ask her nicely, she would read a book to you."

"I don't like her!"

"Sure you do." Mara was having difficulty hiding the exasperation in her voice. The last thing she wanted this morning was a full-blown battle with her child. The guilt about leaving Angie was beginning to get to her. Did all mothers who worked full-time at a career they enjoyed feel the welling sense of guilt that Mara was experiencing? "Come here, Momma's got to find a new pair of panty hose," Mara called to the child as she stepped back into the bedroom and rummaged in her top bureau drawer. The digital clock on the nightstand reminded Mara that she was already twenty minutes late. Somehow, she had to placate Angie. If she left the child and Angie was unhappy, Mara knew that she would have trouble concentrating on the board meeting. And today, more than ever, she needed every drop of concentration she could muster.

"Hey, I've got an idea," Mara hinted in a secretive voice that Angie loved.

Instantly, the child was intrigued. She lowered her small, blond head between her shoulder blades and her dark eyes danced. "What?" Angie asked, in a collusive whisper.

"Why don't you help Mrs. Reardon clean the house?"

Angie's face fell and she eyed her mother suspiciously. Mara ignored Angie's restraint and continued with her idea.

"Here—" she reached into the top drawer again "—is one of Momma's old hankies. You can use it to wash the windows and polish the furniture, and look," Mara retreated into the bathroom, still tugging at the new panty hose. Quickly, she fished under the bathroom sink to retrieve a blue bottle. "This is a bottle of glass spray...you can spray the cleaner on the windows and wipe it off with the hanky...like this." Mara sprayed the cleaner onto the mirror and watched her image become distorted in a froth of bubbles. Then she folded the cloth and wiped the mirror clean.

Angie suspected that she was being conned out of her bad mood by her mother. And although she wanted to continue to whine, she was impressed with her mother's attempts to entertain her. Never had her mother let her touch any of the cleaning supplies. Her enthusiasm was slightly subdued, but she reached a chubby hand out toward the clear glass bottle half-filled with blue liquid. "Will Mrs. Reardon really let me?" Angie asked as she dashed into the bedroom, and after a quick sneaking look at her mother, sprayed a healthy spot of foam on the expensive satin quilt. The look on the child's face was one of expectant defiance.

"Angie Wilcox! What do you think you're doing?" Mara sputtered as she attempted to wipe up the mess on the quilt. "You can't play with this, unless you play with it the right way, with Mrs. Reardon's help! And, never, never spray the furniture or the bedspread again!" Mara admonished her daughter as she furiously wiped at the stain on the quilt. Giving up, she pulled the bedspread from the bed and threw it in a crumpled heap near the laundry hamper.

"You know better!" Mara reprimanded through tight lips, as she guided Angie out of the room and toward the staircase.

Angie paused under a solemn portrait of Peter's grandfather and looked into her room. Mara nearly ran over her. "I think I stay up here," the child mused. "Lolly needs a bath and I give her one."

"Oh, no, you don't," Mara retorted quickly after following the train of the little girl's thoughts. Mara's thin patience was fraying, and she was barely able to hold onto her anger. "If you intend to play with that glass spray, you do it with Mrs. Reardon."

Angie puckered her lips for a moment, seeming to hesitate, but decided against arguing with her mother any further. Clutching the dear bottle of spray as if she was afraid someone might take it from her, she grabbed her tattered blanket and followed Mara down the stairs.

Mrs. Reardon had the vacuum cleaner roaring in the den. The machine went quiet when Mara popped her head into one of her favorite rooms in the house. It was large and comfortable with an informal brick fireplace and knotty pine walls. The varnish had yellowed and aged to give the room a warm, homey look, and the plaid sofa and leather recliner were a welcome relief from the other, more formal furnishings of the house. Large, leafy green plants grew well in this room with its paned windows and view of the gardens to the rear of the grounds. When Mara came home from work to relax and unwind, it was always in this room. It was always casual and warm, and some of her fondest memories included reading to Angie in the den, or sitting on the couch with her child and building with blocks.

"I've got to go now," Mara called to the plump, middle-aged woman with the broad smile and crisp, floral apron. Mrs. Reardon looked up from plumping the pillows on the couch as Mara continued. "Angie's already bathed and had breakfast. And, oh, I gave her a bottle of glass cleaner. She wanted to help you clean the house," Mara lied a little sheepishly.

"So I see!" Mrs. Reardon laughed, exposing gold crowns

over her molars. Mara spun around to see Angie studiously spraying an antique silver coffee service.

"Please, Angie, be careful," Mara pleaded, and kissed the chubby child on the forehead. Turning to Mrs. Reardon, she hoisted the strap of her purse over her shoulder and picked up her briefcase. "I should be in the office all day, if you need me. And June will be back here by early...or at the very latest...mid-afternoon."

"Fine...fine...I'm going to be here all day," Mrs. Reardon agreed distractedly as she wrapped the cord from the vacuum cleaner neatly around her broad forearm. "Don't you worry about a thing."

Mara felt as tightly coiled as a spring as she opened the back door and hurried past the flowering shrubs to her car. Was it her too vivid imagination, or did she hear the shatter of broken glass just as she was stepping into the car? After waiting a couple of extra minutes, knowing that Mrs. Reardon would come out of the house if indeed a calamity had ensued, she started the car. Thankfully, Mrs. Reardon had handled whatever catastrophe had occurred. With a sigh of relief, Mara wound her way past the dozen or so oak trees that were giving merciful shade to the driveway and inched the car onto the highway. Trying to make up for lost time, she pushed the throttle to the floor and began speeding toward the city limits of Asheville. The drive was hot and dusty, and by the time Mara parked in her favorite spot under the building, she felt drained. Why did she dread this board meeting so? An uneasy feeling akin to dread had steadily knotted her stomach.

"You're late," Shane snapped as Mara entered her office. He was leaning against the windowsill, his hands supporting him by propping his long frame against the sill. He looked starched and fresh in his lightweight tan suit and ivory linen shirt. A navy tie, just a shade lighter than his eyes, was staunchly in place. In comparison to Shane's crisp, unruffled look, Mara felt completely wilted.

"I know I'm late."

"The meeting starts in less than ten minutes!"

"I know…I'm sorry."

"Is that all you can say?"

Mara tossed her purse into the closet and put her briefcase down with a thud. "Don't start with me, okay?"

He stood up and straightened his suit. His dark eyes observed her and noted that her usually impeccable appearance was more than a little disheveled. Shane preferred her this way; she seemed so much more vulnerable, so much younger, more as he remembered her, but still he was disturbed. It wasn't like her.

"Bad morning?" he guessed, his dark brows furrowing as he walked toward her.

"It could have been better." She straightened the neatly typed pages of the proposal and counted to make sure that there were enough copies. She avoided his gaze.

"What's wrong?" he asked, echoing the question she had asked of Angie only a half hour before.

"Nothing…everything…I'm not sure."

"It's Angie, isn't it? I think you should tell me about it."

"Let's just forget it until the meeting is over, okay?"

He pulled the reports out of her hands and forced her head upward in order that she meet his gaze squarely. "What's bothering you?" he asked crisply, and his fingers strayed across her arms and throat.

"Shane, don't."

The soft blue silk of her dress brushed against her skin, and through the light fabric, Mara could feel the inviting warmth of Shane's large hands, coaxing her…massaging her…caressing her…

"Look, Mara, if something's wrong with Angie, I think I have a right to know—"

The door flew open. Startled and embarrassed, Mara shrank from Shane's tempting embrace. She felt her face begin to burn guiltily.

"Oh," Dena said, her curious eyebrows arching. Had she just stumbled onto something important? "I...I didn't mean to disturb you..." she began, stepping backward while her green eyes took in the intimate scene.

"You didn't," Shane replied curtly with a polite, but slightly irritated smile. "We were just on our way to the boardroom. Is everything ready?"

"Yes...that's what I came to tell you. Other than Cousin Arnie...everyone is waiting." The look of confusion and incomprehension never left her perfect face, and her dark, almond-shaped eyes puzzled over Shane's features.

For one heart-stopping instant Mara read the expression on Dena's face. *She knows,* Mara thought. *Dear God, Dena knows that Shane is Angie's father!* Surprisingly fast, Mara's composure and common sense took over. If Dena knew about Angie's paternity, she would have already made good use of it, unless she intended to use the information to embarrass Mara at the board meeting! Mara felt her insides churn. Never had she dreaded a board meeting more, but she managed a feeble grin.

"Good." If only she could hide the blush that still burned on her cheeks. "Let's go!" Armed with Shane's proposal, all fifteen copies, and as much confidence as she was able to muster, Mara led Shane and Dena down the stark white hallways into the elegant and slightly overstated boardroom.

Already the captain's chairs around the shining walnut table were, for the most part, occupied. Although a paddle fan circulated lazily over the crowd, a thin cloud of hazy cigarette smoke hung heavily in the air, and the whispered chatter that had buzzed only minutes before stopped as Mara entered the room and took her place at the head of the table. Her stomach lurched perceptively as she placed a strained smile on her face and looked into the eyes of all of the relatives of her late husband, most of whom she hadn't seen since the day of the funeral.

As Mara's eyes swept the interested but cautious faces lining the table, they locked with June's pale blue gaze. Dressed in burdensome black, which had become her only public attire since Peter's death, the older woman smiled tightly at her daughter-in-law and fidgeted with the single strand of natural pearls at her neck. Dena slid into a chair next to her mother, and the contrast between mother and daughter was shocking. Dena seemed devastatingly youthful and glowing with health. Her thick red hair, secured against the nape of her neck, curled softly at her neckline, the understated but elegant ivory silk dress enhanced her slim figure, and the discreet but expensive jewelry sparkled against her flawless skin. It all seemed to give Dena just the right touch of class that made her appear more beautiful than usual.

After informal introductions were made and coffee was offered to all of the board members, Mara called the meeting to order. Somehow she was able to speak, although she felt a painful constriction in her chest. The nervous glances and grim smiles on the faces of Peter's family didn't ease any of her discomfort. Did they all know? Was it possible that they could tell that Shane was Angie's father? Did they think her an impostor—a pretender to the crown? She knew that her restless thoughts bordered on paranoia, but still they plagued her. How in God's name was she going to get out of this? Sooner or later all of the family, June and Dena included, would know that Shane was the father of Peter's child. What would happen? And why, when everything appeared so useless, did she try so vainly to hold Imagination together? It seemed inevitable that, when the truth was learned, the family would contest Peter's will and a horrible, ugly lawsuit would ensue.

Mara wasn't really worried for herself; she knew that she could be as strong as she had to be. But what about Angie, and June? The press would have a field day with the story. How could Mara protect her child and her frail mother-in-law? Was it possible?

A few of the essentials for the board meeting, such as a treasurer's report and a lengthy reading of the minutes of the previous meeting, were accomplished as quickly as possible. Finally, her composure outwardly calm, Mara announced the purpose of the meeting, explaining in detail the financial woes of the toy company, and passed out the typewritten reports to each of the board members.

Shane rose to confront the members of the Wilcox family. He looked exactly what he was: young, tough, and confident. His smile, slightly crooked, seemed genuine, and his dark eyes took in every person in the room at once. He spoke distinctly, cross-referencing his speech with notes from the typewritten pages. After explaining the reasons that Delta Electronics was interested in Imagination and summarizing the contents of his proposal, he smiled confidently at the nervous pairs of eyes that watched him. The fan turned quietly overhead, soft strains of piped-in music melted in the background, the pages rustled as they were turned, and only an occasional cough or click of a lighter disturbed Shane's even monologue.

Mara noticed that the jute-colored open-weave draperies swayed with the movement of air, and that a few of Peter's relatives shifted uncomfortably in their chairs. But for the most part the board seemed to be uniformly concentrating on Shane; he had everyone's attention.

Mara listened and watched the effect of Shane's speech on the members sitting at the table. Some seemed absolutely convinced that Shane knew exactly what he was doing, to the extent that Cousin Arnie even nodded his bald head in agreement with Shane's more elaborate points. A few others were dubious, and the caution in their eyes was an open invitation to questions. And several, at least it seemed from their blank expressions, didn't know quite what to think.

Shane's speech was short and concise. When finished, he tapped the report loudly on the table, closed it, and sat down. "Now," he concluded, taking a long drink from the coffee cup that had been sitting, untouched, in front of him, "does anyone have any questions?"

For a stagnant second there was only silence, and then it seemed as if everyone began to talk at once. Shane smiled to himself in amusement, but Mara's stomach quivered in worried anticipation. Finally, the boardroom quieted.

"Are you trying to tell me…I mean, us," Peter's cousin, Sarah, began after crushing out her cigarette, "that unless we take you, er, Delta Electronics up on their offer, Imagination Toys will…will go bankrupt?" Fear showed in Sarah's ice-blue eyes and her voice was strained with her feelings of incredulity. Never in her thirty-four years had she considered herself being anything but wealthy.

"That's being a little overdramatic," Shane observed with a good-natured smile that was meant to ease Sarah. "But it's obvious from the last financial statements with which Imagination Toys has provided me that the company is in trouble—serious trouble."

"Hogwash!" Peter's aunt Mimi declared, opening her gloved palms in a gracious gesture of explanation. "Imagination is just suffering a little because of the economy, you know, the recession or whatever those buffoons in Washington want to call it." She smiled sweetly, as if she had solved all of the problems, and her third husband patted her knowingly on her arm.

Sarah ignored Aunt Mimi. "But how can that be—that Imagination is in trouble? I thought that the company was worth…several million!" Sarah nervously played with her lighter, rotating it end on end as she asked her worried questions.

Mara's tightly controlled voice interrupted Shane's response. "Of course the company is worth quite a bit, Sarah. But for the past several years, the profits have been falling off, and in order to keep Imagination on its feet, we need an input of more capital into the treasury."

"Excuse me, Mr. Kennedy," Sarah's brother, Rich, argued, "but I really don't like the idea of someone other than the family putting up more funds for Imagination. This has been a Wilcox family venture for generations, and I think we should try and work out our problems among ourselves...no offense, you understand."

Once again the room buzzed with whispered chatter, all seeming to agree with Rich's impassioned speech. It was Mara's turn to speak. "I couldn't agree with you more, Rich," she said with a genuine smile. Rich positively beamed; he was so proud of himself. "Now," Mara continued graciously, "who would like to make the investment? Delta Electronics is willing to put up half a million dollars..." Mara's cobalt eyes skimmed the faces, and most of the eyes upon her avoided her gaze.

The room became hushed, and Mara felt that her point had been driven home. No one in the family was willing to put that much money into the failing toy company. Reluctantly, the family was coming to grips with the uncomfortable financial situation and the fact that Shane's offer was nearly a last-ditch effort.

It was Dena's slow, sultry speech that caught Mara's attention and started the creeping sense of dread that began crawling up her spine. Throughout the meeting, Dena's eyes had been narrowing on Shane, reassessing him, scrutinizing him, and now it was the redhead's move.

"Mara's right, of course," Dena patronized sweetly as she looked from one to the other of the tense faces that lined the table. "Not one of us can afford to put up that kind of money for Imagination, can we? And it's my guess that even combined, the coffers of the Wilcox family couldn't scramble together half a million dollars." Her smile melted to a determined frown. "And why is that?" Dena asked rhetorically. Silence. Shane's eyes had blackened and Mara felt the rush of color to her face, but other than the nervous click of Sarah's lighter, there was no noise. Dena answered her own question. "The answer is simple—for the last three quarters, ever since Peter's death, Imagination Toys hasn't paid any of us one thin dime in dividends! And whose fault is that?"

"You know the reasons for that, Dena. We discussed them last year, and the board approved my decision to withhold the dividends," Mara retorted through clenched teeth. She was conscious of the eyes of Peter's family looking at her, some with empathy, others with accusation. "We all agreed that it would be better to try and turn the company around, rather than bleed it dry with dividends."

"A lot of good it did," Dena snorted, and Cousin Rich smiled in agreement.

Dena tossed her auburn curls, unconvinced by Mara's argument, using the board room as center stage for her simmering dispute with her sister-in-law. Shane's black eyes never left the redhead's arrogantly beautiful face. Dena voiced her opinion. "I guess I just don't understand then, why, if the company is such a burden, don't we just sell it...all of it." She shrugged her thin shoulders theatrically. "From what I understand, Mr. Kennedy offered to buy it out, completely."

An audible gasp escaped from around the table. "Why weren't we notified?" "I never heard that!" "What's going on here, anyway?" Little catch phrases echoed and ricocheted around the small, enclosed room, and several pairs of eyes looked at Mara with unconcealed disbelief.

Mara felt Shane stiffen beside her, but she put a restraining hand on his coat sleeve. An act, she was sure, that everyone in the room noticed and questioned.

"Just a minute!" June's cold voice cracked through the air. She gripped the table severely, her knuckles white, and rose with difficulty. "Don't all of you go blaming Mara…and Dena, you should be ashamed of yourself!" She cut her daughter down with an icy gaze. "The reason that Mara didn't consider Mr. Kennedy's original proposal to buy out the company is that *I* suggested otherwise."

June's proud chin rose a regal inch. "Imagination Toys has been a tradition with the Wilcox family for generations, as Rich so magnanimously pointed out earlier." The color in Rich's round face drained. "Just because things aren't going exactly our way doesn't mean that we should throw in the towel." June's piercing blue eyes moved from one of her husband's relatives to the next in cool, commanding appraisal. There was no question as to who was the matriarch of the family.

"Actually, I do agree with Rich." Her eyes, now more kind, rested upon her nephew. "I wish that there was some way that we could avoid asking for outside help to save the company…but…it appears that we don't have much of a choice. Either we accept Mr. Kennedy's proposal, and I believe it is fair to both parties, or we scale down Imagination from a national toy company to a purely Southeastern endeavor."

Again, the hushed, excited whispers.

June lowered herself into her chair, clearly drained from the ordeal. Dena pursed her lips together petulantly and refused to look in Mara's direction. The rest of the family mumbled and grumbled among themselves. Aunt Mimi appeared positively flabbergasted, Cousin Sarah, appalled and nervous, and Cousin Rich, deflated.

After a few more direct questions about the proposal, the

family was satisfied and voted, albeit somewhat reluctantly, to sell treasury shares in the corporation to Shane and accept a loan from Delta Electronics. It was a long, stifling affair, and nearly two o'clock in the afternoon by the time all of the details were ironed out.

Much later, when all of the board members had gone, having taken a little time to talk with Shane and voice their opinions, doubts, and hopes for the future of the toy company, Mara felt completely drained and worn out. If the morning with Angie had gone poorly, the board meeting was a total, unnerving free-for-all. It was over, and the battle had turned in her favor, but she couldn't help but wonder if it was all worth the effort.

"Let's go to lunch," Shane suggested, once they were alone in Mara's office.

"I'm not hungry," Mara declined, running her fingers through the thick tangle of her blond hair. "I've got a million things to do anyway."

"You should eat something."

She waved her hand in the air dismissively and placed a tight smile on her face. "No, thanks, I'll just have a cup of coffee—really, my stomach's too tied in knots to think about food."

Shane ignored her protests and reached in the closet for her purse. "Well, I'm going out for lunch, and the least you could do is keep me company…come on, it'll do you good."

"But I've got a ton of work to do."

"We all do, but nothing much gets accomplished on an empty stomach."

"All right," she agreed wearily, too tired of battling board members to argue any further.

Shane had been right, of course, and the fresh seafood salad that she had ordered had brightened her mood incredibly. He had been considerate, almost loving, and insisted that they talk about anything other than the company. Mara actually found herself relaxing for the first time that day, and though usually not her custom during a working day, she had indulged herself in a glass of cold Chablis.

The headiness of the wine on her tired body had just begun to tingle her spine when Shane's light mood vanished. He finished his drink, ordered a cup of coffee, and stared into the dark depths of the liquid, as if seeking answers for his life. His frown was commanding, and for a moment he uncharacteristically avoided Mara's gaze.

"I'm going to Atlanta tonight, for the weekend," he began, swirling the coffee in the cup before taking a sip. "I'd like you and Angie to come with me."

Mara ignored the direct invitation. "But I thought you would be here for another week."

Shane smiled grimly at his own black thoughts. "I will, but unfortunately there's some business in Atlanta that can't wait. I'll be there until Monday afternoon."

The invitation lay open between them, if only Mara had the strength and trust to accept it. "I...I don't know..."

"I take it that you haven't told June about my relationship with Angie?" Black eyes delved into her.

"No...not yet..."

Shane's fist thudded down on the table, scattering the silverware and spilling the water glasses.

"Why the hell not?" he demanded.

"You know why not."

"I've heard all your reasons, Mara, and they are nothing more than overblown excuses!"

"But Angie..."

"She would be better off knowing that I'm her real father and that I love her!"

"But...June..."

"This may surprise you, Mara, but I don't give a damn

about June, or any other member of that circus you call a family. I saw them all this afternoon. Any one of them would be glad to sell if they thought they could make a dime out of it.''

''No!''

''Open your eyes, Mara. The longer you wait, the more difficult it is going to be.'' He drew his head closer to hers and whispered hoarsely across the table. ''And if you have any ridiculous notions that I might not insist that Angie become legally mine, you can guess again.''

Mara felt her fingers shaking, but fortunately her voice was strong and didn't betray her turbulent inner emotions.

''You know that I have no intention of betraying you, and I have tried to talk to June, I *really* have.''

''But?'' he snorted, prompting her.

''It's been difficult.''

''You're making it difficult!''

''You know that June hasn't been well…certainly you could see in the meeting today what a strain she's been under.''

''That, Mara, was a show of strength, not weakness.''

''I'm not talking about control of the company, Shane, I'm talking about physical well-being. You don't have to be a doctor to see that the woman is ill!'' Mara stated emphatically, her blue eyes flashing with anger.

''In my opinion, June Wilcox is as strong as she wants to be. The way she handled that meeting today is proof enough for me. If she's ill, it's probably psychosomatic!''

''You're blinded by your own selfish interests!'' Mara charged.

''Is it selfish to want what is rightfully mine?''

''You'll get it, Shane, I promise you.''

''When, Mara? When?''

Mara let her head fall into the heel of her hand, and she rubbed her throbbing temples to ease the headache that had badgered her all day. "I don't know," she said quietly. "I honestly don't know. Can't you please be patient, just a little while longer?" Her blue eyes regarded him through the thick sheen of her lashes. They pleaded with him, and begged him to understand. "It won't be long," she whispered.

Thinking it was one of the most difficult things he had ever done, Shane forced himself to ignore the heartbreaking look of promise in her Dresden eyes. "You've got one more week," he replied in a clipped, well-modulated voice. Was he always in control, Mara wondered, was he always so intense? Was she wrong in denying him his child, if only for another week?

"You're being selfish," she murmured.

A hollow laugh was her answer. "No, sweetheart, if I've made a mistake, it's that I haven't been selfish enough! But, believe me, all that has changed. I only want what is rightfully mine. Angie is my daughter, Mara, and I intend to have her! Soon!"

"And you will."

A grim smile played over his face as he called for the check and paid the bill. They walked in silence back to the building, each wrapped in his own desperate thoughts. Why must it be so difficult, Mara asked herself. Wasn't there an easy solution to the happiness that they both wanted?

Shane left that evening with only a crisp good-bye. He was polite but formal, and although Mara felt a need to reach out to him, to touch him, she remained stoic behind her desk, wondering how they would ever be able to solve their dilemma and become a family. Even the smile that she tried to flash at him failed and fell into a flat, tremblingly dismal line that barely curved upward at the corners.

She waited, and listened to his retreating footsteps as they echoed down the long corridor outside her office. Never had she felt more alone, and never had she felt so hollow and empty.

The drive home in the car was hot and dusty. Even the summer wildflowers seemed to droop along the roadside in the oppressive humidity, and by the time she got home, Mara was damp with perspiration. The giant oaks lining the drive, with their shimmering silver-green leaves reflecting the late summer sun, were a welcome relief to Mara's tired eyes. After a long day at the office, the aggravating board meeting, and the fight with Shane, it was all Mara could do to concentrate on her driving while squinting at the relentless afternoon sun. Now, as she slid the Renault into its usual spot near the garage, she lifted her sunglasses from her nose and wiped away the beads of perspiration that had collected on her cheeks. She paused for one more soul-searching minute in the hot car, her hands still lightly gripping the steering wheel. Was Shane right? Had she avoided the subject of Angie with June in a subconscious attempt to avoid the pain that she might cause Peter's mother? Was she only making excuses, not only to Shane, but also to herself? And was it even possible to tell June about Shane right now and get the truth off her chest? How would her mother-in-law take the news, especially now when Shane had just become a partial owner in Imagination?

The hot sun finally forced Mara to get out of the car and face her mother-in-law. Seeing no alternative to coming right out and telling June the truth, Mara steeled herself for what she knew would be a mental ordeal. Opening the door from the back porch, a cool blast of air from the central air-conditioning revived her and evaporated the clinging dampness from her dress.

"Mommy?" a high-pitched voice called. "That you?" Excited feet hurried toward Mara, and Angie rounded the corner, nearly colliding with her mother.

"Hi, sweetheart. How was your day?" Mara asked, her tired face breaking into a grin at the sight of her child.

Angie lifted her small shoulders in a childish imitation of adult indifference.

"Did Grammie let you go swimming in the wading pool?" Mara asked, bending down to lift the child and noticing that beneath the light pink T-shirt, Angie was wearing her bathing suit.

"That's right...and the kitties, too!" Angie agreed, with a wide, mischievous grin.

"Oh, no," Mara groaned as June, chuckling, hurried into the kitchen to allay any of Mara's fears.

"They're all right now. Don't you worry."

"But the kittens," Mara gasped, envisioning the entire scene vividly in her mind, "they're so small...I don't think they even have all of their eyes open."

"Believe it or not, they can swim...at least for a few minutes," June laughed. "However," she stated on a more sober note, "Southpaw was absolutely beside herself, and against her better judgment she jumped into the pool and dragged the bedraggled things to safety."

"Oh, Angie," Mara sighed, "we never...never, ever put the kitties in the water. They don't like it." Mara's voice was grave.

"They need a bath," Angie explained, innocence lighting up her round face.

"Southpaw will take care of that..." and then noticing that Angie did, for the first time, understand that she had made a terrible mistake, and that tears began to well in the child's eyes, Mara abruptly changed the subject. "What's this?" she asked, poking at a brownish smudge on Angie's cheek.

"Grammie and me made brownies today," Angie announced importantly.

"Did you?" Mara smiled fondly at her child and kissed Angie's tousled blond curls. "And are they any good?"

"Better'n you make!"

"That's because Grammie has a special recipe," Mara replied with a laugh as she set the child back onto the floor. Suddenly Mara felt that all of her cares and worries had melted. She was in her home, with her adorable child, and the problems of the office seemed distant and unnecessary. Angie, wily child that she was, instinctively knew from her mother's expression that the crisis concerning the cats was over, so she contented herself in the den off of the kitchen and played with her plastic building blocks.

"That's a switch," June observed, looking over the top of her reading glasses to watch her granddaughter.

"What is?" Mara opened the refrigerator door and extracted a pitcher.

"For once Angie is playing with a toy from Imagination. That doesn't happen often," the older woman mused thoughtfully.

"No, it doesn't," Mara agreed, pouring herself a tall glass of iced tea and offering one to her mother-in-law. "Unfortunately, Angie is a shining example of the kids in America today, when it comes to choosing toys. Why is that? What's wrong with our line?" Mara asked herself, furrows once again creasing her brow.

"I'm sorry. I didn't mean to bring up all of the worries of the office again," June apologized. She took off the orange apron that she had been wearing over her black knit suit and folded it neatly before placing it back into a drawer. It occurred to Mara, as she studied her mother-in-law over the rim of her glass, that June looked much better than she had earlier in the day. None of the strain or physical weakness that had been so evident at the board meeting was apparent. And, other than the light wrinkles around her eyes, a slightly pale complexion, and a whiteness around her lips, the older woman appeared healthier than she had in months. For just a few short hours to have passed, the transformation was almost impossible. Could Shane possibly be right? Was her mother-in-law's health only a convenient excuse, a psychosomatic act, a weapon that June could turn off and on, to use when she needed it?

Mara had known June for over four years. Although it was evident that the woman wielded her power over her family like a brandished sword, Mara found it impossible to believe that June would knowingly try to deceive anyone, family included.

"How did it go—with Angie?" Mara asked in what she hoped would sound like an off-the-cuff manner.

"Oh, fine. Just fine," June replied. She took a seat at one of the café chairs near the kitchen table and an irritated look settled on her face. "If I were only able to handle the rest of my family as easily as I can Angie, life would be a lot simpler, let me tell you!" The corners of her mouth pulled into a disgusted frown.

"You're referring to the board meeting?" Mara surmised as she settled into a chair opposite June, near the broad bay window of the kitchen nook.

June smiled wistfully. "You know me so well," she whispered. Do I, Mara wondered, do I know you at all? Once again June's agitation lit her face, and she played her fingers over the rim of her tea glass.

"Honestly," June sputtered angrily. "That Rich, what a spoiled cur he's become…and pompous to boot! Where does he get such a 'holier than thou' attitude? Certainly not from Mimi, his mother!" June rolled her eyes heavenward in a supplicating gesture. "And then there's Dena. What can I say about her? She's my own daughter, but I swear, she doesn't have a lick of sense in that gorgeous head of hers!" Pale, watery eyes accosted Mara. "I hope the meeting wasn't too rough on you. The family can be vicious if they all decide to band together.''

"The meeting went just fine," Mara lied, and wondered if June could see through her plastic smile.

"Good! Now, let's just hope we can bring the toy company out of its slump!''

"June," Mara began, looking into the den and noticing that Angie was playing with the doll house, out of earshot. Mara anxiously fingered a spot on the tablecloth and her insides began to knot in dread. "There's something I've been meaning to talk to you about.''

"Oh?" June's spine stiffened, or was it Mara's imagination?

"It's...it's about Shane...''

June clamped her mouth shut, and in the same tone of voice that had effectively controlled the board meeting, she cut Mara off. "I think we've discussed Mr. Kennedy and his proposal to buy a portion of Imagination long enough, don't you?" June rose from the table with regal grace, as if to add physical emphasis to her words.

"It's not about the company." The words were spoken quietly, but they seemed to sizzle, hanging in the air.

June set her lips in a tight line and reached for her purse. "I have to go, and it's not that I'm not interested in what you have to say about Mr. Kennedy, but, well—'' her slender shoulders drooped with the weight of her words "—I'm just not that fond of the man." June noted the pained expression in Mara's eyes, and two points of color stained her cheeks. In all truth, June loved the young woman sitting at the maple table with the checkered cloth as if she were her own daughter. "Perhaps I'm not being fair," June sighed. "But ever since that day that he came bursting in here...*demanding* to see you...I don't know." Her voice caught for a moment, and it was a hoarse whisper, barely controlled when she continued. "You know the day I mean, the day that Peter was buried."

Mara nodded and swallowed her tears of grief for the older woman's pain.

"I've had trouble accepting him," June explained.

"He's trying to help Imagination."

"I know that…and, well, I suppose that when I don't resent it, I do appreciate it. Really I do, in my own way." She took a deep breath, hesitating. "But there's something about him, I don't exactly know how to put my finger on it, but I just don't trust the man."

"Then why did you give your consent to let him invest in Imagination?" Mara asked, stupefied. June's pale blue eyes hardened to ice, and she seemed to talk in circles— never confronting the real crux of the problem.

"Oh," June continued determinedly, "don't get me wrong! I don't think he's fool enough to try and manipulate the company for his own interests entirely. He's too smart for that. But," she waved a suspicious finger in the air knowingly, "I've seen his kind before, and his ruthlessness is something that I don't like, and I can't trust."

"I don't know what you mean," Mara said simply.

"Oh, child." June's eyes closed for a second. "I'm just asking that you be careful with him. It's not hard for me, or anyone else, to see that you're falling in love with him. And I'm giving you my unrequested, and probably unwanted, advice. That man…he's dangerous. Treacherous to women." June's blue eyes, from her imperial position standing over Mara, impaled Mara to the back of the kitchen chair. "Don't let him hurt you…or Angie. That's all I'm asking."

Mara was stunned. June's theatric performance seemed to be exactly that—an act. Yet she played the part with all the vitality of a woman who's experienced the pain and anger of betrayal.

Mara had fully intended to confide in June that Shane was indeed Angie's natural father, but the contempt and disdain that June bore against him stilled Mara's tongue. Without being forthright, June had let Mara know in no uncertain terms that she disliked Shane Kennedy and considered him a threat to everything that she loved, including Angie!

As Mara watched June's sky-blue Lincoln Continental purr down the driveway, she wondered how she would ever be able to summon enough courage to tell the older woman that Angie was Shane's daughter.

Chapter Nine

Shane didn't return. After a long, lonely weekend of soul-searching, Mara was disappointed when he called late Monday afternoon and informed her that his business would keep him in Atlanta until Wednesday or Thursday. The conversation was stilted and the unasked question hung between them on the telephone wires, spreading the distance between them into impossible miles. Shane didn't have to ask. Mara could *feel* the tension and knew that he hoped for her to tell him that she had made the break with Peter's family and told them about Angie. Mara couldn't.

The week stretched before her. At home she would find herself thinking of Shane, wondering where he was and what he was doing. It didn't help that Angie chattered non-stop about him and asked when he would be back—or had he gone forever, like Daddy.

For some reason Mara felt as if her relationship with her mother-in-law was deteriorating. The strain of their conversation about Shane seemed to have pushed the two women farther apart. Although June was still enchanted with Angie, Mara sensed that the easy familiarity that she had shared with her mother-in-law was gone, most likely forever.

Then why was it that Mara found it impossible to summon the strength to quietly tell June that Shane was Angie's natural father and to explain the delicate situation to the older woman. Surely she would understand. The awkward set of circumstances in which they all found themselves entrapped wasn't Mara's fault, was it? Why, then, the guilt? Why did Mara still carry the burden of June's happiness and health upon her shoulders? The questions besieged her nights and disrupted her days.

It was Thursday when Mara noticed how on edge she had become. When Shane hadn't arrived in Asheville the day before, Mara was more than disappointed, she was downright scared. Vivid memories of the past assailed her; pictures of his jet winging into the night across the Atlantic to a troubled and strife-filled nation, the dull ache that had converged upon her when she had learned from his father of Shane's brutal death, the nausea of morning sickness combined with the pain in knowing that she would never see the father of her unborn child, and finally the joy and suspicion of betrayal that had assailed her upon his return. If he didn't come back to her, she wondered if she would have the mental tenacity to continue living. Fortunately, she had Angie. If Shane chose to turn his back on her again, there was always her child...his child to warm her days.

"You're being maudlin," she chastised herself aloud. "It's the heat that has finally got you down." She rummaged in her top drawer for her favorite pen and mentally cursed herself when she noticed that her fingers were trembling. "Damn! If those repairmen don't get here soon to fix the air-conditioning..."

"You'll what?" Dena asked, walking uninvited into Mara's office.

"Oh, I don't know, but they've promised to be here all week…" Mara looked up from her desk drawer and met the redhead's gaze. A dark prickle of apprehension darted up her spine as she noticed the catty smile on Dena's features. "Didn't you leave earlier today?" Mara asked, straightening and leveling her gaze at Dena.

The smile broadened. "That's right," Dena acquiesced and dropped herself onto the couch.

"And you're back?" Mara prodded, noticing that the clock on the wall indicated that it was nearly seven. "Why?"

"I called at the house. Mother said that you were working late, so I thought I'd drop by for a chat." Again the slightly vulgar smile.

"A chat?" Unlikely, Mara thought, and twirled the pen nervously. "What about?"

"Angie!"

Mara froze. The pen stopped twirling and dropped to the desktop.

"What about Angie?" Mara asked hoarsely. Was Angie hurt…or worse? What had happened? Mara's throat went dry before she realized that not even Dena would derive satisfaction from the child's pain. And that was the feeling that was written all over Dena's fine-boned features: satisfaction.

"Well," Dena mused, looking at the ceiling as if lost in thought. Idly she rubbed a corner of her mouth, drawing out the suspense. Dena loved theatrics and she was playing her role well. "It's really not just about Angie…actually it involves Shane as well."

Mara swallowed back the apprehension that threatened to overtake her. "What about Shane?" she asked calmly.

"I've been noticing the way that he acts when he's around the child."

"And?"

"*Possessive* is the word that seems to describe his actions." Dena nodded to herself before her dark green eyes flashed to Mara. "Yes, he's very possessive, I'd say."

"He thinks a great deal of Angie."

"I'll just bet he does!" Dena said sarcastically. Her polished lips curled into a self-satisfied smile.

"Dena," Mara said, her breath catching in her throat. She knew what was coming from the fiery woman, but Mara tried to stem some of the vehemence by appearing in command and in control of the situation. She drew herself up to her full height and, despite the heat, smoothed her dress and hoped to appear cool as she crossed round to the front of the desk and leaned against it. "Why don't you stop beating around the bush and tell me what you wanted to tell me. Then we can both go home."

"Why does Shane seem so possessive about *Peter's* kid?"

"I told you. He loves Angie."

"Hmph! Shane Kennedy doesn't strike me as the kind of man that would be fascinated by children."

It was Mara's turn to smile. "I think you're wrong on that one. Despite his hard business tactics, Shane's a very caring man."

"You should know."

"What's that supposed to mean?"

"Oh, don't play naive with me, Mara. I know you better than that! The dumb virgin routine seems to work on my mother, but it doesn't wash with me! As a matter of fact, it makes me sick!" Her last words were spoken with such a vehemence that Mara was slightly taken aback. Did Dena actually hate her that much? Why?

Mara's face tightened. She thought about telling Dena the

flat out, no holds barred truth, but she hesitated slightly. It would be better to tell June first. Her voice seemed frail, and she knew that drops of perspiration were beading on her forehead, but she forced herself to tell Dena a portion of the truth. Dena deserved that much. No matter how much Dena disliked Mara, she was Peter's sister and entitled to the truth.

"It's true. Shane cares for Angie very much—"

"And you, too," Dena snapped. "I'd be a fool if I couldn't see the way that he looks at you." A sadness seemed to sweep over Dena's features for a minute, and her voice lowered. "He…he looks at you as if he doesn't ever want to stop." She bit at her lip and some of the satisfaction and spunk seemed to have drained out of her.

"He's asked me to marry him. He wants to adopt Angie."

Mara's surprise announcement seemed to startle her.

"Sudden, isn't it?" Dena asked, her eyes calculating.

"A little…I guess…"

"I wonder what all the board members would think about this. First you coerce them into approving sale of stock to Shane Kennedy, and then, quick as a bunny, you marry the guy, giving you, Shane, and Angie's trust control of Imagination. Convenient, wouldn't you say…too convenient!" Dena's green eyes blazed with accusation.

"Oh, no, Dena that's not the way it is…"

"Then what way is it? I'm only telling you what it looks like—a hasty marriage of convenience to get control of Imagination!"

"I've known Shane for years…" Mara attempted to explain, feeling her weight sag a little against the desk. Dena sensed her advantage and unfolded her long, jean-clad legs to stand up and face her sister-in-law.

"I just bet you did…I'll also bet that you've been seeing him on the side for years."

"What do you mean?" Mara said quietly, the meaning of Dena's words all too clear.

"I mean that I think you and Shane are having an affair, and…" Mara began to protest, but Dena shook her red curls and with a look that could turn flesh to stone, continued with her accusations. "I think you've been with him for years, long before Peter died."

Dena had come up to face Mara…so close that Mara could taste the heady scent of Dena's cologne as she licked her lips.

"You think I was unfaithful to Peter?" Mara said, shocked at the cold sound of the words as they stung the air.

"Weren't you?" As far as Dena was concerned, the question, spit with such passion, was purely rhetorical.

"Of course not!" Mara argued, her small fists clenched in frustration. "I…I thought that Shane was dead!"

"So you say," Dena goaded.

"You don't believe me?"

"Not for a minute!"

Mara took the time to close her eyes for just a second, long enough to steady herself and get control of her tattered emotions. She shook her palms and her head in the same dismissive gesture.

"Look, Dena. It doesn't matter if you believe me or not. While Peter was alive, I was faithful to him. I know it and Peter knew it. What you thought then, or think now, doesn't matter." Mara could feel the hot stain of color on her cheeks, but she swore to herself that no matter how catty Dena became, Mara would control the situation and confrontation. If they were going to spar verbally, Mara was not going to lose her dignity nor her self-esteem.

Dena stepped back to put some room between herself and her sister-in-law. She knew the determined glint in Mara's cold, blue eyes was a sign that Mara's back was up against the wall. She only hoped that she hadn't pushed Peter's wife too far. Her purpose was to glean information, not to anger Mara. Dena knew her sister-in-law well enough to realize that if pushed too far, Mara would end this conversation and Dena would never again have the chance to find out if her suspicions were correct.

"All right, all right," Dena murmured, falling into a nearby chair and idly chewing on her fingernail. She averted her green eyes away from Mara's direct gaze and seemed to concentrate on the hem of her mint green plaid blouse. "I'm sorry...I had forgotten that you thought Shane was dead." Her eyes, when they lifted, were shining with pooled tears. Suddenly she looked older than her thirty-seven years.

Mara felt the play of emotions pull at her heartstrings, but she stood, unmoving, behind the desk. If she knew anything at all about Dena, it was that her sister-in-law knew well the art of drama. Were the tears a real sign of distress, or merely a prop in Dena's theatrical show?

"Perhaps...perhaps I'm wrong. But when I see Shane with Angie...the way that he seems to adore her," Dena stopped for a minute. "And it goes both ways. Angie seems to love him, a feeling that she never had for Peter."

"That's not true—"

"Don't lie to me, Mara! I can see it!"

Mara felt herself wavering with pity for Dena, and she damned herself for her own soft-hearted weakness. Dena had turned on Mara so many times in the past that Mara shouldn't ever trust her, and she knew it. But the way that her sister-in-law was slumped in the chair, swayed Mara's resolve, and against her better judgment, she decided to give Dena one more chance.

As the words were out of her mouth, Mara knew that she was making a mistake. "Okay, Dena...what is it, exactly, that you're trying to say?" Mara asked quietly.

Dena dabbed at her eyes with a tissue from the desk.

"Oh, Mara," she sighed with genuine despair. "I know that I've been just awful to you sometimes. And I know it's not your fault that Dad left most of Imagination to Peter. But it all seems so unfair sometimes!"

"I know."

"No, no, you don't. No one could!" Dena asserted, her anger and frustration mounting. "Maybe all this...it wouldn't have been all so important, but it seems wrong to me!"

"What does?"

"The way things turned out! First you had Peter, and whether you were smart enough to know it or not, my brother worshipped the ground that you walked on!"

A lump in Mara's throat began to swell.

"And," Dena continued, "I was foolish enough to think, to hope, that Bruce would feel the same way about me." Her voice quivered. "Or at least that *someone* would."

"Oh, Dena..."

"No, don't interrupt!" Dena cried, gathering strength. The heat in the room seemed to rise a few degrees. "And now, now Shane Kennedy comes along, on the pretense of investing in the company, and falls compliantly into your open arms! And not only that, but he *loves* you, Mara. God, how he loves you!" Dena pointed out, her small face twisting with the pain of thirty-seven unfulfilled, unloved, vanished years. "And...and he even wants Angie." Dena sighed. "Do you know how incredible that is?" She looked up at Mara and let the torture in her face go unsuppressed. "It all seems so incredible...such a storybook romance. It's almost as if..." her voice faded.

"As if what?" Mara asked, sucking in her breath.

"As if Angie were *his* child, for God's sake," Dena whispered.

The silence was electrifying, and the heat in the small, enclosed room pounded relentlessly against Mara's temples.

Several times she attempted to respond to Dena's insinuation, and several times she failed, choking on a denial of the truth. Dena slumped in the chair, her face flushed, and her expectant green eyes the only sign that she wanted a response from Mara. The gaze silently pleaded with Mara for the truth.

Mara reached for her purse and tucked the small, leather bag under her arm. Finally, when the shock of the question had worn thin, Mara looked at Dena and smiled sadly. "You're right, Dena. Angie is Shane's child. I was pregnant with her and before I could reach him to tell him the news, I found out that he was dead. It's…it's a long story, and in the long run the only thing that matters to you is that I married your brother."

"But Peter? Did he know?"

"That the child belonged to another man?" Mara closed her eyes tightly and fought back the tears that began to well every time she remembered those long, desperate days and the feeling of despair that caught hold of her when she thought Shane was gone. It was Peter, young, supple, and strong, who had helped her get over her loss and find a reason for living in the fact that she was carrying Shane's child. "Yes," Mara whispered huskily. "Peter knew, and I believe that in his own way, he cared for and loved Angie."

"But…how could you? How could he…"

Mara shook her head and silenced her sister-in-law. Unwilling tears began to slide down her cheeks. "You have to remember that we, both Peter and I, thought that Shane was dead."

After a thoughtful silence, Dena asked the question that was uppermost on her mind. "What about Mother? Are you going to tell her?" It was more of a demand than a question.

"Of course." Once again Mara was apprehensive.

"When?" Dena demanded.

"I don't know…soon, I hope."

"Would you ever have told her if I hadn't put two and two together and realized that Angie was Shane's kid?" Dena asked, her usual air of sarcasm falling neatly back into place. She got up from the chair, reached in the pocket of her jeans for her keys, and stood, waiting insolently, leaning against the door.

Mara's tone was icy. The very least she expected from Dena was a little compassion after hearing the truth. "I planned on telling her by the end of the week."

"Give me a break!" Dena said with a mirthless laugh. "I bet you planned on marrying Shane before you told Mother the whole sorry story, and then I doubt you would have had the backbone to be honest."

Mara winced at Dena's sharp words. "You're right," she allowed calmly, "I was hesitant to tell June about Angie." Dena smiled wickedly. "But not for the reasons you think. Have you ever taken the time or consideration to talk to your mother and ask her about her health? She's ill."

"Oh, come off it, Mara. Don't give me any of your feeble excuses! You didn't tell mother because you're afraid of her and what she can do to you. Without the Wilcox wealth, honey, you and that kid are practically paupers!" Dena sneered.

Mara rose above the taunts of Dena's insults. "Your mother isn't well, Dena. I've tried to convince her to make an appointment with Dr. Bernard, but so far I'm sure she hasn't seen him."

"Don't change the subject," Dena exploded. "What you and I are talking about is the fact that you have lied to my entire family by passing off your kid as an heir to the Wilcox fortune!" Dena accused viciously. She pointed a long, bejeweled finger at Mara and shook the keys that she had wrapped in her palm to add emphasis to her belabored point. A thin smile of victory curled her lips, and unconsciously her tongue wet her lips. Never in her wildest imaginings had she expected Mara to give her an out-and-out full-blown confession. Green eyes glinted with triumph at the thought!

"No. I never intended to—"

"Oh, yeah, I know," Dena interrupted icily. "Your intentions were honorable. Well, just try and explain all that to the board. All of the family is involved here, and we've all been deceived. The board is going to be in an uproar, and you can bet that they will find some legal loophole to contest Peter's will! What you've done is considered fraud!"

Mara's initial shock at Dena's impassioned speech had faded and boiling anger and indignation took over. Her thin, worn patience gave way. "Are you threatening me?" she challenged.

"You bet I am!"

"Why?"

"Because I want it, Mara. I want it all! It's my birthright. Imagination Toys is in my blood—"

"In your blood?" Mara managed with a laugh. "Are you kidding? You were willing to sell the entire company to the first interested buyer. Don't try to convince me of your loyalty."

Dena's grin spread slowly over her face. "Oh, but that was before I was sure that Angie wasn't Peter's child. Before, it was only conjecture—now, I know the facts!"

"And you plan on using 'the facts' against me, is that it?"

Dena's face froze in an overdramatized affront. She looked positively stricken, but just for the moment. "Against you—heavens, no." Once again the evil grin. "For me—yes!"

"How?" Mara asked, wondering why she was even listening to her sister-in-law. Clearly, Dena was obsessed with gaining control of Imagination.

"Do you know how long I've waited for this?" Dena

asked, her eyes narrowing. "Years! All the time that we were growing up, I lived with the obvious fact that Peter was Father's favorite child. And then, when Dad died, his will was another slap in my face! He gave me less than a quarter of the estate, while Peter got it all! That wasn't bad enough, though. The topper came when Peter died young and his wife, a woman not even related to the family, inherited the bulk of the company along with the house. Do you know how angry I was? How unfair it all was? Of course not! No one could." Dena's lips drew back tightly, white against the even row of her teeth.

For the first time in over four years, Mara saw her sister-in-law clearly. And despite Dena's threats and power plays, Mara felt a rush of pity for the obsessed woman. "Dena," she suggested gently, "have you ever talked this over with someone professionally?"

"What do you mean?" Dena asked, but she guessed Mara's unspoken thoughts.

"I mean…I think that you should talk your feelings over with a psychiatrist."

"Wouldn't you just love that, though?" Dena sneered, as if the idea were totally absurd. She shook her head in disgust. "I can't believe how transparent you can be sometimes. *I* don't need psychiatric help, and Mother doesn't need a doctor, so you can just quit dreaming up excuses to have us both committed, because it won't work!"

"I never—" Mara gasped.

"Oh, sure you did, Mara. You're just like me, only you won't admit it. You and I have been locking horns over the control of Imagination for years, and now I have the upper hand because, unless you give up all of your interest in Imagination and step down as president, I'm going to let this sordid little story of Angie's dubious paternity leak out to the papers. I think the social editor and maybe the financial editor would find it incredibly amusing."

"You wouldn't."

"Try me!" Dena cocked her head and looked at the ceiling as if lost in thought. "How does this headline grab you," she mused, "'Local socialite uses child for control of toy company, or better yet, Imagination toys in shambles: Paternity of child heir in question.'"

"I know that you might find this hard to believe," Mara replied, her chin inching upward defiantly, "but I'm not really concerned what the newspapers might make of the story."

"But, think of your social standing in Asheville."

"I told you, I really don't care about anything like that," Mara repeated. She had heard enough of Dena's threats and accusations. She clutched her purse tightly in the well of her arm and moved closer to Dena and the doorway. "I'm leaving, now, Dena," Mara stated calmly. "If you want to stay here any longer, it's fine with me, but I'm not going to stay and argue uselessly with you. We're getting nowhere, and I'm tired of wasting my time. You've heard my side of the story, and you can do with it what you want. Obviously, I can't stop you. But I really do think that you should take your mother's feelings into consideration. I...I wasn't joking when I told you that I think she's seriously ill, and I'm worried about her."

"Why do you care so much about Mother?" Dena asked with renewed suspicion.

Mara sighed. "Because June has been very good to me and she loves Angie very much."

"Oh, yeah?" Dena inquired with a smirk of disbelief cast on her face. "Then the least you could have done, once Peter was gone, was be honest with her and let her know that the child she has prized as her only grandchild was fathered by another man! Instead you hid behind a lie, Mara!"

"That may be," Mara granted wistfully. She sighed to herself and somehow managed a feeble smile. "But I never expected to see Shane again."

"So what? The kid was his, whether he was alive or dead!"

"Look, Dena, I'm not denying any of that. What I'm asking from you is that you please don't say or do anything that might upset your mother. I'm going to try and persuade her to see Dr. Bernard, and once I know that she's not seriously ill, then I promise, I'll tell her all of the truth."

Mara didn't wait for Dena's response. She started walking down the long corridor to the elevator shaft and snapped off the lights to the offices of Imagination. As the darkness closed in on her she heard Dena's well-modulated Southern drawl echoing in the hallway behind her. "You're copping out, dear sister-in-law," it accused, and then, just as the elevator door opened and Mara stepped into its gaping interior, she heard Dena's high-pitched, pleased laughter. An involuntary shudder skittered down Mara's spine at the sound. Just how desperate, how obsessed, how neurotic was the scheming redhead?

The parking lot under the building was peacefully quiet and was succumbing to darkness in the ever-lengthening shadows of the early evening. Blissfully cool air greeted Mara as she made a hasty exit from the elevator and headed toward her reserved parking space near the entrance to the building. She slid her tired body into the soft vinyl seat of the Renault and let out a nearly inaudible sigh. For a moment, allowing herself a few seconds of precious time to calm down, she rested her head on the steering wheel, and let her tawny hair fall forward around her face.

How did it all get so crazy, she wondered silently to herself as she attempted to shake off the feelings of apprehension and anger that still hung cloyingly around her. She found no answer to the enigma that had become her life.

"Damn," she muttered to herself, as she switched on the ignition of the car and started worrying about what action Dena might take after hearing Mara's confession. "Damn, damn, damn." How could everything in her life have gotten so suddenly complicated? All because of one little lie.

"Oh, don't worry about me," June had replied to Mara's request that she check in with Dr. Bernard. "You have enough problems of your own without bothering yourself about my health. I'm fine. *Really.* You worry too much."

It had taken a considerable amount of gentle persuasion, and Mara wasn't entirely convinced that the older woman would do as she promised, but June had finally, though reluctantly, agreed to have a checkup. When pressed for a date, June was uncharacteristically vague, but Mara left well enough alone. At least June had promised to visit the local medical clinic. Even that small victory was more than Mara could have hoped for.

It was late by the time Angie had taken her bath. But the sight of the young child with her fresh scrubbed face, laughing dark eyes, and halo of wet, golden ringlets made Mara forget, at least momentarily, about the pressures of her job and problems with Dena. There was something about Angie, dressed head to toe in animal-print pajamas, that made everything else in the world seem insignificant. Mara had taken time to put a rather complicated puzzle together for Angie, and the child laughed delightedly when she recognized that the picture was taking the shape of two adorable kittens.

The doorbell rang, and Angie scrambled off of her chair, nearly slipping on the tile in the kitchen and calling importantly over her shoulder, "I get it, Mommy."

Mara hurried from the kitchen just as Angie was tugging at the brass handle of one of the twin front doors. With a grunt, she was able to open it and there, on the darkened

porch, was Shane, and Mara felt her heart leap at the sight
of him. He looked tired, worn out. His black hair was disheveled, and the light touch of silver near his temples stood
out in the darkness of the night. At the sight of his daughter
the fatigue seemed to leave his face, and he bent down on
one knee to scoop up the youngster and hold her against his
chest as if he would never let go.

Angie clung to Shane, just as desperately as he held her,
and Shane's face, buried against the tiny neck of his child,
was a tortured display of emotions. His love was so open
and honest that Mara discovered she had to turn away from
the poignant scene to avoid bursting into tears of frustration
and self-reproach. How could she deny Shane the small but
inherent right of a father to claim his child?

Shane set Angie back on the floor reluctantly, and answered every one of the child's endless questions.

"We doing a puzzle of kitties," Angie jabbered excitedly. "Do you want to see them?"

"Of course," Shane replied seriously. "Maybe I can
help."

"I don't know," Angie said, her brows puckering in
thought. "Even Momma has trouble..."

Shane shot Mara a glance full of amusement and delight
with his child. "All the more reason for me to try," he
bantered back at Angie, who was racing down the hall, back
toward the kitchen.

"She missed you," Mara whispered quietly.

"Not half as much as I missed her," Shane muttered, and
deep pangs of guilt twisted Mara's heart.

Angie, perched precariously on the edge of one of the
chairs around the cozy kitchen table, had already managed
to scramble several of the pieces of the puzzle by the time
that Mara and Shane had reached the kitchen. Shane laughed
good-naturedly, picked up the mischievous little imp, and
plopped her squarely down on his lap. She giggled with

mirth, and father and daughter began working on the puzzle, interlocking the intricate cardboard shapes.

While Shane and Angie huddled together under the Tiffany lamp, Mara put on a pot of fresh coffee, and the rich scent of java eventually permeated the kitchen and small dining nook where Shane and Angie were studiously arranging the puzzle. Mara watched with envy and pride as father and daughter became caught up in a world uniquely their own: Shane's muscular shoulders—Angie's small, busy hands; Shane's thick, rumpled, raven-black hair—Angie's tousled, slightly damp, blond curls; Shane's rough, deep-timbred laughter—Angie's musical, tinkling imitation; and both of them with their deep, black, knowing eyes.

Just as Mara was pouring the coffee into cups, they finished with their project. Within minutes, the jagged pieces of the simple jigsaw had, to Angie's amazement and pleasure, been rejoined and the two playful kittens in the picture once again stared back at Angie.

"Does Imagination have much of a market for these things?" Shane asked, eyeing the puzzle box.

Mara handed him a cup of steaming coffee. "Some..."

"Don't tell me, let me guess—the competition does much better than we do?"

A self-derisive smile curved over Mara's lips. "I wish I could disagree with you, but unfortunately, once again, you're right. San Franciscan has outdone Imagination three to one in puzzle sales, along with dolls, clay, balls...you name it."

"Not computer games for children?"

"I don't know," Mara sighed. "Until you came into the company, we weren't even in the electronics market."

Angie interrupted as a sudden, important thought struck her. "Mommy—is Snoopy on tonight?"

"Oh, honey, I'm sorry. I forgot all about it!" Mara

glanced at her watch. ''You're still in luck; if you hurry, you can see the last twenty minutes.''

Angie darted into the den and snapped on the TV while her parents joined her at a slower pace. Angie insisted that Shane sit on the couch, and after racing through the house to find her blanket and Lolly doll, she hurried back to the den to scramble onto Shane's lap and reclaim her important position.

It had been a long, fatiguing day, filled with unsettling and turbulent emotions that had torn at Mara for hours. The outburst with Dena had been the worst, and Mara wanted to tell Shane about it, but the unspoken tension in the air stopped her. Although Mara was already emotionally drained and exhausted, she could feel the threat of another confrontation with Shane in the air. It wasn't so much what he said, as what he didn't say, and the dark, impenetrable looks that he passed in her direction. Deep lines of concern knotted his brow and indicated to Mara that he was ready for a showdown. Only Angie's presence had kept him from demanding answers to the questions that were hovering in the black depths of his eyes.

The Snoopy special was long over. While sitting near Shane on the couch, pretending interest in a dull variety show, Mara could feel the tension between them building, minute by minute. She wanted to close her eyes and transform the cozy den, with its paneled walls and shelves of books, into her favorite room with the two people that she loved most in the world filling it. But, although both Angie and Shane were only inches from her, she felt isolated and cold with dread; she knew that soon Shane would demand to know why she hadn't come out and told June the truth about Angie. Nervously, Mara played with her coffee cup, an action not lost on Shane. Only the softness and innocence of the heavy-lidded blond child cuddled in Shane's lap kept the imminent argument at bay.

Within a few silent, uncomfortable minutes, Angie had fallen into a deep, dreamless sleep. Mara reached for the tired child, intent upon taking her upstairs to bed, but Shane shook his head and pushed Mara's arm gently aside as he rose from the couch still clutching Angie. When he walked out of the den, Mara could see the top of Angie's curly head nestled securely against Shane's chest. Mara had to restrain herself from following them, but she knew intuitively that Shane wanted to spend a few quiet moments alone with his child.

Mara took the coffee cups and placed them in the sink in the kitchen. Shane was still with Angie, and rather than disturb the long-denied intimacy between father and daughter, Mara stuck her hands into the pockets of her jeans and walked out past the back porch, into the darkness of the night. Although the temperature had dropped considerably since late afternoon, the air was still cloyingly warm, unusually thick, heavy with humidity. The dark sky was hazy, with only a few winking stars lighting the black expanse overhead; a hot, sultry, late-summer night. The promise of rain hung heavy in the air.

The only relief from a night that stole the breath from her was a slight, pine-scented breeze which lifted Mara's hair away from her face and neck, cooling the small, dewy beads of perspiration that had gathered on her skin. Silently, wrapped in her own, private thoughts, she strode down the garden path, not noticing the heady scent of the late-blooming flowers or the murmuring buzz of the evening's insects. Finally, after crossing a broad expanse of slightly dry lawn, she reached the white fence that separated the manicured grounds from the paddock. She stood, her arms folded over the top wooden plank of the fence, her left foot poised against the bottom rail. In the meadow beyond, she saw the shadow of a cat stalking field mice. In the distance, Mara heard the soft call of a night owl, and the rumble of an eighteen-wheeler on a remote highway. It was a hot, restless summer night.

Mara felt Shane's presence before she heard the familiar creak of the screen door as it scraped over the floor of the porch, and before he coughed quietly. Looking upward, to the imposing second story of the house, she noticed that the light in Angie's bedroom was out, and surmised that the child was sleeping soundly in her bed.

Mara's image, a dark womanly form, thrown in relief by the white fence, reminded Shane of a younger, more care-free period of his life—an existence that they had shared happily together. There was a childlike quality in the way that Mara hung against the fence, as if she were still an adolescent school girl daydreaming in the darkness. It was her form, a silhouette of innocent womanhood, that played dangerous games with his mind and beckoned him to walk closer to her.

He stopped short of her, his hands pushed to the back pockets of his jeans, and watched as she turned to face him in the shifting moonlight. Soft strands of golden hair were lifted by the breeze and shimmered to silver in the hazy moonglow. In the quiet solitude of that summer night, their gazes locked, dusky blue with darkest ebony. In the distance, thunder growled.

His hand, as if in slow motion, reached out and outlined the curve of her jaw, the length of her throat, the swell of her breast to drop in frustration at his side. Mara felt the hardening of her nipples straining for release against the soft imprisonment of her clothes. Her breath became constricted in her throat, and when she attempted to speak, to try and bridge the abysmal gap that she knew was growing between them, she was unable to. The words of love failed her. The apology that she felt straining inside her—to amend for the fact that she had denied him his right to claim his daughter—was lost in the darkness. She needed him…wanted him...ached for his touch, and yet the words that would help heal the wounds and bind the two of them together were lost somewhere in the deepest part of her.

"Mara...oh, baby," he moaned, his hands on her shoulders, holding her at a distance from him and yet teasing her with their warm promise. A shudder ripped through her, a shudder of a need so deep that it inflamed all parts of her as she felt his fingers enticing warm circles of passion against her skin. Even through the light fabric of her blouse, his touch aroused her to the depth of his longing.

His lips descended hungrily to the welcome invitation of her open mouth. In an explosive, long-withheld union of flesh, Shane's tongue rimmed her anxious lips and delved into the sweet, moist cavern of her mouth. Softly she moaned and slumped against him, letting the heat of the summer night scorch her body by his passionate, hungry touch. Spiraling circles of desire wound upward through her veins from the most womanly core of her body. Her fingers touched and wound themselves in his thick, wavy black hair, communicating without words how desperately she wanted him...how much she needed him.

"Why do you make me ache so badly?" Shane asked, forcing her against him with a fierce power born of denial. Her supple body molded willingly to the throbbing contours of his. "Why do you torture me?" he whispered against the skin of her cheek. His lips roved seductively to the shell of her ear. "And why, why do I *need* you?" He buried his face in her soft, honey-touched tresses, and his hot breath caressed the very center of her being. "I *want* you, Mara," he murmured in hot, desperate longing. "God, how I want you!" His voice and hands seemed to embrace every part of her, and Mara could feel the insistent tips of his fingertips rubbing the taut muscles of her back, kneading them with urgent persuasion.

Far off, lightning paled the late summer sky, and for one

breathless instant, Mara saw Shane's face as clearly as if it were early dawn. The muscles in his face were set and hard. The look in his shadowed eyes was that of a man plagued by his own traitorous thoughts.

"I...I don't mean to play games with you," she asserted, reading the anger and frustration on his features. "Surely you must know that." Her light eyes were probing, delving deeply into his black gaze. Once again, his lips sought and found the supple curve of her mouth, and any words that may have been forming in his mind were instantly forgotten with the fever of his embrace.

Mara found herself clinging to him, clutching him, holding on to him as if she thought he might, once more, disappear into the night and be lost to her. *Don't leave me*, she thought desperately. *Please, Shane, don't leave me ever again*, but the words were lost in the passion of the night. The tears that had been threatening to spill all day came at last, unwanted. Her eyes filled, and although she fought to push them back, the salty droplets slid down the soft hills of her cheeks to moisten her lips and give the heated kiss the tangy flavor of her despair.

His body stiffened as he recognized that she was quietly crying. After a pause, as if he was trying to restrain himself, he moaned, and then softly, gently, never allowing their bodies to drift apart, he folded his knees against hers and drew her down to the dry, soft carpet of grass. Far away, a pale, craggy streak of lightning flashed against the mountains and the dull, echoing sound of thunder reverberated through the surrounding hills.

"What's wrong?" Shane asked, his eyes guarded while his hands, with gentle strokes, smoothed the hair away from her face. With a wistful smile, he captured a tear from her eye on his finger and touched it to his lips.

She returned his smile with a wan imitation, and lay on her back, her crossed arms cradling her head. Shane lay,

half sat next to her, his face bent over hers so closely that
she could feel the warmth of his breath ruffling her hair and
taste his heady, masculine scent that laced the air and lingered against her lips. His dark eyes showed nothing but
genuine, intense concern, and all at once she saw the
younger man that she had always loved so desperately. Did
he know, *could he feel,* just how desperately she had loved
him and agonized over him for the past few days...how
much she had wanted him for the last four years?

"What isn't wrong?" she countered, finally able to answer his probing question.

"Nothing is," he corrected her and pressed a finger to
her mouth, at first to silence her. But finally he surrendered
to the longings in his body, and enticed her to open her lips
and let him touch the inside of her. Slowly she complied,
opening her mouth and accepting the exploring finger, letting the wild, suggestive impulses spark her blood. He
touched her teeth, her gums, her tongue, and she reveled in
the salty, bittersweet masculine taste.

His groan of surrender was primeval in intensity, and
Mara felt him tremble with repressed passion. As the space
of minutes lapsed he levered himself up on one elbow and
with his free hand, opened the buttons of her blouse. The
sheer fabric fluttered in the breeze to gape open in the filtered moonlight, an open invitation. He was entranced, filled
with a need only she could fill, and while thunder rolled
against the Blue Ridge, Shane moved over Mara and pressed
his face into the dusky hollow of her breasts. "Oh, God,
Mara," he moaned, letting his weight press against her,
"you're beautiful!" With hands that trembled, he lifted the
blouse away from her breasts and looked with naked yearning at the uneven pattern of her ragged breathing. Even
through the flimsy fabric of her bra, the dark circles of her
nipples pushed tautly upward, an anxious invitation to his
hands and mouth.

Before touching either of the warm, supple peaks, he placed the palm of his hand over Mara's trip-hammering heart, and felt the rush of desire coursing through her veins in its erratic, pulsating beat.

Gradually Shane's hand moved. And while his eyes held hers, his hand slid over the lace of Mara's bra, and brushed against the tip of her straining nipple. A long, low sigh escaped from Mara's lips. And when through the soft fabric she felt his hot breath and warm, coaxing lips tease and brush her breast, she could stand no more of the bittersweet yearning. She arched her body up to meet his and let her fingers push his head more tightly to her breast, drowning in the sweet, warm, melting sensations that were oozing throughout her body.

"Oh, Shane," she murmured, calling his name over and over into the furious night. His answering groan and shudder of surrender further added to the heightened feeling of desire that was making her lose all thoughts of anything other than fulfilling the burning need that was flaming within her.

And his lips, after suckling tentatively at each of her nipples, left wet shadows of passion against her bra, and made the heat of her need smolder to new summits of desire.

The power of her hunger was dizzying, and without thought she found the buttons of his shirt and began slipping them through the buttonholes to expose the taut muscles of his chest and the powerful shoulders. Her fingers slid even more boldly to the waistband of his jeans before he took a long, steadying breath and held both of her hands in his. "Oh, Mara," he breathed raggedly, "don't do this to me." His eyes closed in agony.

Confused and disappointed, she pulled her hands from his and turned away from his dark gaze. "I…I…guess I don't understand," she admitted, torn by the depth of her need for him and the pain of his rejection.

"Neither do I," he conceded, in one long, lingering

breath. Disgusted with himself for the breakdown in his willpower and angry because of the pain he was causing her, he let himself fall back onto the grass to gaze, searchingly, at the few winking stars that could be seen in the restless, dark sky. "I'm sorry," he breathed, wondering why he always felt such a need to apologize. "I told you before—I can't have you on these terms—Peter Wilcox's terms."

"Peter has nothing to do with us…"

The unasked question burned in the air, and though unspoken, Mara could feel the question in Shane's gaze.

"You don't have to say anything, Mara," he whispered. "I know that you haven't told June about Angie." Shane's words sounded dead with disappointment.

"I tried," she offered, somewhat apologetically. A gray-green flash of jagged electricity sizzled across the sky, lighting the mountain tops, and thunder rumbled ominously near.

"That's not good enough," he accused. "She has to be told!"

"She's…she's going to the doctor, sometime next week, I think. Once I know that she's all right, I'll tell her…everything."

"Too late." Shane's voice was as distant as the approaching summer storm.

"Shane, be reasonable…"

"*Reasonable?*" he repeated incredulously, throwing the word back into her face. "Reasonable? I think *I've* been more than reasonable." In a quieter tone, "It was my mistake." He pulled himself up into a sitting position, and his eyes traveled over the tortured expression on her face. His shirt gaped open, exposing the tense, rock-hard muscles of his chest and the dark mat of hair that swirled roughly between his taut male nipples. The ripple of his muscles in the warm night was electrifying, and Mara felt the feminine urges of her body once again responding to his enticingly male physique.

"You're insinuating that I haven't been fair...." she charged, though her voice sounded frail.

A dark eyebrow quirked attentively. "No, I'm not. What I'm telling you is that you can't expect to have it both ways." He silently let his eyes run down the length of her body. Her blouse was still parted, and the sculpted form of her breasts heaving in the moonlight made his ache for her increase. Reluctantly, he moved his eyes away from the soft curve of her abdomen...

"You're wrong—I don't expect anything to work both ways," she pouted.

"Sure you do! Admit it, Mara, you want everything— Angie, the toy company, the Wilcox fortune, social standing, this house, and me. And I hate being last on the list!" His dark eyes narrowed.

"You're wrong...you're not last. Oh, Shane, don't you know that much, at the very least?"

"I know that you're hedging."

"I'm not trying to..."

"Well, then, dear," he teased, his face moving to within inches of hers, "you have to be willing to pay the price, and it won't be easy."

"The price?" she asked. "What price are you talking about?" Even in the shadows of the night, under the black cloud-filled sky, Shane could see that she was honestly confused.

"Can't you see what is bound to happen?" he asked. "Once you make your surprise announcement to your mother-in-law that Angie is my child, can't you see what is bound to come crashing down on you, on us? The whole damned roof will cave in! All of that Wilcox family will go running to their lawyers in an attempt to save what they consider to be rightfully theirs. There is going to be one helluva mess, darling, and you'll be right in the middle of it.''

He stopped for a moment to note her reaction to his thoughts. She had propped herself up on her elbows and was hanging on his every word.

''And what about the press?'' he continued. ''The newspapers will have a field day with this one, don't you think?'' he asked.

Dena's taunts, issued earlier in the evening, came thundering back. ''Oh, God,'' Mara moaned with the impact of his statement.

''And that's not the worst of it. There will probably be charges of collusion between you and me, as if we had planned the entire stock takeover. And,'' his voice grew even more sober, ''Angie will be the target of it all!''

''No!'' Thunder, closer now, clapped threateningly.

''You won't be able to avoid it.''

''But…if you knew all of this…why did you take such a chance and invest half a million dollars into Imagination?''

''It's a sound investment, believe it or not,'' he stated with a grim smile. ''And Imagination Toys needs me much more than I need them.''

''Oh, Shane,'' she murmured. ''I don't know if I'm up to battling with the family anymore.''

''Sure you are. And any story they might dream up about collusion won't wash with the courts. Don't worry about it, I've already done the groundwork.''

''You don't know Dena…''

Shane's eyes narrowed wickedly in a brilliant flash of lightning. ''I saw her in action last Friday at the board meeting, and don't worry about Dena, I'm sure I can handle her…''

The rain, thick droplets, began to fall in a late summer deluge. Quickly, Shane pulled Mara to her feet and together they dashed toward the house. Once in the safety of the screened portion of the porch, they stood close, not touching, but together watched the fury of the storm unleash.

Shane's thoughts, deep and troubled, were as ominous as the black night itself. The rain beat a steady rhythm against the roof of the porch, and the downpour, still dusty with summer grit, gurgled with the sound of running water. Mara's clothes clung to her, and tiny droplets of rain, reflecting in the light from the kitchen window, ran in jeweled rivulets down the tanned length of Shane's neck.

"I expect that you'll tell June tomorrow," Shane announced, wiping the moisture from his face with the back of his hand.

"I don't know if I can..."

"You don't have a choice." His tone was even more cutting than his words. He rested his hands on his hips and looked off into the mountains before turning to face Mara. When he did, he crossed his arms over his chest. His hooded gaze pinned Mara against the screen, and involuntarily, expecting the worst, she felt her spine become rigid with dread. What she didn't realize was how alluring she appeared, her hair and face freshly doused with rainwater and her clothes clinging to her slim figure.

Shane's words came out slowly, as if with measured intent. "You should know that while I was in Atlanta, I spent a lot of time with Henderson...my attorney."

"Yes?" she returned stiffly. Apprehension tightened her features.

"We talked about a lot of things, such as the collusion and fraud that the Wilcox family will no doubt charge us with."

"Go on," she coaxed, steadying herself for the final blow that she was expecting.

"And besides all of that, I told him about Angie."

Genuine fear took hold of Mara. Her fingers tightened on

the screen. "And?" she prodded, her breathing irregular and constricted. "What did he say?"

"Well," he began, rubbing the back of his neck. "What it all boils down to is this—either you marry me right away and I adopt Angie, changing the records to indicate that she is my natural, biological child, or I'll start custody proceedings against you."

Mara's knees began to buckle under the weight of his threat. "No! Oh, Shane, you...you wouldn't!" Mara cried, unbelieving. "You can't...take her away..."

"I don't want to. You know that, but—"

"Don't do this to me!" she wailed over the pitch of the storm.

"You don't really leave me much of a choice, do you? I've set up a trust fund for her, but that's not enough. Damn it, Mara, it's just not enough!" His fist crashed into the screen. "I want her, damn it, and I intend to have her!"

"I told you that I would marry you," Mara pleaded.

"When?" he demanded, and the lightning crackled in the air.

"After I know for certain that June is well."

"There are no certainties in this life, Mara. I gave you two weeks, and they're gone!"

"But, Shane—"

"There's no more room for argument!" His eyes glinted in the night like tempered obsidian. "This is what's going to happen—I'm going to fight you tooth and nail for custody of my child unless you marry me tomorrow. And if you think that you can handle a legal battle—fine, I'll see you in court. But just be aware that I'll spare no expense, and I'll leave no stone unturned in order that I get at least partial custody of *my* child!"

"Shane, please...don't do this to us. Please, don't threaten me," she pleaded, her frightened eyes beseeching him.

"It wasn't my decision, Mara. It was yours!"

"I'll tell June next week, I swear..." she began, half-sobbing, the tears glistening in her eyes. "...but please don't take my baby away from me!" Mara's face twisted in fear and agony—why did he demand so much and give so little? She loved him with a passion that wouldn't, even after four long years, subside, and yet she felt as if he had never loved her. Why couldn't he understand and wait, just a little longer?

Lightning cracked across the sky and the thunder pealed loudly enough to shake the timbers of the old Southern mansion. The wind had picked up, but above the clamor of the storm, Mara thought she heard the faint sound of a child screaming...

"Angie!" Mara gasped, realizing that the girl was probably terrified. She turned toward the kitchen, but Shane was ahead of her, running through the house and dashing up the stairs two at a time. The thunder roared again, and the little girl shrieked.

Shane reached Angie's room before a minute had passed, and by the time that Mara had made it, breathlessly running to the bedroom, Shane held the sobbing, frightened child in his arms. He was whispering soft words to her and fondly stroking her hair with his hands. "It's all right, precious," he murmured against her small head. "*Daddy* is here now, and he's never, never going to let you get scared again."

Mara froze in the doorway, and Shane's dark gaze defied her to deny the words of comfort and love that he, as Angie's father, was giving to his child.

Chapter Ten

Shane's vigil didn't end until early morning. He refused to leave, even long after the wrath of the storm had passed and Angie had fallen to sleep, cradled in his arms. It was a sight that, under a different set of circumstances, would have warmed Mara's heart. As it was, Shane's powerful presence as he dozed restlessly with his child in his arms reminded Mara of his threats. She found it impossible to believe that the man she loved, with his rumpled black hair and dark beard, would go so far as to take her child from her unless she married him. Never once had he asked her to live with him for love. No, it was only to give him back what he considered rightfully his.

Although Mara loved him deeply, and she knew that people were married for far less noble reasons, the thought that he was coercing her...with her child as bait, began to anger her. And so, as he sat in the leather recliner near the fireplace with the sleepy Angie on his lap, Mara found herself resenting the fact that he would do anything to have his way. It was several hours before she finally dozed.

When the first few silent rays of dawn crept over the high plateau and the sun cast fresh shadows on the wet lawn, Shane roused himself, and with a pleased expression on his face, carried Angie up to her room. Assured that the tired little girl would sleep until late in the morning, he stretched and went back downstairs. Mara was where he had left her, curled up under a plaid blanket on the couch in the den. He knew that she hadn't slept much the night before, and he also knew that he was the cause of her sleeplessness. If he had thought that the reason for her restlessness was a simmering passion for him, he would have been pleased. But as it was, he knew that it was his threats that had kept her awake, and he briefly wondered if he had pushed her too far. Was he asking too much? As he watched her in the early morning light, sunbeams filtered through the paned windows and her tousled hair glistened with gilded highlights. The strain that had aged the contours of her face last night had lifted in the peaceful repose of slumber.

For the first time since he had read Peter Wilcox's obituary, Shane Kennedy was unsure. Was he making a vast, irreparable mistake with not only Mara but also his daughter? Was Mara right when she charged him with being selfish to the point that he was interested in only *his* happiness. For a moment, he wavered. And then the picture of Angie's terrified face, starkly illuminated in a flash of lightning, burned in his memory. His lips curled in a grim smile. No, he was right, damn it, he was right!

Shane was gone when Mara finally stirred. She squinted against the bright sun, and it took her a minute to realize that she was in her clothes in the den. It must have been after three o'clock when she had finally dozed off. She stretched and counted each of the chimes from the grandfather's clock...five, six, seven, eight. She got up with a start—June would be at the house within fifteen minutes!

Thoughts of the storm, Angie's terror, Shane's threats, and unfulfilled passion whirled in Mara's head as she straightened the den and began to put on a pot of coffee. Gravel crunched in the driveway, and Mara knew that she had to face her mother-in-law. The thought that Shane had issued her an ultimatum still bothered her, but, Mara promised herself, she owed it to June to tell her the truth. Today was the day.

However, her resolve shook a little as she saw the stoop of June's shoulders and the tight whiteness of June's lips.

"Good morning," she called with feigned cheerfulness to the older woman.

"Same to you," June replied. "Aren't you going to work today?" June's pale blue eyes traveled up Mara's body, noting the rumpled jeans and wrinkled blouse.

"Yes...it's...just that Angie didn't sleep well last night, and well, we sort of camped out in the den."

Relief relaxed June's face. "I know what you mean; that storm kept me awake for hours!"

"How...how are you feeling this morning?"

The question made June straighten her shoulders sharply and stare, unblinking into Mara's concerned gaze. "I told you, I'm a little tired, but other than that I'm feeling just fine." The tone of June's voice indicated that the subject was closed. Mara wasn't convinced that lack of sleep caused June's pale complexion, nor curved her thin lips into a tight, uncomfortable frown. To Mara, it was obvious that June was in pain.

After handing June a cup of coffee, Mara went upstairs and checked on Angie, who was still sleeping soundly. Then, after a quick shower, she changed into a soft, lilac print dress, and went back downstairs to the kitchen, intent on telling June the truth. But, apparently Peter's mother hadn't heard the approaching footsteps, and when Mara reentered the kitchen, she found June sitting at the table, swallowing several brightly colored pills from a variety of vials.

June's features mirrored her guilt as she looked up and saw Mara standing in the doorway. Quickly, she recovered herself and, with an effort at dignity, recapped the bottles and put them back into her purse.

Mara's blue eyes took in the entire situation, and she found that she had difficulty swallowing. June's condition must be far worse than even Mara had realized.

"Are those the nerve pills that Dr. Bernard prescribed for you?" Mara asked. She poured herself a cup of coffee, and although she was already late, took the time to sit across from her mother-in-law, hoping to communicate with her.

"Yes," June admitted, dusting the lapel of her moss-green jacket nervously. "Among others."

Mara took a scalding sip of the dark liquid and observed June over the rim of her cup. Why did the older woman look so defeated? Just how ill was she? Mara scowled into the cup and then, in a soothing voice, tried to broach the painful subject again.

"June," she reproached, "you would tell me if you were seriously ill, wouldn't you?"

"Of course," the gray-haired woman snapped, but she couldn't find the strength to meet Mara's concerned, intense gaze.

"And you would let me know if watching Angie was too much of a burden?"

"Yes, Mara, I would." This time, watery blue eyes reached out to Mara and begged her to understand.

"But, this morning…because you didn't sleep well… don't you think Angie might be too much trouble for you?"

"Nonsense! She's never any trouble for me! And…

and…well, if I do get tired, today, Sylvia Reardon comes in to clean, doesn't she…I'm sure she'd give me a hand.''

''Of course she would,'' Mara agreed thoughtfully. June's eyes pleaded with her, and Mara couldn't find the heart to refuse. Putting her coffee cup down on the table, Mara rose and grabbed her purse. ''You will call me, won't you, if you need help. Shane's in the office today. So, if you need me, I can run home…''

June's smile seemed frozen on her face at the mention of Shane, and fleetingly Mara wondered if Dena had told her mother the truth. All during the drive into Asheville and for most of the morning, Mara was wrapped in worried thoughts about her mother-in-law. She stayed close to the telephone and waited in case June should need her.

It was late in the afternoon when Shane walked into her office. Although he had been in the building since early in the morning, he had been busy making sure that the computer was functioning properly and that the conversion of space in the factory for assembly of the new line of video games he hoped to promote was complete.

''I'm leaving for Atlanta,'' he said after closing the door to her office and dropping into a chair opposite her desk. He folded his fingers under his chin and studied every emotion that traversed her face. ''Are you coming with me?''

''For the weekend?'' she asked, hedging. She had been writing on her memo pad, but she stopped doodling, and her blue eyes fastened on his.

''For the rest of your life.''

Mara took a deep swallow of air, let it out wearily and dropped her pen, before leaning back in her chair.

''You know that I want to Shane,'' and she seemed as if she meant every word she breathed.

''Then what's stopping you?''

''I just can't…not yet.''

Shane's jaw tightened, and his dark eyes promised that he would carry out his threats of the night before.

"I tried to talk to June this morning, but…I caught her taking some pills. And I'm very worried about her," Mara explained.

"How can I make you understand that June Wilcox's problems aren't yours?" he asked. "And as for popping a few pills…don't you ever read the papers. Drug addiction, whether it's Valium, uppers, downers, whatever, isn't confined to California. Lots of men and women, wealthy or not, use—"

"That's not the way it is!" Mara shouted, interrupting him. Her tired nerves were stretched as tautly as a bow string. "She's ill, for God's sake!"

"Then she should see a doctor!"

"She will!"

"And until then, whenever it may be, I should content myself in the thought that it will probably be soon?" he inquired, disbelieving.

"It's only a few more days…"

"You think! And what if your suspicions prove true? What if the doctors do find that there is something seriously wrong with June, what then? How long will you expect me to wait then?"

"I'm not asking for much," she pleaded quietly, inching her chin upward in a show of dignity.

"Too much, Mara," he hurled back at her as he rose from his position in front of her expansive desk. He whirled toward the door and began to leave, but Mara's soft voice stopped him.

"Shane, wait…" she commanded, rising from her chair and reaching for him.

He spun on his heel to face her, but refused to capture her extended hand. All of the anger and pent-up rage of four years of frustration showed on the bladed contours of his masculine face as he stood before her. His dark eyes narrowed, almost wicked in their arrogance, and he looked down at her with his lips curling in undisguised contempt. "I've waited, Mara. God, how I've waited. And I won't, *I can't* wait any longer! It seems as if you've made your choice!"

He left her standing helpless in the middle of the room, and he didn't turn back to face her. No "goodbye," no "I'm sorry," no "I'll understand," and no "I love you." Nothing but a helpless, empty feeling that crept into her heart.

"Mrs. Wilcox…Mrs. Wilcox?" Lynda was inquiring through the intercom on Mara's desk. "Did you want me to come in for that dictation now? Mrs. Wilcox?" Lynda's voice brought Mara crashing back to reality.

"Yes, Lynda…but, make it in about five minutes, okay?" Mara asked into the black receiver. She needed a few minutes to gather her poise.

"You're the boss," Lynda quipped back lightheartedly.

Mara lifted her finger from the intercom and let the hot, fresh tears run unrestricted down her face. She was tired, not only from lack of sleep, but with worry. And she was frustrated, caught in the middle of a situation she couldn't control, torn with concern for a woman whose own family cared little for her, and in love with a man she didn't entirely understand. Mara let the bitter tears run unchecked, if only for a moment. "I'm not going to lose, Shane," she murmured to herself as she dabbed at the corners of her eyes with the tissue. "I absolutely refuse to lose to you…or to June. Somehow, I swear, we're going to find our way out of this!"

"Pardon me?" Lynda asked, standing in the doorway. Color washed over her face as she noticed that her employer had been crying. "Oh…well…if you want to do this… later…I'll come back," Lynda stammered, backing out of the office. Mara took command of the situation.

"It's all right, Lynda. Come in. I've got quite a lot of correspondence to get out before we go home tonight." Mara smiled sincerely at the young girl as Lynda took a seat near the corner of the desk and poised her pencil in readiness over her stenographer's tablet. With as much authority and poise as she could pull together, Mara began the dictation, and was relieved to see that Lynda's embarrassment faded. Somehow, Mara promised herself, she would get through this day and straighten out the problems she faced. It couldn't be impossible, she reasoned, her spine stiffening at the thought of the challenge. It was going to work!

With her new confidence neatly in place, Mara finished work at the office for the weekend. It was the first Friday in many that she was able to leave by five o'clock. Although the traffic in downtown Asheville was snarled and the evening was slightly warm, Mara refused to have her spirits deflated. Rather than use the air-conditioning in the car, Mara rolled down her window and listened to the sounds of the busy city. A few horns blared impatiently, an occasional motorist mouthed a stream of invectives, but for the most part, even in the height of rush hour, the feeling in the air was of calm equanimity. It was as if, by finally deciding to somehow solve her own problems, Mara had begun to defeat them. When she finally maneuvered her car out of the city limits, and the tree-lined streets broke from suburbia into the quiet of the mountain countryside, Mara pushed her sandaled foot more heavily on the accelerator and let the sporty car race toward home. The wind whipped and twisted her hair, the radio played lighthearted, soothing music, and soon she would be able to spend a quiet, warm summer weekend with Angie. She smiled at the thought of a picnic near the river.

As for June, Mara had convinced herself that she could deal with the older woman gently and fairly. Her plan was simple: it was time that she took the bull by the horns and began handling her own life. Whether June agreed or not, Mara was going to call Dr. Bernard and request a complete physical for her mother-in-law. And then, if June was strong enough, Mara would tell Angie's grandmother the truth of her identity. If June's health prevented a forthright confession, Mara would find a gentler way to break the news.

With her spirits soaring higher than the tops of the ancient oaks that welcomed her home, she hurried into the house and called out her usual greeting. "Angie...June, I'm home."

But the house sounded incredibly empty. No running footsteps or laughing chatter warned of Angie's arrival. The television had been turned off, and there was no noise in the house except for the regular ticking of the great old clock and the smooth hum of the air conditioner. Mara's voice echoed back to her, and though she tried to ignore it, a small tremor of anxiety taunted her. The house didn't *feel* right. "Angie?" Mara called a little louder.

The house was immaculately clean, evidence that Mrs. Reardon had been working earlier in the day. And the grass was freshly cut, Mara noted, her eyes scanning the lawn. Mr. Staples, the gardener, had worked outdoors. June's sky-blue Lincoln was parked in its usual spot in the garage. But the house was empty. Mara checked all the rooms—Angie's bed was freshly made. Hadn't she napped? Still, no sign of grandmother and child.

Rather than panic, Mara went back downstairs to the kitchen. Perhaps June left a note. Maybe someone came and took them for a drive...or a walk. Unlikely. No note. The only evidence that anyone had been in the deserted house since Mrs. Reardon had been in was a tiny, neat pile of dishes in the sink.

Mara, with real dread beginning to take hold of her, walked out onto the porch, and noted, with a slight sense of relief, that Southpaw and her family were snoozing in the late afternoon sun. But there was no sight or sound of Angie.

"Mara, is that you?" June's familiar voice called out as the screen door scraped against the boards of the porch. Mara nearly jumped at the sound, but was relieved when she saw June propped up on the yellow chaise lounge in a shaded portion of the broad expanse of porch. Sunlight, filtered through the chestnut tree in the back yard, cast moving shadows over June's delicate features.

"Didn't you hear me calling you?" Mara asked with a laugh as she approached the older woman and noted the open magazine that had dropped to the floor.

"Well, I must have dozed off," June apologized and attempted to stretch. She grimaced in pain as her cramped muscles refused to straighten. "I was reading this article on floral arrangements, and I guess my lack of sleep caught up with me," she admitted with a sheepish frown. She tugged the reading glasses off of her nose and tucked them into her purse.

"It's been a long day for everyone," Mara agreed, her eyes skimming the hedge where Angie sometimes hid. The sun was still bright, and she was forced to squint. "Where's Angie?"

June stiffened, and her eyes snapped with fear. "What?" she asked. "I thought she was with you..."

"But I've been at work," Mara reminded her, wondering if her mother-in-law's tired mind was beginning to play tricks on her. "I left her with you...this morning."

"I know, I know," June snapped almost hysterically as she looked from Mara to the back yard, and back to Mara. She wrung her thin hands nervously. Mara swallowed the dread that was rising in her throat as June began to speak. "But I thought...I mean, that man told me that the three of you were going out somewhere...to the park or something...for the afternoon."

"What?" Mara gasped, and then controlled herself when she saw her own fear reflected in June's pale eyes. "What man?" she tried not to look desperate as she grasped the older woman's arm.

"Shane Kennedy!"

"He was here?"

"That's what I'm trying to tell you!" June retorted. "He was here, earlier...around two-thirty, I think." Nervous, trembling fingers were toying with the strand of pearls at her neck. "It was just before Angie's nap." A fast calculation indicated to Mara that Shane must have come to the estate directly after the argument in the office. "And he told me that the three of you were going to take the afternoon off and go see some sort of jazz festival in the park...or something like that. I honestly don't remember," she sighed, filled with hatred for Shane and self-remorse that she hadn't stood up to him and kept the child. June's stern eyes impaled Mara. "He lied to me, didn't he? He deliberately tricked me into giving him the child!"

"I...I don't know," Mara answered as honestly as she could, hoping that the fear that was beginning to take hold of her wasn't being conveyed to her mother-in-law.

June slumped back onto the plump, yellow pillows of the chaise. "I didn't want to let her go, you know," she admitted in a tight voice. "I wanted to call you, but he insisted that you had already left the office and were probably waiting for him at the park. It was a lie, wasn't it?"

"I don't remember making any plans with Shane..."

"Damn that man!" June hissed, slamming her small, bony fist into the soft cushions. "Oh, dear god, Mara. What have I done?" she whispered, and the fist unclasped to fall over her small breasts.

Mara was scared, but not for the safety of her child. She knew the power of Shane's love for the little girl, and she knew that he wouldn't allow anything or anyone to hurt

Angie. As long as Angie was with Shane, the child was safe. But of course, June knew nothing of Shane's devotion to his child, and coupled with that, Peter's mother disliked Shane intensely. Mara read the fears on June's worried face, and somehow, she knew that she had to calm the older woman.

"It's all right," Mara began, placing a comforting hand on June's thin shoulders. June averted her gaze.

"No, it's not…I should never have let her go!" Self-doubt tortured her. "If anything happens to Angie, I'll never forgive myself!"

"Nothing's going to happen, don't worry," Mara said with a thin smile, knowing that her words didn't ring true. "There's just been a mix-up of some kind. That's all!"

June's watery blue eyes impaled Mara with the lie.

"Come on, now," Mara insisted, ignoring June's rueful stare and helping the older woman to her feet. "Let's go into the kitchen and I'll make you some lemonade. I'm sure that Shane will call shortly, or bring Angie back very soon." She smiled confidently at her pale mother-in-law as they made their way back to the inside of the house, and she hoped that June wouldn't notice the nervous collection of moisture that had beaded in the palms of her hands. What was Shane doing with Angie? He was supposed to be on his way back to Atlanta! And what, if anything, was all this nonsense about a jazz festival in the park?

June sat rigidly on the couch in the den. Her forehead was creased with a worried scowl, and she watched, unseeing, through the paned windows, out past the gardens. Mara hurried back into the kitchen, obsessed with her worries for Angie and her mother-in-law. What kind of game was Shane playing? Was he hoping to force a confrontation between Mara and her mother-in-law by abducting his child for the afternoon? Did he just need some time alone with Angie? Why would he take her away from Mara? The words froze in her mind, and thoughtlessly she cut her finger on the can of lemonade she had been opening. Without realizing what she was doing, she took a paper napkin and wrapped it over the finger.

The shrill ring of the telephone startled her from her dark thoughts, and in her anxious attempt to pick up the receiver, she spilled some of the lemonade onto the counter. Ignoring the mess, she grabbed the phone and answered it breathlessly.

"Hello? Shane?" *Dear God, please let it be him,* she prayed, closing her eyes.

"Mara!" Shane's controlled voice came to her over the wires. Mara's weak knees buckled and she slumped against the counter, unconscious of the dripping lemonade.

"Shane," she whispered, after swallowing with difficulty. "I've been half out of my mind! Where are you? Where's Angie?" Her fingers tightened around the ivory-colored plastic receiver.

A thick pause. Mara felt the seconds creep by. "I'm home."

"In Atlanta?" she nearly shouted. Then, thinking about June in the next room, she hushed her voice. "And Angie?"

"She's with me." His voice sounded cold, indifferent.

"Why?" she asked. "Why would you do this to me?"

"Let's not go through all of that all over again."

"But, I don't understand..."

She heard his deep, resigned sigh. "Neither do I. Not really," he admitted. "But I felt that I had to do something to get your attention."

"Get my attention? By stealing my child?" she hissed vehemently, and glanced furtively toward the den. How much of the conversation could June hear, piece together? Surely the older woman had heard the telephone ring and might wonder if it was news of Angie. Another fear assailed Mara. Perhaps June was, at this moment, listening on the extension, but she pushed the thought aside. It was ludicrous. June was, above all else, a lady, and she wouldn't stoop to listening in on someone else's call.

"Bring her back, Shane," Mara demanded.

"No."

"What?"

"I said 'no,'" he repeated quietly. "If you want her, come and get her."

"*If* I want her?" Mara gasped. "Oh, Shane, don't do this. Don't play games with me, and please, please, don't use Angie…don't put her between us. It's not fair to her!" Mara pleaded desperately.

"And living with one parent, and a lie, is?" he asked, his voice rough.

"That could all be changed, very soon."

"I've heard that one before!" His voice sounded dead, emotionless.

"Shane, for God's sake, what are you doing? Can't you see what you're asking of our child?"

"If you'll listen, I'll explain," Shane retorted. Mara clung with both hands to the phone. Her eyes were closed as she concentrated on what he was saying.

"I did lie to June," he admitted, "and I'm not proud of it. But I knew that she wouldn't let Angie go with me unless she thought I was meeting you.

"I really hadn't planned on taking her with me. I just stopped by to say goodbye, and there Angie was, so glad to see me. She was filthy, covered with dirt from head to foot from chasing those cats, and…and it was impossible for me to leave her…I just couldn't."

"I…I understand," Mara whispered, her eyes shining with pooled tears as she imagined the vivid, touching picture he was painting.

He continued. "And of course there was June Wilcox, standing guard over *my* child—standing in the way of what should be ours alone, Mara. *Our* family. *Our* happiness. She had *my* child, and I couldn't stand it, not one minute more.''

There was a pause, thick with agony. Mara heard Shane draw in a long, deep breath before he continued.

''And so you have it. I took Angie on impulse, but during the drive home, while she was sleeping in the car, I had time to do a lot of thinking, and I've decided to keep her.'' Mara's breath stopped. ''She's safe, and she's happy. If you want to see her, then you'll have to come to Atlanta.''

''That's blackmail!''

''No, kidnapping,'' he retorted angrily. ''I've talked with Henderson, my attorney, and instructed him to start custody proceedings for Angie.''

''No,'' she interrupted as panic gripped her, but Shane continued.

''And unless you get down here as fast as you can, I'm going to call the local paper, along with a few syndicated gossip sheets, and tell them the whole story from the father's viewpoint, of course, including the fact that I had to kidnap my own child.''

''Shane don't—''

''I just don't want you to be under any illusions, Mara. You know that I mean what I say, and I'm telling you that I'm going to fight you tooth and nail for custody of Angie, if that's the way you want it. I mean it, I don't care what it costs to get the best attorney in the country, I'm willing to take my chances in court! Are you?'' he asked, brashly. In the background, Mara could hear Angie chattering away.

''It…it doesn't have to be this way…''

''The choice is yours. If you don't want the fight in court, then prove it!''

''How?'' she asked weakly.

She heard his naked sigh on the other end of the line, somewhere deep in Atlanta. ''Oh, Mara, baby,'' he whispered, ''it's all so simple, if you want it to be. If you're really concerned with June's health, I understand that. But I think that the solution to the problem is to tell her the truth, as soon as possible. She's stronger than you think, and I'm sure she can handle the news. The sooner you tell her, the better.'' His voice, raw with emotion, became soothing, coaxing. ''It would hurt the least, coming from you…''

The click in her ear indicated that he had hung up, but Mara still clung to the phone, unwilling to believe that the fragile connection, that had bound them tenuously together, had been severed. ''No,'' she whispered into the receiver. ''No…no…''

Finally, realizing that she had to take some kind of action, she numbly hung up the phone and turned back toward the den. But June was in the doorway, grasping the molding for support.

''That was Shane, wasn't it?'' she accused, blue eyes unblinking.

''Yes…and Angie's with him…safe.'' Mara tried to sound cheerful, and in an effort to meet June's inquisitive gaze, she began pouring lemonade. If June's sharp eyes noticed the mess on the counter that had dripped to the floor, she didn't comment.

''Why did he lie to me?'' The question knifed Mara in the back.

''He didn't…I mean it seems that he and I had a slight misunderstanding. That's all.'' Mara shrugged, reaching for the tall, frosty glasses of lemonade and handing one to June. The glass was visibly shaking.

''You're not telling me all of it!''

Mara took a sip of the liquid. ''Mmm…no, but I will,'' she said, moving toward the den and hoping to appear calm. Mara flopped down on the recliner, in a position she hoped looked worry-free and unconcerned. ''Shane took Angie to Atlanta…and I had forgotten all about it.''

June studied her daughter-in-law dubiously, and the ashen

color of her complexion didn't improve. Mara didn't blame the older woman for seeming suspicious; her story sounded too much like the hastily contrived lie that it was. She tried to amend it.

"Shane had talked about it with me earlier in the week, but with all of the fuss at work, you know, the new computer, those formidable video games, quarterly reports...it slipped my mind. I really didn't think that we had anything firmly planned." She shrugged her shoulders, smiled at her mother-in-law, and took a long sip from her glass.

"Then why didn't he tell me about it when he was here. I would have packed Angie's bag..."

"Oh, well," Mara gulped, "he thought I was bringing her extra clothes, and I suppose...that he thought you already knew about the trip. It wasn't a lie—he did plan to meet me at the park. I guess he left a message with the receptionist or something, and I just didn't get it." Mara almost cringed visibly at her ridiculous excuses.

"Lynda seems more efficient than that," June commented dryly, but the fear in her eyes seemed to have lightened a little and her stiff, fragile shoulders relaxed slightly.

"It doesn't matter how the mix-up occurred," Mara answered with a wan smile. "The important thing is that Angie's safe!"

"You're right, of course," June agreed. "Perhaps I overreacted, a little. It's just that I love Angie so much." Mara's heart began to bleed for the little old woman. "And...that Shane Kennedy, he has a way of unnerving me." June rose with difficulty, reaching for her purse. Mara swallowed, and before June could leave, tried once again to tell the older woman about her relationship with Shane.

"He's an...unsettling man," Mara observed, bracing herself. June's entire body tensed, but Mara continued. "I thought so when I first met him...nearly five years ago..."

"Some people are just like that, aren't they...always putting you on edge," June commented nervously as she started out of the den toward the back door. "I'll see you on Monday, if not before," she said, and then added, "Have a nice time in Atlanta."

"June, wait!" Mara nearly shouted. "I need to talk to you. There's something I've been meaning to tell you…"

June turned on her heel, her eyes cold as ice as she looked through Mara and donned her mantle of easy, Southern sophistication. "Can't it wait, dear?" she asked without waiting for a reply. "I'm really very late already, and I have a bridge game scheduled for seven." She looked pointedly at her watch, and Mara noticed the sharp edge of impatience in her eyes.

"It…it can keep," Mara whispered, and June gave her a smile that reminded Mara of the way a person looks when they pat a dog on the head after it had obeyed an order.

"Good," June called cheerily…too cheerily. "I'll see you Monday."

"Sure," Mara whispered to herself, and mentally kicked herself for her own lack of courage. She watched June walk slowly to the garage and noticed her uneven gait. And with the same well-measured stiff carriage, June got into her car, pressed the throttle so heavily that the Lincoln's large motor raced in the garage, and turned the wheel of the car until it rolled awkwardly down the drive.

Mara waved as she watched June's lumbering vehicle roll lazily down the drive. Once the car was out of sight, Mara propelled herself into a whirlwind of action. She raced through the house, throwing whatever she could think of for herself and Angie into a suitcase. She only paused when she came to her daughter's room and found the tattered blanket and bedraggled Lolly Doll. Clutching both to her chest, she looked around the frilly empty room with its green and white gingham accents, the chest full of forgotten, unused toys, and the large, comfortable bed where Angie slept.

Shane couldn't take the child away from her, Mara thought desperately. He wouldn't! And yet his promise of just that was what she most feared.

A custody battle that she might have won a few years ago wouldn't necessarily be in her favor today, not with all of the national attention given to the father's rights. And the fact that she had lied and had hidden the paternity of her child, whatever the motivation, wouldn't look good to judge and jury, especially since she, as Angie's mother, had inherited the bulk of the Wilcox fortune. Of course there were Peter's relatives, all of them to consider. When they found out what deception she had planned, innocent or not, they would be more than willing to testify against her. Mara clutched the tattered piece of blanket as if it were her child. No matter how innocent her intentions, she would appear guilty by all who judged her!

The other option open to her was to marry Shane as he had suggested. God, if only she could! She would have to tell the truth and get it out—end the speculation and the misery. Soon, no doubt, Dena would make good her threats.

That she wanted to marry Shane, Mara had no doubt. How many years had she wished for just that? The thought of uniting their small family sounded perfect, if only for one, vital flaw. Never in the last few weeks had Shane whispered one word of love to her. She wouldn't deny the depth of his passion for her, it was never in question. But still she doubted his love.

Her marriage to Peter, by the time that he had fallen ill, had become a sham. Mara had married once for the sake of her child, and she had survived that one loveless marriage vowing never to enter another. Now she was confronted with the same problem. Mara knew that Shane loved Angie, just as much as she loved her child, but she also realized that love for a child wasn't enough to support a marriage. What about the relationship between husband and wife?

Could a marriage with Shane possibly work after all of the battles they had suffered together, after all of the wounds they had inflicted upon one another?

Questions, doubts, and fears kept nagging at her all the while that she fed the cats, locked the house, and threw her baggage in the little yellow Renault. Shane's address was wadded up tightly in her clenched fist, but she had already committed it to memory.

Knowing that she was in for the most heart-wrenching battle of her life, Mara twisted the key in the ignition, eased off the parking brake, and after expelling a long, uneasy breath, raced down the driveway. The drive to Atlanta would take over three hours. Mara bit her lip and ripped through the gears with renewed determination. Somehow, no matter what, she had to have Angie back...forever!

Chapter Eleven

Despite the dread that threatened to overtake her, Mara tried to remain calm during the tiresome four-hour drive Southwest toward Atlanta. Although she had left Asheville in broad daylight, as Mara continued toward her destination the sun settled behind the mountains, shadowing the rolling hills of the Piedmont Plateau in a rosy dusk. Central Georgia was just as beautiful as she had remembered it, and the heavy scent of Georgia pine trees filtered in through her open window. Mara tried to keep her mind on her driving and staying within the boundaries of the speed limits. But as the minutes stretched into hours, and evening began to gather, she involuntarily treaded more heavily on the throttle of the racing sports car.

As each road sign along the drive had passed, illuminated milestones of her journey and the towns and cities themselves had come and gone as if they were green flags urging her on toward Atlanta; Flat Rock, Tuxedo, Greenville,

Lavonia…Mara had read them and forgotten them, knowing only that putting the towns behind her brought her closer to her child…and Shane.

Mara's stomach knotted at the thought of him. He was playing a dangerous game, and Angie was in a precarious position—the rope in a tug of war between mother and father. The anger that had overcome her after the initial shock of Shane's phone call had slowly given way to dread. How serious was he? How far would he go to claim Angie? And a deeper, more frightening question—how far would she go to stop him from taking her only child from her? If only the marriage could work, if only they could be reunited, if only this battle between them could be resolved. The night closed in on her and the questions and fears flashed through her mind as rapidly as the endless stream of approaching headlights.

Mara was more than nervous when she finally saw the winking lights of Atlanta. She was downright scared! In the past she had always thought of Atlanta fondly, remembering pleasant springs with warm sunshine, the scent of peach blossoms, and the beauty of the pink dogwoods in bloom. But tonight, as her car raced nearer to its destination, she felt only despair and loneliness. How could she ever make her life with Shane? How could it ever possibly work? The nearer she got to the glimmering lights, the more her dread mounted, and she looked upon the city as if it were a devious, well-lit leviathan, waiting for her in the surrounding darkness.

It wasn't difficult to find the section of town where Shane lived. Located just off of Tuxedo Road, the most prestigious area of Atlanta, Shane's home was an enormous, red-brick mansion that rose three stories into the night. The grounds around the estate, well-lit with lamp posts near the long drive, were immense and meticulously well-tended. Pine trees, ancient oaks, magnolias, and the ever-present dogwoods flanked the mansion, softening the straight lines of the massive brick structure.

Mara stopped the car and gazed quietly up at the immense mansion that Shane called home. Warm light from eight-foot windows melted into the darkness and was reflected in the large white columns of expansive front porch. Clean, black shutters lined the windows, and glowing sconces near the door seemed to invite her into the house. She hesitated only slightly before stepping into the night and marching proudly up the three brick steps to the massive front door. Narrow paned windows on each side of the white door tempted her to look inside, but she refused, preferring to meet Shane's gaze squarely.

It took all of her courage to ring the doorbell, but the knowledge that Angie was inside the stately manor encouraged her. After pressing a trembling finger to the bell, she listened, and over the quiet hum of slow traffic she heard the sound of chimes announcing her arrival. The sound of her own heartbeat pounded in her ears, and then another, louder noise interrupted the soft city sounds. It was the reverberating drum of running footsteps. Excited, small feet were hurrying to the door. Mara set down the suitcase and bent down on one knee expectantly. The lump that was forming in her throat began to swell as the door was pulled open, and in the crack of the interior lights, Angie's expectant black eyes reached out and found her mother's teary gaze.

"It *is* Mommy!" Angie called over her shoulder as she burst through the door and, in a scrambling pile of soft arms and legs, crawled into Mara's waiting arms. "Daddy said you were coming," Angie volunteered as she clung to her mother's neck.

"Did he?" Mara whispered thickly.

Angie paused, as if a sudden important thought struck her, and held Mara's chin in her chubby hands. Her concerned eyes probed Mara's. "You hurt Mommy?" she asked innocently. "You crying?"

"No, no, I'm fine," Mara sniffed and managed a trembling, and slightly feeble smile. "I'm…just glad to see you, that's all."

A frown crossed Angie's face. "Shane said I could call him Daddy," Angie said matter-of-factly.

Mara bit her lip and looked deeply into Angie's dark eyes. "And what do *you* think about that?" she asked. Shane's approaching footsteps forced Mara's gaze upward past his slightly worn jeans and casual T-shirt, past the rigid lines of his chest and neck to the powerful, determined set of his jaw. When her eyes touched his, she felt a shiver of ice slide down her back, for nowhere in his commanding gaze did she see even the slightest hint of compassion. His eyes were those of a stranger, and the slightest hope that she held for them, that they could learn to love again, flickered and died.

From Mara's position, kneeling on the cool bricks of the front porch, Shane appeared larger than his natural six feet. And his stony gaze watched the intimate reunion of mother and daughter as if from a distance.

"What *do* you think about calling me Daddy?" Shane asked Angie, a trace of kindness lighting his eyes as his daughter turned to rain a smile upon him.

Angie lifted her small shoulders indifferently. Her eyes, large, round, innocent black orbs scrutinized her father, and her small face drew into a studious frown. "I not like my daddy," she admitted.

Shane stiffened, and the child continued with a curt nod of her head. "He not nice at all. I'm glad he's gone!"

"Angie!" Mara whispered reproachfully.

"No, no!" Shane interrupted, waving off Mara's soft rebuke. "I'd like to hear this. Why are you glad?" he asked Angie.

"He don't like me," Angie pointed out without any trace of emotion.

"How did you know?" Shane questioned, and Mara felt her stomach tighten in anticipation.

"He yelled at me. All the time." Angie squirmed out of her mother's arms, as if struck by a sudden thought. She began to race down the hall, giggling. "Come on, Mommy. Look what we got here!" The small child, sliding on the patina of the warm oak floor in her footed pajamas, slipped out of view as she rounded a corner down the long hallway.

Mara stood up slowly and reached for her suitcase, but Shane's hand intervened. Long fingers coiled around the soft fabric of her rose-colored jersey sleeve.

"Is that right...what Angie said. Did your *husband* mistreat *my* child?" The fingers tightened their grip.

Mara found her breath constricted in her lungs. Shane gave her arm an impatient shake and his nostrils flared in the half-light of the porch. "Did he hurt her?" His voice was low, almost a growl. "Was he cruel?"

"Of course not," she shot back, trying to retrieve her arm from his manacling grip and failing. Her blue eyes sparked with the quiet rage she had tried to dispel for the last few hours. "You should know that I would never allow anyone to hurt her. Not Peter. Not even *you!*"

"But what Angie said..."

"He was cross with her, nothing more." She pulled her hand away in a desperate tug.

"Often?"

"Enough."

"How could you...let a situation like that endure?" he charged, reaching for the suitcase and pulling the bag upward in a jerking motion that flexed the muscles in his arms and showed, emphatically, the extent of his long-repressed anger.

"*I* did what *I* had to do. What I thought was right!"

"By allowing a man who obviously hated her to be her father?" he ridiculed, as his lips curled in disdain. "What kind of mother are you?"

"A damned sight better mother than you were a father!" she spat back at him. "Remember, you were the one who disappeared for four years, letting me think that you were dead. And now I know the real reason, don't I?"

"What's that…the *real* reason?" he asked sarcastically.

"It's obvious," she began, her gaze taking in all of the interior of the house at once—the expensive period pieces that lined the walls, the plush carpeting that covered warm hardwood, the crystal chandelier, the entire estate. "You were too busy finding your fortune to have time for your family!"

"My family was married to someone else!"

"Because you left me!"

"I called, damn it…and I wrote to you, but you chose to ignore my letters!"

"*I* never got your letters, if you really did write them!"

"Oh, I wrote them, all right. And you can bet that someone, maybe your dear husband, got them…or just maybe you got them but decided to gamble with Wilcox. Because at the time he was a damned sight wealthier than I."

"That's ludicrous!"

"I don't think so," he accused. "And what's more, I think that now you're a desperate woman caught in her own web of lies!"

"At least I would never stoop so low as to kidnap a baby!"

"My baby, Mara…*Mine!*" he bit out as he spun on his heel and walked back to the interior of the house, swinging the suitcase as if it weighed nothing.

Angie's voice broke into the heated discussion and halted the sarcastic retort that was forming on Mara's lips. "Come on, Mommy…look what we got!"

Mara walked stoically behind Shane, and tried to ignore the way that his jeans pulled against the back of his thighs and buttocks while he walked. She tried not to watch the move of his forearms and shoulders as he carried the suitcase and set it down near the base of the stairs. Why, she wondered to herself, when she was so incensed with him, when her wrath was at its highest fury, did he still assail all of her senses?

Mara passed from the immense entry hall to a large room near the back of the manor. It seemed to be both a family room and a study. The room was decorated in masculine accents of rust and brown, and the furniture, unlike the entry hall and the other rooms that Mara had glimpsed, was contemporary. Shane's desk of polished walnut stood in the recessed alcove of a bay window, and a modern, cherry-wood filing cabinet served as a small room divider, giving the desk a small bit of privacy. Despite the warmth of the surrounding temperature, there was an intimate fire glowing in the marble fireplace, and a worn, oxblood leather couch with an afghan, hand-knit in hues of gold and brown, tossed carelessly over the back. In the midst of the furniture, right before the fireplace, was an incredible pile of toys scattered all over the braided rug.

"What's this?" Mara asked, her hot temper fading to incredulity at the sight of her daughter entranced by the sight of the colorful toys.

"Look, Mommy, here's a new Lolly," Angie pointed out by holding up the latest version of the popular doll. "And here's an 'lectric train, and...and some talking horsies..." Angie began rummaging through the pile of toys, holding up those of particular interest to her. All of the toys were brand-new, and the one imposing factor that Mara noticed was that none, not one, held the trademark of Imagination.

"Did Christmas come early this year?" she asked as she turned to find Shane leaning against the doorway, surveying both her and child, and obviously enjoying the look of frustration in her eyes. "And if Santa did come, why didn't he bring home anything from the assembly lines of Imagination?"

"It's an experiment," Shane shrugged, seemingly amused at her confusion.

"In frustration?" she guessed. "You find a way to get me down here to show off your collection of toys from the competition?"

Shane's deep, rumbling laughter broke down the wall of misunderstanding that had grown between them. "Of course not," he said as he walked into the room and settled himself down in the midst of the mess. He tossed a foam rubber soccer ball into the air and watched distractedly as it bounced off the ceiling. "I bought all of these toys while I was down here last weekend. According to the figures I've run up in my computer, these things are the thirty most popular toys sold in America today...not one of them is from Imagination."

"I could have told you that much." Mara sighed, dropping down onto the couch and fingering a toy dump truck.

"But," he contended, his eyes locking with hers, "you couldn't have told me why *these* toys are popular." He pointed to the pile of toys.

"Heaven only knows," Mara murmured, looking wistfully at Angie, who was beside herself with the toys. The new Lolly was being dragged upside down as she examined each of the other toys.

"Well, I thought that if I brought some of the toys home and studied them, perhaps I could find out what makes them the leaders in sales."

"While lining the pockets of the competition," Mara whispered.

"Sour grapes, darling," he retorted with the hint of a

smile. "Besides, you can see for yourself, Angie's fascinated with them."

"Oh, she likes just about any new toy," Mara countered, cynically, "as long as it isn't made by Imagination."

"Exactly my point," Shane agreed, raising himself from the rug and pushing his hands into the pockets of his jeans. The motion tightened the muscles of his forearms, and his eyes darkened. Mara felt the change in mood, and all at once the room began to close in on her. She felt his presence, his intensity, his physical magnetism drawing her toward him.

For a moment, as their gazes locked and the questions and doubts that separated them loomed between them again, Mara felt suspended in motion, breathless. The furrow between his brows deepened and the line of his jaw seemed to protrude. "Are you hungry?" he asked, breaking the uncomfortable, shifting silence. He, too, was aware of the subtle change in atmosphere. "Angie and I were just about to sit down. Come on, Angie, let's fix Mommy some dinner." Angie's blond head bobbed expectantly.

The dinner only took a few moments to prepare. Shane's kitchen, with its airy country charm, tiled floor, hanging brass pots, and indoor barbecue, was easy to work in, and within minutes, the steaks were broiled, the salad was tossed, and the potatoes came steaming from the microwave. They sat in a formal dining room, and while Shane poured from a vintage bottle of Cabernet Savignon, Mara lit the five, white tallow candles in the candelabrum. Angie's dark eyes danced with the festivities, and Mara realized, as she watched her child over the rim of her wine glass, just how much the little girl adored Shane. It was so apparent that he reciprocated that adoration, and that he would do nothing but the best for her. The intimate surroundings, the love of father and daughter, the warm, stately old house—it all seemed so right to Mara. And the laughter. God, how long had it been since she had heard the sweet sounds of Angie's laughter, so free and uninhibited? Mara felt as if, at long last, she had come home.

After a dinner that her daughter seemed to dominate, Mara caught Angie yawning. "Come on, pumpkin," she said, picking up her child, "let's get you up to bed."

Above Angie's predictable but insincere protests, Mara picked up her daughter and headed up the stairs. Shane followed her and carried the suitcase up to a room at the head of the stairs.

The room was twice the size of Angie's room in Asheville, and Mara eyed Shane suspiciously as she entered it. The walls were newly papered in a delicate yellow rosebud print, and the matching canopy bed and dresser looked as if they had been delivered very recently. The room was complete, down to a writing desk in the same dark pine as the posters of the bed and a full length, free-standing mirror.

"It looks as if you were expecting her," Mara whispered.

"I was," he agreed, and pulled pensively on his lower lip.

Angie snuggled deep into the folds of the down comforter and closed her eyes against the soft, clean new sheets. Shane left the room after a few moments, but Mara stayed, waiting until she was assured by Angie's deep, rhythmic breathing that the child was soundly asleep. "Oh, Angie," she murmured to herself as she brushed an errant blond curl from her daughter's face. "What are we going to do?"

As Mara descended the polished oak staircase she noticed that most of the lights in the house had been extinguished. Only the glow from the fire in the den illuminated her way back to Shane. Now that Angie was peacefully asleep, it was time to iron out all of the problems that they faced and hope that some of the damage of the last lonely years could be bridged.

Shane was sitting on the couch, staring into the fire, holding a half-empty glass of Scotch in his hand. At Mara's entrance, he barely looked up but contented himself with reading the blood-red coals of the smoldering embers. He raised his glass in a gesture of invitation for her to join him. She declined by shaking her head and stood uncomfortably in the doorway.

"We...we can't live like this, you know," she admitted, slowly crossing the room to stand directly in his gaze, before the fire. Heat from its glow warmed the back of her calves. The house was already warm, and the fire only added to its simmering heat.

"You're damned right we can't," he agreed forcefully. His dark eyes traveled upward, from the toes peeking out of her sandals, up the length of her calf to the curve of her hips and the swell of her breasts, to rest on her face—the face that had haunted his nights and, more often than not, awakened him in the darkness with burning need and longing. God, how long had he waited to make her his again?

Mara felt as if, with the touch of his eyes, he was undressing her, and that not only her heated skin was in his view, but also the very soul of her. The farthest reaches of her mind were being explored by the intensity of his gaze, the rake of his eyes on her body. Gradually, he stood, taking one final swallow of his drink before coming over to within inches of her. Her face tilted upward to meet his probing gaze. An uneasy awkward silence fell upon them, and the flames threw shadowed patterns across Shane's proud face.

"You had no right to take her," Mara whispered, her eyes searching his.

"I had every right."

Again the heavy silence.

"You *used* her."

A self-derisive smile, hard and cold, curled his lips. "I didn't. What I did was tell her the truth."

"The truth that you were her real father?"

"That's right." He braced himself against the mantle with one strong hand and touched a lock of Mara's hair with the other.

"And how did she take the news?"

His face softened with a smile. "She seems to like the idea. She's too young to really understand."

Mara let out the breath she had been holding, and felt the subtle pressure of Shane's fingers as they traveled from her hair to her throat. Her heart began to clamor for his touch, and when his fingers brushed the hollow of her throat, moving in slow, seductive circles, he found her racing pulse. His fingers lingered for a second, and then dropped to toy with the neckline of her dress.

"I'm glad you came," he murmured thickly into the deep golden silk of her hair. "I've waited so long..." His lips, warm and sensitive, found hers and captured her entire being in a kiss that promised unrestrained passion and fulfillment.

"I...I'm glad to be here," she admitted, feeling the gentle pressure of his hands as they guided her to the floor. Willingly, she yielded. "Oh, God, Shane," Mara whispered. "I'm so glad to be here."

As they dropped to the floor, Shane managed to pull off his shirt, and the shadowed flames seemed to flicker and dance upon his rugged, masculine chest. Mara felt the tiny beads of anxious perspiration begin to moisten her skin, and her heart was pounding within the walls of her rib cage. His hands found the wrap-tie of her dress, and in one swift movement the rose dress opened, exposing the feverish rising and falling of her chest that was protected by only the thin fabric of her slip. "It's so hot in here," she murmured, the touch of his hands and the heat from the fire igniting molten flames of desire within her. "I...I feel as if I'm going to melt..."

"Let's hope so," he murmured, his voice husky with

yearning. "I *need* you so badly," he moaned as his lips
rained dew-soft kisses upon her, across the gentle hill of her
cheeks, over her eyes, and lower, past her throat to whisper
against the French lace of her slip. Her breasts strained
within the confinement of the sheer garment. His hot breath,
laced with the tingle of Scotch, heated the dewy drops of
perspiration on her body and made her ache for him with a
primeval urgency that took control of her mind and soul.
"Oh, Mara, baby, let me make love to you here, in our
home...away from all of our problems."

Her answering sigh of surrender, and the anxious fingers
caressing his skin, heating his flesh, were all the encourage-
ment that Shane needed. Slowly he slid the dress over her
shoulders, and let one strap of her slip fall to expose her
breast, proud and round in the firelight. He closed his
eyes as if in agonized pain. "Why do I want you so
badly...why?" he sighed, almost to himself. When he
opened his eyes to gaze deeply into hers, the passion that
he tried so hard to deny smoldered in his gaze.

With trembling hands, Mara reached up and put her palms
on either side of his head, until the pressure of her fingertips
drew him down, closer to her, until his lips brushed against
and finally captured the ripe and aching tip of her breast.
"Love me, Shane," she pleaded. "Please...love me..."

His weight shifted until he lay boldly over her. Her fingers found the zipper to his jeans, and she knew, in an
instant, how strong his passion had become. Within minutes
he had found the most intimate part of her. She felt herself
yielding, melting, softening to his touch in warm liquid
waves of fulfillment.

"Marry me, Shane," she demanded, and the naked plead-
ing in her eyes found the black passion of his. "Marry me,"
she whispered over and over again as she felt herself blend
into him.

When at last his passion had subsided, he held her quietly

in his arms and stared into the few final coals that still glowed in the fire. His fingers still rubbed her shoulder and breast, but he seemed lost in thought...distant.

Finally, with a groan, he sat up and pulled her into a sitting position as well. She felt warm and glowing as she gazed silently into the fire and felt the security of Shane's powerful arms holding her.

"I want you to marry me," he sighed, and she felt the muscles in his arms flex.

"I will." The answer was honest. "I...want it, too."

"When?" The question stung the air and Mara paused, but for only a moment. No matter what else she had learned and understood tonight, she realized that she could never deny Shane the right to his child. And in time, she hoped, once that she had proven her love for him, he would love her.

"I'll tell June the entire story on Monday...and this time I'll force her to listen. We can be married next week."

His thumbs cupped her chin and forced her to look into his eyes. "You're sure?"

"I've never been more sure of anything in my life," she returned, contentedly snuggling closer to him.

"June and the Wilcox family...they might give us a battle for Imagination..."

"I know," she murmured, "but let's cross that bridge when we come to it."

"Would you be willing to live here, in Atlanta?" he asked.

"If that's where you're going to be..."

He smiled crookedly and placed a kiss on the top of her head. "All right...good. But you have to realize that we might lose the toy company, or at least your portion of it."

Mara sighed deeply. "I know that, and I know that I've worked hard to keep that company afloat. But to be perfectly honest, I haven't done a good enough job to turn it around, and it *is* part of the Wilcox family estate. Perhaps it should belong to them…''

"We'll see," he murmured, but once again the strong lines of determination hardened his expression. "We'll see…"

The morning dawned bright with the promise of hot weather. After a quick breakfast Shane insisted upon showing Mara the sights and pleasures of Atlanta. The drive toward Peachtree Street took only a few minutes, and after Shane parked the car he insisted that Mara and Angie join him for a walking tour of the city. The walk included a tour of some of Atlanta's finest and newest hotels, the fabulous Peachtree Plaza with its array of shops and the Toy Museum of Atlanta. The cool interior of the museum was welcome relief from the bustle of the busy city and the warm Georgia sun.

Mara and Angie were fascinated with the museum and the incredible display of antique toys, some dating from early in the nineteenth century. There was a collection of toys from around the world that particularly fascinated Angie, who stated quite emphatically that some of the dolls, especially the dolls from Holland in their wooden shoes and painted faces, were even prettier than Lolly.

By early afternoon, Angie had to be carried, and then, while Shane held her, she fell asleep, exhausted. The child was disappointed when she learned that she was being taken back home for a nap, but Shane avoided hurting her feelings by offering to take her to the zoo the next day. The pout on the little girl's face disappeared, and she settled into the back seat of the car with only mild protest.

Mara, too, was exhausted, but the feeling of serenity that she had found with Shane the night before never left her. The drive home was quiet, with Angie snoozing in the back seat. Shane took a long way back, pointing out spots of interest to Mara as they passed, and for the first time in years, Mara felt completely at ease, and the problems facing her with the Wilcox family seemed remote and distant. All of her awareness was focused upon Shane and how deeply she loved him. He had been right all along, she admitted ruefully to herself. She should have told June the truth about Shane the minute she saw him again.

The phone was ringing when they got out of the car. Shane quickly made his way into the house, but by the time he picked up the receiver, the line was dead. For some reason, an uneasy feeling swept over Mara, and she had difficulty shaking it.

After cleaning the breakfast dishes, Mara, led by Angie, toured the grounds. They were gorgeously groomed, and even though it was early fall, Mara could visualize what the gardens of azaleas and rhododendron would look like in the spring, flanked by stately pink dogwood trees.

"I wonder who takes care of all this," Mara mused to herself.

"Don't look at me," Shane laughed, joining Mara and Angie. "I'm incredibly poor at this sort of thing—black thumb, or something like that."

"Then you have a gardener?"

"Yes. A retired groundskeeper for a golf course. He comes here twice, maybe three times a week, to keep up the grounds and his wife takes care of the inside of the house."

Mara's eyes traveled up the three stories to the roof top. In the daylight the house seemed more immense and grand than it had in the night. "One woman takes care of all that?"

"I'm not messy..."

"But still. The house is so *huge*."

A smile cracked across his face, and he bent down to whisper into her ear. "We need a big house. We'll have to have enough room for all of Angie's brothers."

Mara giggled despite herself. "I think we can wait a little while on that one," she teased as she and Shane started back toward the house. "Angie," Mara called at the child attempting to climb a small tree. "Don't hurt yourself! We're going inside…are you coming?"

"I coming in just a minute."

As Mara walked back into the kitchen, Shane headed toward his study. "There are a couple of things I want to finish up in my office," he explained, "and then we'll go out to dinner!"

Mara watched him stride down the hall with his easy, familiar gait. Yes, she thought to herself, I could be quite happy here. From her vantage point, near the center island in the kitchen, she could look out the window and see Angie playing outside, scampering near a shallow goldfish pond. Mara could see it coming. Angie was about to go wading and try to catch a fish!

The phone rang just as Mara got to the door and warned Angie about staying out of the pool. Just as she had contented herself that Angie would stay out of the water, she heard Shane's footsteps approaching.

"It's for you," he stated, curtly.

"What?"

"The phone…it's that sister-in-law of yours, what's her name, Dana?"

"Dena," Mara answered, and wondered why Dena would be tracking her down. Her stomach tightened as she thought of all of Dena's threats. "Oh, God," she moaned quietly to herself.

"Mara, for God's sake, is that you?" Dena shrieked over the wires when Mara answered the phone.

"Yes…yes…Dena?" Mara asked, hearing what she construed to be sobs on the other end of the connection. "What's wrong?" she asked, and swallowed with difficulty. "Dena?"

"It's...it's Mother," Dena blurted out.

"What about her?"

"She's...she's in the hospital...that's where I'm calling from. I've been trying to reach you all day!"

"Just calm down," Mara whispered, but felt her own heart thudding with dread. "Now, explain everything to me. What happened?"

"I...I don't know..." Dena admitted through her sobs. "She was at some bridge thing last night...and, well...she just collapsed. An ambulance brought her here."

"And has she seen Dr. Bernard?"

"Along with about five others."

"How ill is she?" Mara asked, not daring to take a breath.

"They say...that she'll be all right...apparently she's suffered a series of slight strokes...they've finished with most of the tests and Dr. Bernard is letting her go home, as long as we can find a nurse to take care of her." Dena's voice was calmer, and her sobbing had subsided slightly.

"Have you found one?"

"Dr. Bernard gave me a name...Anne Hamilton."

"Have you called her?"

"Not yet...I thought I should call you first."

"Okay, look," Mara commanded. Her voice was firm as she took control of the situation. If the doctors were releasing June from the hospital, she certainly wasn't as ill as Dena thought. "Call the nurse and get her over to June's apartment as soon as they release your mother. I can be at the apartment in about four hours. Can you handle everything until I get there?"

"I...I think so."

"Good, I'll see you later." Mara hung up the phone with numb hands. She turned toward the hallway and noticed Shane standing near the stairs, her suitcase in his hands. His eyes were dark, unreadable.

"It's June, isn't it?" he asked, grimly.

"She's in the hospital...she suffered a series of slight strokes, or something..."

"Let's go," he commanded. "Angie, come on," he said more loudly through the open door.

"You don't have to come," Mara offered.

"Of course I do."

The drive to Asheville was hampered by Saturday afternoon tourists, leisurely plodding along and gazing at the quiet beauty of the Indian summer day. Mara thought that she would be torn to pieces by the concern she felt for her mother-in-law and the guilt that she was carrying. What could have set off the strokes? A gnawing thought chilled her to the bone as she concluded it must have been because of Mara's reaction to the fact that June had let Angie leave with Shane without asking for Mara's permission. Somehow, the dread that had overcome Mara must have passed to her mother-in-law, leading to the grave turn in her illness.

The quiet, tense hours passed with the miles, and when Mara saw the Asheville skyline, her stomach had knotted to the point that a sharp pain of dread and fear passed over her. Shane parked the car in front of June's town house and helped Mara out of the car.

"Are you going to be all right?" he asked, his concern reflected in his dark eyes.

"As soon as I see for myself that June is getting better."

"Do you want me to come in with you?"

Mara shook her head. "No...I don't think so, not at first anyway. She...is nervous around you, anyway, and I wouldn't want to shock her. Besides, I think it would be better if Angie doesn't see her...not until I know that June's all right."

"It's my bet that she's done this on purpose," Shane commented, helping Angie from the car. "I don't trust her or any of the rest of the family, either."

"How can you say anything of the sort. She's ill, Shane!" Mara retorted, her frayed emotions getting the better of her.

"Are we going to see Grammie?" Angie asked, heading up the stairs.

"In a few minutes," Shane replied, and squatted down to face his daughter. "Grammie's a little sick, and she needs a little time to recover…" His dark gaze sent Mara a dubious, incomprehensible look. "So why don't you and I go over to the park for an ice-cream cone?"

Angie puzzled the question for a moment. "And then I can see Grammie?"

"Of course you can, sweetheart," Mara said with a wan smile, before quickly hurrying up the stairs.

"Mara?" Shane called, pushing his hands into his pockets.

"Yes?"

A pause. "Good luck."

Mara smiled before knocking softly on the door and entering June's home. Everything was just as she had left it, the cool blue hues of the interior, the overstuffed floral couch, and everywhere, pictures of the family.

A door whispered closed and Mara looked up to meet the questioning gaze of a professional-looking, robust woman of about fifty. "You're June's nurse," Mara guessed. "Ms. Hamilton?"

"That's right. Who are you?"

Strong forearms folded tightly over her bosom.

"I'm Mara Wilcox, June's daughter-in-law," Mara explained with a polite though stiff smile. "How is she?"

"She's much better," the nurse began, relaxing slightly. "Dena said that you would be coming."

"Is Dena here, now?" Mara asked.

"I asked her to go home. She was absolutely beside herself!" The nurse took a seat on the sofa. "You can call her if you like."

"No...no, what I would really like to do is see my mother-in-law, and offer to help her any way I can. How serious is her condition?"

"Dr. Bernard thinks she'll be up and around in a few weeks."

"But I thought she had several strokes..."

"Yes, but, fortunately only minor ones, and if she's careful, with her diet and exercise, she'll be fine. She'll just have to slow down a bit, that's all." Mara listened while the nurse continued to describe June's condition, and a feeling of relief washed over her as she realized that June could, quite possibly, live a normal, healthy life. "She's awake, now. Would you like to see her."

"Yes," Mara said, walking after Anne Hamilton toward June's bedroom.

The woman in the bed was hardly recognizable to Mara. Thin, drawn, and frail, without a trace of color on her cheeks, June looked much worse than Mara had expected. Pale blue eyes focused on Mara as she entered the room.

"Mara...is that you?" June asked weakly.

"I...I came as quickly as I could. Oh, June, how are you?"

"Still kicking," June allowed with a thin smile. She turned her eyes toward the nurse. "Could you give us some time alone?" she requested. The nurse smiled her agreement, but in a guarded look that she passed to Mara, she said more clearly than words, Don't upset her.

"June," Mara began, trying to think of a gentle way to break the news of her forthcoming marriage. "There's something I want to tell you." She stepped more closely to the bed and June raised a bony hand to wave off the words that were suspended in Mara's throat.

"No, Mara, it's my turn," the elderly woman stated with a raspy breath. "I've spent the last day waiting for you to show up, because I have to tell you...something I should have done a long time ago.'' For a moment the tired eyes closed, and Mara felt stifled and confined. The smell of antiseptic, the vials of pills, the thinly draped figure on the bed—it all seemed so cloyingly and disturbingly unreal.

The old woman continued. ''I know that Shane is Angie's father,'' June said with a sigh.

''What...but how...''

June ignored Mara's question and continued with her own confession. ''I've known about it for several years. When Peter found out about his illness...''—her voice caught—''...that it was terminal, and that he couldn't father any children of his own, he told me that another man, one presumed dead, was Angie's real father. And if he seemed harsh with Angie, it was because he knew that he couldn't have children of his own.''

''Oh, June,'' Mara sighed, slumping into a chair near the bed.

''Don't worry, I had already guessed that Angie wasn't Peter's child. I took a few courses in genetics when I was in school, and I know the odds against two blue-eyed people having a dark-eyed child. Nearly impossible. And,'' she sighed wearily, ''I...I intercepted some letters that were forwarded to the house four years ago...I just had the feeling that Angie's natural father was alive somewhere.'' Tears began to pool in June's aging blue eyes. ''I...still have the letters, and I didn't open them...I wanted to, but I just couldn't...''

''It's all right,'' Mara said, touching June's arm.

''No...no, it's not. I'm just a foolish old woman looking out for my own best interests, fooling myself, telling myself that I was helping everyone else...but it's just not so. And when, on the day of Peter's funeral, Shane Kennedy appeared on the doorstep, I remembered the name on the return address of the envelopes, and knew that he was Angie's father. I...I hoped that he would go away, disappear again, but I knew he wouldn't…he was so damned insistent that he see you."

Mara's throat seemed to have swollen shut, and she found it difficult to blink back the tears of pain she felt for her mother-in-law.

"I did it because I love Angie so much," June sobbed. "I…couldn't bear the thought of losing her…and you. I was afraid of becoming one of those lonely old women that you see walking in the park…all alone." She breathed heavily. "Oh, Mara, I'm so sorry…I put my happiness before yours…"

Mara looked up to see Shane standing in the doorway, holding Angie. How much of June's confession had he heard? He set the little girl down, and she scampered over to her grandmother's bedside. "Grammie, you okay? Look, I brought you flowers!" she said excitedly and held up a bedraggled bunch of daisies and dandelions.

"Thank you, sweetheart," June mumbled.

Shane strode to her bedside and watched the older woman. "I heard what you said to Mara."

"I'm sorry," June admitted.

"I just want you to know that I will never interfere with your relationship with Angie. I realize how important she is to you, and how much she loves you. I don't condone what you did, but I do understand it."

"Go…Mara…in the desk in the living room," June commanded. "The letters are in the bottom drawer."

"I don't know…"

"Get them," June insisted, some of her color returning. "Angie can stay in here with me."

Unsteadily, Mara walked back into the living room toward the antique secretary that June used as a desk. She knew that her fingers were trembling, and it was with difficulty that she found the unopened letters, addressed to her in Shane's bold scrawl.

"Oh, dear God," she moaned, and opened the first of three. Tears stained her cheeks and dropped onto the sheets of paper that swept her back in time four long years: Words of love dominated the pages and in the last letter was a proposal of marriage, dated over four years in the past. "If only I had known," she sobbed, looking into Shane's eyes. "If only I had known. I loved you so much…"

Shane folded his arms around her and pressed his chin against her head.

"You know now," he murmured, and his arms tightened around her, securing her to him. "God, Mara, I loved you…and I still do…and nothing matters but that we're together again."

"What about June…and the toy company?"

"It doesn't matter. I've bought up some of the shares from family members, and I think, now that Dena and June have reexamined their lives, that they won't object to moving the company to Atlanta, as long as they retain part interest."

"Are you sure?"

"We'll cross that bridge when we come to it," he said with a knowing smile. "As for right now, let's go in and tell Angie and June that we're getting married…I have a feeling that neither will object."

* * * * *

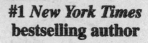

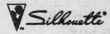

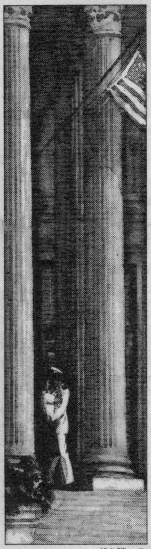
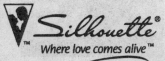